the NAKED MAN FESTIVAL

To my two favourite girls

BRIAN THACKER

the NAKED MAN FESTIVAL

and other excuses to fly around the world

ALLEN&UNWIN

First published in 2004

Allen & Unwin
83 Alexander Street
Crows Nest NSW 2065
Australia
Phone: (61 2) 8425 0100
Fax: (61 2) 9906 2218
Email: info@allenandunwin.com
Web: www.allenandunwin.com

National Library of Australia
Cataloguing-in-Publication entry:

Thacker, Brian, 1962- .
   The naked man festival : (and other excuses to fly around
   the world).

   ISBN 1 74114 399 3.

   1. Thacker, Brian, 1962- - Journeys. 2. Travel - Anecdotes.
   3. Festivals - Anecdotes. I. Title.

910.4

Set in 10.5/15 pt Minion by Bookhouse, Sydney
Printed in Australia by McPherson's Printing Group, Victoria

10 9 8 7 6 5 4 3 2

Contents

A festival odyssey

As I stepped out of Frankfurt airport as a young, naive backpacker on my first Big Trip OS, I noticed a couple of people dressed as clowns. In the underground train station I saw two more clowns drinking large cans of beer. Sitting opposite me on the train was another clown having an animated conversation with a court jester. I had no idea what was going on (my first thought was that— because Europe is a season ahead in fashion—this was the latest look and everyone would be dressing like clowns in the Australian winter).

After seeing another dozen or so clowns, I finally found out that the Germans weren't clown fetishists after all. It was acutally part of an ancient festival called Fasching and, as well as dressing up, people danced, sang and drank massive steins of beer for three days straight. Fasching, which takes place immediately before Lent, is celebrated under various names and in different guises (so to speak) all over the world. You'll find people getting dressed up and pissed up at Carnaval in Rio, Mardi Gras in New Orleans, Carnevale in Venice and countless other drunken parties around the globe.

By evening, half the population of Frankfurt was rolling drunk, which meant there were a lot of very happy clowns. I saw them collapsed in doorways and throwing up in gutters. I even saw two clowns on the riverbank trying to make little clowns. I had the most marvellous time and, by midnight of my first day in Europe, I had three clowns, an ape and a nun as my new best friends.

Since then, whenever I've attended a festival or celebration, it's quite often turned out to be the highlight of my trip. Not only do festivals provide a fascinating insight into a people and culture, they're often a great party—and I've suffered through many a killer hangover to prove it. During my travels I've danced, sung and drunk my way through Oktoberfest in Munich to an Elephant Festival in Thailand to a Potato Festival in Thorpdale, country Victoria (which was a bit light on the dancing, singing and drinking part—and a bit heavy on the potatoes).

I've even managed to stumble across an unplanned and unrepeatable festival—an impromptu Swiss imitation of an imaginary Australian festival. While on a ski holiday in Davos, Switzerland, a few years back I was quite surprised to learn that Lifesaver Day is the biggest and most important holiday in Australia. It's the last official day on which lifesavers patrol the beaches for the summer and the entire country throws a massive party. Or at least that's what Phil, a lawyer from Sydney, told the 20 Dutch people in the chalet we were sharing.

I was on my way down to dinner one evening when Phil called me into his room and asked if I had a pair of board shorts and thongs with me. Phil, who was in his early forties, was on a skiing holiday with three of his lawyer mates. All four of them were standing in his room wearing boardies, singlets and thongs, and had their noses smeared with zinc cream.

Phil then went on to explain that he wanted to 'have a bit of fun' with the Dutch guests in our chalet. The first thing we did, after Phil had explained the importance of Lifesaver Day in Australia to the Dutch contingent, was to crown the Lifesaver Queen. Naturally Phil picked the most gorgeous girl in the room. Hanneke, a 25-year-old blonde from Amsterdam, was dragged up and placed on a chair that was balanced on a table in the centre of the dining room. We beach-going Aussies then gathered around in a circle, crouched down on one knee with our hand on our hearts and, just as we had rehearsed it earlier, broke into the song 'Little Surfer Girl'. Hanneke's face soon turned a fetching shade of sunburn. Particularly so when we took it in turns to kiss her hand.

After dinner, Phil managed—rather impressively, I thought—to talk all the Dutch men into an eating race with their apple pie and cream dessert. The impressive bit was that he got them to do this with their hands firmly tucked under their legs. The winner, Phil gushed excitedly, would become the Lifesaver King for the day. Jaap, a lanky 40-year-old bespectacled fellow from Utrecht, scoffed down his entire plate in less than 30 seconds. He was so thrilled to be named the Lifesaver King that he didn't even realise his face was an absolute mess of pastry and cream.

As we downed a few more glasses of wine after dinner and Phil regaled them with more stories, I almost started to believe him too. Oh, except when he told a group of them that all the dogs in Australia had been wiped out in a plague and we now have pet kangaroos hopping around our backyards.

So, with all these great experiences under my belt, it wasn't too difficult coming up with an idea for this book. I would go on a festival odyssey. In a six-month period I would attend as many festivals and celebrations as distance, time and, more importantly, money would permit. There was only one small (or rather large) problem, though: there are literally thousands of festivals to choose from. When I began my research into festivals and celebrations, I was totally blown away by the sheer number and variety of events that take place around the world. And that was just for one day. I typed 'festivals February 22nd' (a random date, by the way) into a Google search and was presented with an absolute plethora of parties. On February 22nd you could shake your booty at, among others, the Islamic New Year Festival in Indonesia; the Annual Bob Marley Day Festival in San Francisco, USA; the Hucknall Real Ale Festival in Nottingham, England; the Andes Heavy Rock Festival in Chile; the Cuchillo Pecan Festival in New Mexico, USA; the Ouagadougou Film Festival in Burkina Faso (I kid you not); the Abu Simbel Nubian Festival in Egypt and the Festival of Sexual Diversity in São Paulo, Brazil.

Then again, if I wanted to (and couldn't be bothered moving around too much) I could attend an entire yearful of festivals in the one country. Nepal has a major festival every single day of the year (the festival for February 22nd, by the way, is the Maha Shivratri Festival which celebrates the birthday of Lord Shiva—it's a popular one, because it is the only day of the year on which the consumption of hashish is legal).

So what sort of festival was I after? Most traditional festivals have their origins in religion. Back in the good old days they had a good old time, too. Most of the ancient religious festivals listed in the *Dictionary of Festivals* tended to involve lots of orgies. Oh, plus lots of sacrificing of pigs, goats, sheep, rams, horses and even a few people.

The humans sacrificed were generally 'a person of no benefit to society'. Gee, they'd have plenty to choose from today, including—but by no means limited to—parking inspectors, people who pose as statues in shopping malls, TV evangelists, rap artists and shopfront spruikers.

Although religious festivals account for many of the largest and most important festivals today, other non-religious festivals easily outnumber them. People will find any old excuse for a festival. There are festivals devoted to frogs' legs, crossword puzzles, tubas, chicken clucking, slugs, butterfly migration, coffins, bog snorkelling, nude night-surfing and even absolutely nothing. The Telluride Nothing Festival in July 2004 promised the following events: sunrises and sunsets; gravity; and a rotating Earth. Their slogan is, 'Thank you for not participating'.

The Nothing Festival is not the only festival at which very little happens. One large supermarket chain in Australia has a Food Festival every Friday. You won't find much partying going on there (although it may be worth calling in to pick up some bananas, which are a bargain at only $1.79 a kilo).

I had only just begun investigating the festivals most likely to provide me with some colourful stories when it became clear that two countries have a mortgage on the most interesting (read kooky) and varied (read kooky) celebrations. Only in Japan could you attend (and participate in) a Penis Festival, a Used Pins and Needles Festival, a Crying Baby Festival, a Staring Festival, a Quarreling Festival and a Knickers Festival. The King of Kook crown, however, belongs to the good ol' US of A, where you can party on at the Testicle Festival, the Snowman Burning Festival, the Barbed Wire Festival, the Big Whopper Liars' Festival, the Roadkill Festival and the Rotten Sneaker Festival.

Japan and America became my two biggest festival targets and with a couple more in Australia I fulfilled my festival odyssey. Or, so I thought. I'd almost finished writing the book when, while on a brief visit to London, I legged it up to Scotland for Hogmanay (New Year's Eve) so I could end the book on the final day of the year and write about the rich cultural heritage of this ancient celebration. Okay, I'm lying. It was just an excuse to get rolling drunk again.

Country Music Festival

Tamworth, Australia
January 17th

Country & Western music drives me to drink. With all that cheatin'
and losin' loved ones goin' on, it's so damn depressing. And if just
listening to it makes me feel like downing a few, imagine the benders
the writers and singers must go on. Gee, they must have a hard life.
Not only do they regularly get cheated on; they somehow always
manage to lose their girlfriends or boyfriends, and sometimes their
dog, house, car, hat, gun or left sock (and quite often all in the course
of one three-minute song). Consequently, if I have the misfortune
of listening to country music, I need a large jug of beer. If it's Kenny
Rogers, I need an entire barrel. But, technically at least, I'm a huge
country music fan. My favourite singer of all time had 17 no. 1 hits
on the American Country Music charts, was inducted into the

Country Music Hall of Fame, was a regular performer at the Grand Ole Opry in Nashville (the mecca of country music) and sometimes even wore a cowboy hat.

I'm talking about the King. Elvis Presley. Not only do I listen to his records (too often, too loud and for too long, my wife says), but I also like belting out a few of his numbers on my guitar. I love his early stuff (which is basically all country songs and, more importantly, pretty easy to play). Needless to say, I don't get much of an audience for my rendition of 'Lonesome Cowboy'. I do have one big fan, though: my 11-month-old daughter, Jasmine, loves me. When I play, she dances and claps along with a huge beaming smile on her face. Admittedly, it doesn't make me feel that special—she also dances and claps along to my mobile phone ring tone and the sound of my electric toothbrush.

So when my wife suggested we go to the Tamworth Country Music Festival (she's been known to Yee-ha! along to a few Country & Western songs and even owns a pair of cowboy boots), I thought this could be my chance to play to an audience of more than one— and one who is quite often strapped into a chair so she can't escape. I decided to try busking in the main street of Tamworth. People would love me. All I needed was a bit of practice. Oh, and a hat.

·

'Don't take your guitar. Everyone will laugh at you,' my friend Richo told me. To be honest, I wasn't too worried about people laughing at me. I was actually more worried about getting lynched and thrown into the guitar-shaped swimming pool. Richo also said, 'Don't take the piss out of the Country & Western crowd.' He was the fifth person to tell me that. Just because I was planning to call myself Slim Elvis (a cross between Elvis and Slim Dusty—Australia's most successful country artist), wear the most ridiculously large cowboy hat I could find, don Elvis sunglasses, and mutter, 'Thang you. Thang you very much', a lot.

He was right about the guitar, though. I own a $150 three-quarter size Korean copy (copied, that is, from a cheap Japanese copy). The music folk at Tamworth use guitars like mine as kindling.

'Take mine,' Richo said.

'You're kidding!' I gasped. 'How much is it worth?'

'Oh, two thousand dollars.'

I was totally amazed. Richo owns an acoustic guitar shop and every time I visit him, he follows me around the store saying, 'Don't touch that one, it costs too much.' If I want to have a strum of a 'nice' guitar, he makes me sit down. Then he very carefully hands it to me and won't go back to work till I've finished playing and he's put it safely back on the shelf.

'Are you sure?' I asked uneasily.

'Yeah, just take care of it.' I'd be careful all right—but that wouldn't be much use if someone were to beat me over the head with it, I thought. The guitar had a beautiful sound; it almost made even me sound half-decent. What a nice gesture, I thought, especially when Richo also lent me the ridiculously large cowboy hat he'd bought in Texas and a black satin cowboy shirt. To show him how much I appreciated it I stole a couple of plectrums from behind the counter when he wasn't looking.

·

The day before I was due to fly up to Tamworth (for those of you who don't know where Tamworth is, it's somewhere in the middle of New South Wales), my friend Tony came to see me.

'You'd better not see this,' he said. He was holding a copy of *The Australian* newspaper.

'See what?' I asked.

'You don't want the pressure.'

'What pressure?' I had no idea what he was talking about.

I grabbed it from him (which of course is what he wanted me to do, or he wouldn't have said anything in the first place). The headline on the front page said 'Country road to stardom'. The story was about a 21-year-old girl who had driven 3800 kilometres (it took four days) across the country from Western Australia to busk at the Tamworth Country Music Festival. 'It's not about fame or money,' she said. 'It's about passion.' She had arrived a week early to reserve a good spot on Peel Street (Tamworth's main street). The article went on to say that two of Australia's biggest country artists (Kasey Chambers and Troy Cassar-Daley) were 'discovered' busking in Peel Street (referred to as the 'Boulevard of Dreams').

'You'd better be good,' Tony said.

'I've got a good hat!' I said cheerfully.

The thing is, I hadn't really had much chance to practise. Richo had told me weeks ago that I should practise for at least half an hour every night so my finger tips would get hard. 'If you don't,' he said, 'you won't last 10 minutes.' I'd practised four times for a total of about an hour. I doubted there would be much chance of me getting picked up for a recording contract. I'd be more likely to get picked up for loitering.

·

I had quite an entourage for my Tamworth debut. There was my wife Natalie (my Finance Manager), my daughter Jasmine (President of my fan club), Natalie's mum Caz (the Nanny), and we were meeting my friend Chris (my Manager—although he didn't know this yet), who was driving up from Sydney.

'Which gate are we?' I asked. (I can wander around airports for hours looking for the right gate.)

'Just follow her,' Natalie said pointing to a girl in front of us. She was wearing cowboy boots, cowboy hat, denim skirt and a denim jacket with 'Cowboys are my weakness' emblazoned across the back in large pink letters.

From Melbourne we flew to Sydney where we changed planes onto a regional airline for the hour's trip to Tamworth. About half the people on the flight had hats on. According to the Official Tamworth website: 'You're as good as naked if you come to country music week without a good hat on your head.'

From the air, the town of Tamworth looked tiny. The whole area was in the middle of a terrible drought and the surrounding fields, as far as the eye could see, were bleached almost white from the relentless sun. It may be tiny, but Tamworth is the country music capital of Australia—the Nashville of the Antipodes. The Tamworth Country Music Festival is one of the biggest in the world. Every day for two weeks, 40 000 people turn up for a heap of toe-tappin', boot-scootin' and yee-haain'—there are over 2500 events staged over 100 venues around town.

As soon as we stepped off the plane I put my hat on. I didn't want to be 'as good as naked'. I did feel rather silly though; I kept expecting someone to laugh at me. The carousel at Tamworth airport had a pile of guitar cases on it. They all looked the same. Willie Nelson grabbed the guitar I had in my hand and said, 'I think that's mine, mate.' Shania Twain grabbed another one from the carousel and Garth Brooks walked away with two. With everyone wearing hats, they all looked like someone famous. John Denver, the cab driver, drove us to our motel. Two people were checking in when we arrived. They both had guitars.

Our motel room was a broom closet. A double bed, two singles and a cot were somehow squeezed into a tiny space about the size of a large cupboard. The one good thing about it was that you could change TV channels, put on the kettle, grab a drink from the fridge and kiss everyone goodnight without getting out of bed.

We headed straight out to the opening concert. We were only in town for two nights and we wanted to get in as much yee-haain' as possible. The concert was being held in the local park and, to be honest, I was expecting only a handful of people sitting near the playground swings watching someone as bad as me playing. But it was huge. There were thousands of people, all wearing cowboy hats and all sitting in their BYO chairs. A band was just starting on the impressively large stage as we found a spot on the ground among all the chairs. It was dark already, but it was still stinking hot. The band's first number was 'You're A Cheatin' Honky Tonk Angel'.

I went for an amble, along with all the local teenagers who were out in force strutting their stuff, trying to impress each other. Their clothes were quite an odd mix. The boys were dressed like New York rap artists from the waist down (extra baggy cargo pants and over-sized runners), and Willie Nelson on top (checked shirts and cowboy hats). The girls were wearing cowboy boots, jeans, big-buckled belts and tiny midriff-flashing titty-tops.

The band was now playing a song called 'Cheating.com' (who said country folk weren't keeping up with the times?). When they'd finished, the Mayor of Tamworth officially opened the Tamworth Country Music Festival. 'For those of you who have been to Tamworth before, you will notice a big change,' he said. 'The Mitre 10 hardware store has moved.'

A Telstra spokesman (Telstra were the official sponsor) spoke next. 'Don't be frightened by the internet,' he said. 'Go play with it. If you want to know how to grow better tomatoes, there are websites.' He didn't say anything about Cheating.com, though.

A very camp-looking cowboy in tight leather pants began the next set by prancing around the stage singing about how his 'backside was sore'. When the next band started playing 'You're A Cheatin' Yodeller', we'd had enough. Well, Jasmine had at least. She was doing a bit of high-pitched yodelling herself.

We wanted to hear some more country music so we went to the pub. Okay, I tell a lie—we wanted to drink some beer. Caz took the yodeller to bed while the rest of my posse mosied on down to the Tamworth RSL (Returned & Services League) club. The place was packed with people wearing hats playing pokies. A band was playing a song called 'We Know What You Do On The Weekends. You Drink Tequila Cos You're The Queen Of The Trailer Park'. Country music may be a bit samey and whiny but, gee, some of the songs have wonderful titles. Another of my favourites is 'I've Never Gone To Bed With An Ugly Woman, But I Sure As Hell Have Woken Up With A Few'. Another I like is 'I Don't Know Whether To Kill Myself Or Go Bowling'.

On our way to the RSL I told Chris that I had appointed him my manager.

'Okay,' he said.

'There's one small problem, though,' I added. 'You'll need a hat.'

•

I was so excited the next morning that I got up early. Well, okay, Jasmine woke up early and got everyone else up. After going for a walk, then pottering around the room for two hours, I decided to get some practice in. Halfway through my first song there was a loud banging on the wall from next door. That was followed by an even louder, 'Shut the fuck up!'

'I'm not that bad, am I?' I whimpered to Natalie.

'It's still only eight o'clock in the morning!' she whispered.

Oops.

We made our way to Pixie's Big Breakfast Cabaret for an 'All-you-can-eat $8.95 breakfast'. A massive circus tent had been set up next to the Tamworth RSL. There were a few hundred (mostly old) folk sitting at long tables near the stage. Everyone was clapping and hollering along with Pixie, which seemed like a bit too much frivolity for eight-thirty in the morning. Pixie was a fiddler (and a pretty good one, too). He was fiddlin' standard fiddlin' stuff like 'The Devil Went Down To Georgia'. After listening to the third fiddlin' song, though, it did become a tad tedious. Mind you, if you're heavily into fiddlin' you could always go to the world's biggest Fiddlers Festival in Galax, Virginia. Every August, over 2000 fiddlers fiddle for four days straight. It could be a lot worse, though. And I know. I once attended (well, more like I was dragged to) a Middle Ages Music Festival in Melbourne. It was full of middle-aged people listening to harpsichords and other instruments that made me want to joust with someone—preferably one of the musicians. Almost as torturous would be the Polka Festival held in Tabor, South Dakota, every July. They promise you will listen to 'some of the hottest polka in the nation' (isn't that an oxymoron?). However, the real jewel in the 'get me the hell outta here' music festival stakes is the Swiss Yodelling Festival—which is not held in Switzerland. The world's largest yodelling festival takes place in that other well-known international yodelling hot spot—Salt Lake City, Utah. Over 1000 Mormon yodellers take part. That wouldn't just drive you to drink, you'd be calling for a general anaesthetic.

While we queued for our 'All-you-can-eat $8.95 breakfast' (which seemed to consist mostly of baked beans), Pixie—who had stopped fiddlin' for a second—told us that Tchaikovsky was a poof.

On the way into town we passed a hat shop. Chris bought a large black one. 'Now do I look like a manager?' he asked.

'You look like a cattle rustler,' I said. 'But that's close enough.'

It was only ten in the morning, but the mercury had already crept up into the mid-thirties. I had planned on wearing jeans and boots with my black satin shirt, but, with the onset of the stifling heat, I had opted for boardies and thongs instead. I now looked like a cross between Elvis Presley, Slim Dusty and one of the Beach Boys.

The girls headed for an air-conditioned café while I dragged Chris through town to the *Northern Daily Reader* offices to register for busking (I had rung them a couple of weeks earlier and they had told me I could still register as late as the opening day).

'Do I really need to go?' Chris moaned. He quite liked the sound of the air-conditioned café.

'Yes,' I said. 'You're my manager.' If I told him how much Colonel Tom Parker made out of managing Elvis, he might have been a bit keener. But somehow I didn't think my earnings as a busker would be able to support the two of us.

The offices were closed. Gee, it would have been nice of them to tell me that, although I could register up to the opening day, they were actually closed on Saturdays. It looked as if I was going to have to find my own spot on Peel Street.

'You haven't done a very good job,' I told my newly appointed manager as Peel Street was already abuzz. Every 10 metres or so there was someone busking. They all had elaborate set-ups, with amps, microphones, posters and their own CDs for sale. Some even had rugs and chairs set up in front of them. All I had was my guitar. Damn, if only I'd thought to bring our lounge suite . . .

We went for an exploratory stroll up the street to check out the competition and secure a good busking spot. The first fellow we passed was playing a song called 'Cheatin' Truck-driving Cowboy'. His name was 'Hank the Cowboy'. He had quite a pile of CDs, which his wife was selling from a coffee table next to him. He was already up to volume 10. Actually, it's not that odd (having lots of CDs, that is, not being called Hank the Cowboy). The Country & Western crowd are quite prolific. Just to put that in perspective, before his death last year, Slim Dusty released his 100th album. Gosh, that's a lot of cheatin'.

Set up next to Hank was a 10-year-old girl. She hadn't been in the game very long: she only had three CDs for sale and was singing along to a tape. Even though she had a microphone, you could barely hear her, but her hat was still full of money. Maybe I would do all right, after all.

I thought no one else would have had the brilliant idea of doing Elvis songs. Boy, was I wrong. The first 'Elvis' we saw was a bald guy with no teeth. He was singing 'Teddy Bear'. Just up from him was an Indonesian-looking fellow with stuck-on sideburns singing 'All Shook Up'. I should have known, though. I once read that Elvis impersonators are growing at such a rate that, by the year 2050, the entire population of the planet will be Elvis impersonators. The Indonesian guy finished his song and said, 'Sank you, sank you very much.'

I couldn't find a free spot anywhere. We crossed the street to try the other side. Ron and Ray, dressed in matching shirts and hats, were having a break and sitting down smoking cigarettes. Their ashtray was overflowing (they smoked a cigarette after *every* song).

'How ya doin'?' I asked. They were both 79 years old and had been coming to Tamworth for nine years.

'We took up singing at seventy,' Ray told me. They had four CDs for sale.

Next to Ron and Ray was an entire family. Mum and dad were singing while their four kids (aged between 7 and 12) were line dancing. I made a mental note to call Child Welfare: what they were doing to those poor kids was a crime.

I finally found a spot and it was quite a good one, too. I set up (well, I took my guitar out of its case and put the case on the ground in front of me). I was the only person in the entire street that didn't have an amp. My first song (I only had six, by the way. I was going to repeat the same set over and over) was 'Blue Moon Of Kentucky'. Blue moons were a bit of a theme I had going. I was also doing 'When My Blue Moon Turns To Gold'. Naturally, I had to throw in one 'losin' loved ones' song so I had learnt 'I'm Left, You're Right, She's Gone'. Elvis had some great song titles. They were mostly shite songs from his films, but they had good titles nevertheless. He sang his way through 'Song Of The Shrimp', 'There's No Room To Rhumba In A Sports Car' and the particularly poignant 'Yoga Is As Yoga Does'.

I had almost made it to the end of 'Blue Moon Of Kentucky' when a bunch of bad-arses on Harleys noisily (and I mean *fucking* noisily) pulled up in front of me. I was standing at the pick-up spot for 'Harley Rides'. They then sat there idling, waiting for their next fare. I could have, and may as well have, been singing 'Harley Riders Are A Bunch Of Big Girly Pansies' for all anyone could hear me.

Things took a more hopeful turn when I found an ideal position right in front of the ANZ bank. After I wowed the crowd with my six songs I had a rest.

'I'm doing all right! Did you see the crowd?' I gushed to the girls, who'd turned up as I was finishing my set.

'I think they're queuing for the ATM, dear,' Natalie said.

Okay, she was right. I didn't have one single cent in my guitar case and not one single person had even glanced at me.

My second set (which was a repeat of the first set) fared even worse. The ATM queue had disappeared, so there was no one there at all now. It was then that Natalie had a brilliant (although potentially putting-us-under-the-scrutiny-of-Child-Welfare) idea. She put Jasmine in the guitar case. As soon my little girl was seated she started dancing and clapping along to my singing. Almost instantly, a crowd began to gather. They would walk past and ignore me as per usual, then suddenly spot Jasmine and stop dead in their tracks. Cameras and videos came out and, best of all, people started throwing money. One lady walked up and put $2 in the case and said, 'It's for the baby, not you.' Jasmine loved it. She lapped up the attention. She was now singing along—well, more like gurgling along. I finished my set to rapturous applause (although everyone was looking at Jasmine).

I (um . . . I mean, Jasmine) made $9.45—just enough to buy my lunch. After a focaccia in a trendy café (which had a John Denver tribute band playing), the girls headed back to the motel pool, taking my star attraction along with them.

I thought I'd have one more bash at the solo thing and hit the streets again. We (my dutiful manager and I) passed one busker who also had a gimmick. He had a chicken standing on his head. Another chicken was standing on a table next to him (they must take turns doing shifts on his head). I later read that he went a step further in the gimmick stakes and married the two chickens off. Apparently, hundreds of onlookers watched as the feathery nuptials took place.

A good spot was still hard to find. Every nook and cranny of Peel Street had someone singing, strumming, plucking, fiddling, dancing, whipping (some guy was doing strange things with a bullwhip) or talking—a handful of 'Bush Poets' were waxing lyrical about sunburnt deserts and big blue skies with some cheatin' thrown in for good measure.

'Maybe I could do that,' I pointed out to Chris. 'How about this: There once was a man from Horsham, who took out his balls to warsh 'em. His mum said: Jack, if you don't put 'em back, I'll take out a hammer and squorsh 'em.'

A bit further down the street we spotted the first busker (besides me) who didn't have an amp. He was sitting on a stool playing his acoustic guitar so softly that you'd have to be sitting on his knee to hear him. Then it clicked who it was—Monty, the ex-weatherman from the 'Today' show. He gave me a big smile and waved us over. I was almost going to say, 'Didn't you used to be Monty?' but instead I said, 'Hi, how's it going?'

'We are the only ones in the entire street without an amp!' he squeaked.

'We don't have any CDs for sale, either,' I added.

'Are you part of the act?' he said to Chris.

'No. I'm his manager.'

Monty looked very impressed. As we walked away a couple sat down next to him and the bloke said, 'Didn't you used to be Monty?'

'Fuck it,' I said to Chris. 'Let's go to the pub.' It was too hot, too hard to find a decent busking spot, and—who was I kidding?—I was nothing without Jasmine.

There was more country music in the pub (funny, that). A very large girl was singing that her boyfriend (Snowy, the guitarist in the band) was very well hung. We grabbed a beer and moved to the beer garden. Just as we were sitting down, we overheard a fellow with a Spanish accent chatting up a woman old enough to be his mum. 'Enough of thees talking,' he said, 'let's go fuck.' When she stormed off, he turned around to chat to us. His name was Jaime and he was from Chile. He, too, was a busker and played Chilean Country & Western music (whatever that was). Jaime had certainly mastered the art of cussin'. In the five minutes he spent talking to us, he told us the following people were cunts: the police, the army, Catholics, Jews and Argentinians.

When Jaime left to do some more talking (or fucking—whichever came first), I hauled out my *Official Guide to Tamworth* to find out who we could go to see play. Just about everyone, by the look of it: between midday and five o'clock alone, there were 94 different acts performing around town. All up, 285 acts would be on a stage somewhere during the day (and night). Among them were countless tribute bands: John Denver, Garth Brooks, Dolly Parton (we contemplated seeing that one—just for the singing, of course), Willie Nelson and Johnny Cash. There were some great bands' names, too, including The Toe Sucking Cowgirls, SNACs (Sensitive New Age Cowboys), Fat Men Don't Line Dance, Drunk But Not Intoxicated and, my favourite, Spurs for Jesus. Oddly, there was a plethora of Cashes. Johnny must have had a big family. There was Joanne Cash, Sam Cash, Davey Cash, The Cash Boys and Bobby Cash.

'I saw Bobby Cash sing on the 'Today' show,' Chris said. 'He's the most popular Country & Western singer in India.'

'What was he like?' I asked.

'Um, not bad. He sang a bit of a song in Hindi as well.'

'How'd that sound?'

'Pretty terrible.'

'Let's go see him then.'

Bobby was playing in two hours' time at the imaginatively named The Pub on Goonoo Goonoo Road (I kid you not) on the outskirts of town. In the car on the way there we tried to guess what songs he would be playing. We came up with these:

'Take Me Home Country Road, To The Place I Belong, West Pinjabi'

'The Curry Of The County'

'Oh, Give Me A Home Where The Sacred Cows Roam'

'Thank God I'm A Hindi Boy'

Bobby was sitting outside in the beer garden (well, I assumed it was Bobby— he *was* Indian and he *was* holding a guitar). We introduced ourselves ('I'm busking and this is my manager').

'I hear you're the most popular Country & Western singer in India,' I said.

'That's because, out of one billion people, I'm the only one,' he laughed.

Quite a crowd had gathered to watch him play, including a dozen or so who were either members of his family or his fan club from India. Even though it was probably close to 40 degrees, they were wearing slacks and long-sleeved polyester shirts. Bobby sang like Glen Campbell (which was impressive, because when he spoke he had an Indian accent). He even had the country drawl thang going. His first song was about how he was going to quit drinkin' and quit cheatin'. Chris was right, though. When he sang a song in Hindi, it sounded terrible. And thankfully he never did sing 'Thank God I'm A Hindi Boy'.

.

We met the girls back at the motel and headed out to dinner. I'd seen a poster up in the motel advertising a steak and ribs place that, because of its fantastic name, we had to visit. The only trouble is I've forgotten what it was called. I thought I'd written the name down, but I hadn't. I'm not joking, it was something like The Good Ol' Boys Yee-ha Bar and Grill Barn. Maybe not that, but similar. It looked like a barn (with straw on the floor), and the ribs and steak were piled so high on my plate that they touched the rim of my hat. I couldn't even look at the bowl of coleslaw. I did finish the fries, though. I can always polish off fries, even when my stomach pleads with me to stop eating.

Weighed down with a few kilos of meat (and fries), we waddled over to Peel Street. There were still a few buskers about, including one bloke who'd been in the same spot since ten that morning. He'd been strumming away for almost 12 hours (he sure wasn't going to lose his place).

The busking scene was a bit more subdued at night. There was a fellow gently plucking a mandolin, another on a violin and an old bloke with a karaoke machine softly singing some Kenny Rogers song. A band of young guys with long greasy hair and ripped jeans were setting up their amps, drum kit and mike stands. 'That's nice,' I said. 'Young fellows like that playing Country & Western music.' When they started playing they almost blew me over. They were deafening—and definitely not Country & Western. It was hardcore thrash. They were singing (well, screaming) about 'Destroying everything (and everyone)'. The noise reverberated up the entire street. The old bloke with the karaoke machine kept on singing. He was oblivious to the fact that he was getting totally and utterly drowned out by 'DESTROY, DESTROY, DESTROY!!'

We ended the night at the Tamworth *East* RSL. A band was playing upstairs in the nightclub to a packed crowd that were *all* boisterously singing along to a song I'd never heard before. A cute girl walked up to me and said, 'Hi, you're not a local, are you?'

'Um . . . no,' I said.

'Locals don't wear their hats in nightclubs,' she explained.

•

The next morning we were all a little grumpy and tired. Jasmine had been restless all night and had woken up just about every hour, on the hour. 'She's got performance anxiety,' Natalie said.

We contemplated another breakfast extravaganza (besides 'Pixie's Big Breakfast Cabaret' there was also the choice of 'Jim Hayne's Big Bush Brekky', 'Big Barry's Bluegrass Breakfast' and 'Freddy's Fiddlin' Fry-up for Fat Fuckers'—sorry, I made that last one up), but I really needed a wee break from country music. We'd listened to it almost non-stop since we'd arrived. Not only were there bands and performers playing *everywhere*, but there was country music blasting out in taxis, cafés and the corridors of our motel, on every single radio station, and even in the public toilets (try doing a crap to 'Am I Not Pretty Enough'). Thus we were found 15 minutes later in a café playing some soothing cool jazz. Then again, a day of listening to Country & Western music would be heaven compared to the All-Night Gospel Singing Festival held in Bonifay, Florida. Over 10 000 bible-belting songsters sing along to groups like The Gospel Enforcers. But wait, it gets worse. This goes on (and boy would it go on) for 24 hours. Non-stop. Pass me the drugs, please. Personally, I'd much prefer to go to the Trance Music Festival held in Essaouria in Morocco. The music may be shite and go on for a couple of days, but at least you would be in a trance so you'd miss most of it anyway. They have quite the opposite problem at the Lower Keys Underwater Music Festival held (er . . . underwater) in Florida. You'd get very wrinkly skin if you stayed too long. Apparently, sound travels through water four times as fast as air and people dive or snorkel around underwater listening to such bands as The Snorkelling Elvises (I told you—they're taking over the world).

Being underwater sounded like a lovely idea at that particular moment. It was only nine-thirty, but it was already 36 degrees outside. I tried to talk my manager into finding a busking spot for me while I sat in the air-conditioned café, but he told me to fuck off (a sacking could be on the cards, I thought). I trudged up the street in search of that elusive spot. Buskers were out in force again. Ron and Ray looked like they were just about to expire. Only Ron was singing. Ray was already onto her 14th cigarette for the day.

I eventually found a spot and rushed back to get my star. I plonked Jasmine down in the case again, but this time round the jaded veteran wasn't interested in performing. She didn't dance. She didn't clap. In fact, she kept trying to crawl out of the case. We really would have Child Welfare after us now. It was dangerously hot and I was trying to get my 11-month-old baby to perform circus tricks for money.

'Do you know why she won't perform?' Caz said. 'Because yesterday *she* made all the money and *you* kept it.'

Well, we weren't making any money today. I was hoping it was going to pay for my breakfast. We made 50 cents (and that was only because the person who threw it in felt sorry for Jasmine). That wouldn't even cover my orange juice.

The heat was stifling. Before Child Welfare turned up, we decided to escape to the only air-conditioned place not playing country music: the Grace Bros department store. It was wonderfully quiet and wonderfully cool. We found some seats next to Women's Apparel and (literally) chilled out. All of a sudden, our blissful oasis was interrupted by the sound of a band starting up—playing, you guessed it, country music. Behind Women's Apparel, and next to Manchester, was a large stage and The Anne Conway Country Music Show. Quite a crowd (mostly old folk escaping the heat) had gathered and were sitting in lines of plastic chairs. And do you know what? I loved it. The young band (not including Anne Conway, who was the host) were actually quite good and played quite a few Eagles songs (I was a huge Eagles fan when I was a teenager—can we just keep that between you and me, though, if you don't mind?). Chris had to leave to get back to Sydney (he had some big record deals to broker), but we were content to stay in Grace Bros till we had to leave for the airport at three-thirty. Anyway, they a had a nice sandwich bar and I was more than happy to watch the next act—a cute 21-year-old girl who kept wiggling her bottom.

Walking out of the store was like walking into an oven. The temperature gauge at the post office was sitting on a fry-your-bottom-off 42 degrees. Yet, here's the remarkable thing, people were line dancing in the middle of the street. In the full sun. The heat would be killing brain cells by the minute (which was probably what got them into line dancing in the first place, when I think about it).

•

'How'd you go?' the bloke at the airport check-in asked me.

'Not bad,' I said.

'So, did you have a good time?'

'Yeah, it was great!' And I meant it too. I might not have come away a total C&W convert, but I'd quite warmed to the friendly locals, the beer, the buzz and even some of the music.

'Um, there's a problem with your ticket,' the check-in bloke said. 'It's for tomorrow afternoon, not today.'

Oh, shit. I'm hopeless. I'd booked the flights on the internet and, somehow (probably connected to the fact that I'm hopeless), I'd got the date wrong. 'This flight is full, too,' he added.

Caz and Natalie gave me a look that could only be described as icy. You know how I just said I was warming to country music? Well, that's true, but after spending every waking hour for two days listening to it, I couldn't possibly do another day.

'Can we get a stand-by?' I stammered. 'My wife will divorce me if we don't get on.'

'I can only try,' he said.

Thankfully my marriage was saved and we were squeezed onto the flight. We did almost lose Jasmine, though. We found her crawling out of the terminal, on her way back to Tamworth. She was looking for another guitar case to hop into. One whose owner would let her keep the money.

Tet (Lunar New Year)

Ho Chi Minh City, Vietnam
January 31st

Tet is New Year's Eve, Christmas Day and every single person in Vietnam's birthday all rolled into 24 hours of feasting, drinking and making as much noise as is humanly possible. It is the most important and sacred date in the Vietnamese calendar because locals believe that the first day of the New Year determines your fortune for the rest of the year.

Fortune was certainly on my side when I was invited to the home of a Vietnamese family to celebrate this extraordinary day. Unfortunately, however, there was a good chance I would be eating such delicacies as cauliflower fried with pig's skin, dried turnips soaked in fish sauce and pig's head meat pies. I'd also have to share these tasty delights, not just with the living Vietnamese family, but with their deceased family members as well. Dead ancestors are invited along as special guests. Apparently, the Kitchen God would be making a brief visit, too. That's all right, he could have my cauliflower fried with pig's skin.

In Vietnam, the week leading up to Tet is called *Tat Nien*: a time 'to extinguish the year'. A lot of peculiar rituals and events take place over this time and I was keen to experience them before flying into Ho Chi Minh City where I would join my Vietnamese hosts for Tet.

Seven days before Tet

I arrived in Vietnam just in time to witness the start of the Kitchen God's journey to heaven. He gets there by hitching a ride on the back of a carp. On this day, people all over Vietnam release live carp into rivers and lakes so the Kitchen God can ascend to the heavenly palace to report to the Jade Emperor on the affairs of the household. The Kitchen God is privy to the family's most intimate business and domestic secrets for the ending year. That's all very well, but does he help with the dishes?

As soon as I stepped out of the taxi into the bustling streets of Hoi An I fell hopelessly in love with the place. I fell hopelessly in love a dozen more times as I went in search of a hotel. Young Vietnamese women with high cheekbones and long dark hair, dressed in traditional *ao dai* (long flowing tunics of fabric worn over pairs of loose-fitting white pants) almost knocked me over with their bicycles and their beauty. One deliciously gorgeous girl even tried to chat me up. Well, sort of—she actually stopped to try and talk me into going to her aunt's tailor shop.

Hoi An was simply enchanting. Not much of the town has changed since it was built in the 19th century. It was once one of

Southeast Asia's largest ports, but when Da Nang took over as the area's main trading destination, Hoi An returned to its peaceful backwater existence. The majority of the simple wooden buildings are shops or restaurants now, but there are still hand-painted silk lanterns hanging from dark, oily timber beams outside. Inside, the weathered timber floors slope unevenly as if rolling over a gentle sea.

After checking into a simple riverfront guesthouse, set snug against the bridge over the Thu Bon River, I went for a wander in the bright sunshine. The fishing boats were out to sea, but a few women were propelling crude, flat timber boats upriver with bamboo poles. Their faces were shaded, hidden by conical straw hats. I walked past all the riverfront restaurants till I was on a track that meandered through tall reeds right on the river's edge. Alas, luck was not with me; I didn't see a single carp (or Kitchen God for that matter) being launched on its celestial journey. I did see quite a few carp, though. They just happened to be headless and lying on plates in the market ready to be launched on a culinary journey. More women in conical hats were squatting in a quagmire of water, guts, fish bones and blood, selling their catch by the waterfront. Each woman had a single plate set on the ground and, by the look of it, some had not seen much action with the hook that morning. Among the offerings was a plate of fish heads. As I was eyeing them off, the lady kindly offered to sell me some: 'You want?'

'No, thanks,' I said. 'I'm right for fish heads at the moment.'

One woman had caught only one fish, so to make it look like more, she had cut it up into slices and spread them out evenly on the plate. Even so, there sure was a lot of carp for sale. Carp, I imagine, that had probably been released upstream earlier in the day. Which meant, of course, that the Jade Emperor wouldn't get those all-important reports and the family would have bad luck for the coming year. Gee, I hope the fish-head soup was worth a year of heart-break, financial ruin and damnation for some poor family.

I dropped into the tailor shop, which I'd promised to visit to get a shirt made. It was squashed in among lines and lines of identical shops and they were all selling tailored shirts, suits and 'Good Morning Vietnam' T-shirts.

The gorgeous girl I'd met earlier, whose name was Giang, kept saying, 'You are a very handsome man,' and rubbing my hand.

'I only want *one* shirt,' I whimpered. I ended up ordering four. Any more rubbing and I would have bought the shop.

After exceeding her sales quota for the day, Giang kindly took me to her friend's restaurant on the waterfront for lunch. I was so looking forward to my first meal in Vietnam, but I have to admit I was little worried when we stepped inside. We were the only diners and the waitress looked a little *too* surprised to have someone to serve. That tends not to be a good sign. As it turned out, I wasn't disappointed at all. I somehow managed to devour an entire plate of delicately made fried won tons followed by some sort of chicken dish with lemongrass served, still sizzling, on a banana leaf. It was a veritable feast. Best of all, it only cost me $2. Giang was a cheap date, too. She only had a juice. That came to the bank-breaking total of 21 cents.

Afterwards, as I sat feeling bloated with beer in hand, Giang moaned about the age-old problem of buying gifts for the family. 'I have many presents to buy and I leave tomorrow back to my village,' she said. Like most Vietnamese Giang had been saving for Tet for months.

'Why don't you just give them all "Good Morning Vietnam" T-shirts?' I suggested.

'No, all my family want is wine and whisky.'

After I left the restaurant, I saw plenty of bottles of wine for sale in the street. Each bottle had an entire snake in it (I'm hazarding a guess they were dead). Temporary shops were set up everywhere around town selling snake wine and all sorts of other tipples. Each and every bottle was wrapped in red cellophane with 'Chúc Mùng Nam Mói' (Happy New Year) printed on it. That very traditional Vietnamese company Coca-Cola had also jumped on the Tet bandwagon. Special cans had been made for the occasion with 'Chúc Mùng Nam Mói' emblazoned across the can.

'Hey, you want postcard?' A boy of about 10 had sidled up beside me on a pushbike and shoved a pile of tacky postcards in my face.

'No, thanks,' I said. 'I'm right for tacky postcards at the moment.' Then I had an idea. 'But . . . can I hire your bike for the afternoon?'

'Yes, okay,' he said without hesitation. 'Um . . . it cost you one thousand dong.' Now he had a hopeful maybe-I-can-fleece-him look in his eye.

'Sure,' I said and handed him 1000 dong. His eyes lit up. He'd just made the deal of his life. So had I. One thousand dong is about 12 cents.

Speaking of money, I have to say it's pretty hard to take a currency seriously when it has a name like dong. To be fair, though, Vietnam isn't the only country with seriously silly sounding currency. In Zambia people walk around with ngwees in their wallet. In Gambia they have bututs, in Guatemala it's quetzals, Malawians hand over kwachas and the folk in Costa Rica have piles of colons (bad pun intended). Mind you, a currency doesn't need to have a silly name to be treated as a joke. Look at the New Zealand dollar.

I devoted the afternoon to riding idly around the suburbs of Hoi An having a good old-fashioned stickybeak. I love to observe how local people live, play, eat, work, relax and watch TV (everyone everywhere watches lots of TV). I was having a little trouble with the bike, though. My wife says I look like Kermit the Frog any time I ride a bike. Well, I certainly did now. My knobbly knees were poking right out (it *was* a 10-year-old's bike) and I had to pedal like mad to get anywhere. Even then, I was barely moving. Luckily, I was quite happy to make slow progress along streets lined with square concrete houses that had been painted in fantastic shades of periwinkle and aquamarine, as the houses were ideal for stickybeaking. They had wide wooden shutters in the front that were opened to reveal simply furnished interiors and more open shutters at the back of the house to let the cooling air pass through. In most of these homes, prominently displayed smack in the middle of the living room, was a kumquat tree in a pot. This is a New Year's tree or *cay neu*, which is a bit like our Christmas tree—but without the angel on top. It is used to ward off evil spirits and is decorated with the same cheap Chinese-made tinsel we buy and use. And, just as our wealthier citizens do at Christmas, the cashed-up Vietnamese had gee-look-how-wealthy-we-are-because-we-can-afford-this massive trees.

When I returned a few hours later, my entrepreneurial little mate was waiting for me. 'So,' he said, 'now you want postcard?'

•

Later that afternoon I met up with a bloke called Nick. A fellow Melbourne boy, he is the co-owner of Hai's Scout Café, one of the most popular cafés in town. Nick is one of those friend of a friend's of a friend's grandma's cat's friend. I always feel a touch of trepidation when someone tells me: 'It's okay, he'd *love* to have you as a guest.' Anyway, it was better than okay; Nick was the perfect host. Even if he did try and get me killed. Twice.

The first time was on Nick's moped. I sat on the back. 'Hold on tight,' Nick said. I sure did. He rode like a real local: very fast, slightly out of control and always honking the horn. Not to mention constantly looking back over his shoulder to chat to me. I was quite relieved when we stopped at a simple roadside café. And when I say simple, I mean simple. There were a few old tables and a collection of mix-and-unmatch chairs. A small gas stove was set up in the middle of the footpath. This was just one of many identical street cafés found on most of the street corners.

'I've tried 'em all,' Nick said. 'And this one is the best.'

We each ordered a plate of *cao lau*, the local speciality. Not that we had a lot of choice, mind you—it was the only thing on the menu. Two minutes later I was handed a plate piled high with steaming noodles, pork slices, bean sprouts, coriander and all sorts of other leafy green stuff I couldn't identify. It wasn't just the best street-stall food I'd tried; it was the best Vietnamese food I'd ever eaten.

'Do you want another plate?' Nick mumbled through a mouthful of noodles.

'Erggh,' I groaned. I was full. 'Yeah, okay.' What the heck, I thought. It was not only delicious, it was less than a dollar a plate.

Hoi An's main park had been taken over by a B-grade carnival for Tet celebrations. It was filled with scary kids' rides (as in scary because they all looked as if they could fall apart any minute). There was also an impressive collection of sideshow amusements (including a hoop-throwing game where the lucky winner won an *entire* bottle of water) and, tucked in the corner, a stage where a band was playing to a packed crowd of teenagers. The band was sort of Duran Duran meets Engelbert Humperdinck: three guys playing keyboards, all with dodgy eighties' New Wave suits and haircuts, each playing a totally different tune, while the Vietnamese Engelbert crooned softly along to a tune of his own.

For a B-grade carnival, it had a lot of very satisfied customers. In the beer garden, set up smack in the middle of the kiddies' rides, everyone looked deliriously happy. Or very pissed. To continue the kiddie theme, everyone was sitting on kindergarten furniture—it looked as if the finger-painting class was just about to start. We found two tiny vacant chairs at a tiny table already occupied by two blitheringly drunken locals. Not that they stood out at all, mind you. *Everyone* was blithering drunk.

'The locals stay pissed for the entire week of Tet,' Nick shouted into my ear over loud Vietnamese pop music, which was being produced by a suave looking dude singing along to a backing tape. It was a wonder people had managed to get pissed at all—they were all throwing copious amounts of beer over each other.

The most beautiful 'beer maids' hovered around the perimeter of the beer garden, ready to pounce and top up any drink that had more than a sip taken out of it. It was a very warm night and the beer was also very warm, so the beer maids were unceremoniously throwing large blocks of ice into the glass with each refill.

Our blithering new friends kept offering us snacks, including snails and a delicacy that unnervingly looked like rabbit droppings on a stick. They also repeatedly screamed out '*Yo!*' ('Cheers!' in Vietnamese) and pushed our glasses to our mouths to make us skol, then laughed their heads off like a pair of lunatics. In fact, everyone was screaming out '*Yo!*' so much that I felt as if I was at a New York rappers' convention (albeit one held at the East Brooklyn kindergarten). I had to stop myself from shouting, 'Yo, motherfucker!'

It was at this point that Nick tried to get me killed for the second time. One of our—formerly happy, but now mightily pissed off— new best buddies suddenly started slapping Nick in the face and screaming at him in Vietnamese. Nick tried to calm him down, but the fellow just got angrier. Now Nick is quite a big fellow but these blokes were not only pissed, they were a few won tons short of your full Vietnamese picnic.

'What's goin' on?' I stammered to Nick in a lull between slapping.

'They're pissed off because I speak Vietnamese,' he said. Gee, it was lucky that I hadn't used my full repertoire of Vietnamese—hello, goodbye, thank you, Happy New Year and the names of a few assorted dishes—or I'd be getting a slapping, too.

'Yeah, but what were you saying in Vietnamese?' I asked.

'Nothing!' he said as he took another slap to the head.

I'm guessing it was more than nothing. These guys weren't happy. I'm pretty sure he wasn't complimenting them on their stylish polyester jackets.

It was when the guy stood up and took off his stylish polyester jacket that Nick motioned subtly to me that we get the fuck outta there.

We made our way to the other side of the beer garden, where we bumped into Nick's business partner Hai and a couple of his friends. Nick rushed off to the loo while I downed a beer in one gulp. I was just about to explain to Hai what had happened when our drunken, angry friend staggered over and shook hands with Hai. They chatted in Vietnamese for a minute (well, the guy shouted and Hai talked), then the drunk guy tottered off back to his mate.

'Do you know him?' I asked incredulously.

'Yeah, he's a dickhead I went to school with.'

'What did he say?'

'He said that there was a westerner here who he really hates.' I was just about to explain that the dickhead was talking about his business partner Nick, when Hai laughed and said, 'I told him that he should kill him.'

Hai may not have been entirely sober.

'He was talking about Nick!' I said.

'Ohhh fuck!'

Nick returned just as our drunken friend staggered over again. He had a scary, deranged look in his eyes. Oh fuck all right. He was going to kill Nick. He lunged at him, but—quite spectacularly—fell forward as stiffly as a board, with his arms still at his side. His head made a loud (and very impressive) THWACK! as it hit the edge of the plastic kindergarten table. As he lay collapsed in a heap on the ground, I noticed a huge and horrible red line had already appeared on his forehead. But now *I* was angry. The bugger had knocked over all our beers.

We left him lying on the ground and, before the Tet Offensive could start again, staggered back to Nick and Hai's café. We ended the night lying back in lounge chairs listening to Hai play his guitar and sing beautiful, melodic Vietnamese love songs. Or he could have been singing in English. I don't know. I'd had about a dozen whiskies by then.

Six days before Tet

Just what I needed to see (and smell) with a terrible hangover: severed pigs' heads covered in blood and flies. I had inadvertently wandered into the severed pigs' heads (and other odd chunks of meat) section of the market and spent the next five minutes trying to hold back a good chuck while fighting my way through the crowds to get out. The market was filled with people in a Tet-inspired buying frenzy. Locals were weighed down with huge baskets filled with all types of food, and bags stuffed with presents and new clothes (as part of starting the New Year afresh, everyone buys new clothes to wear on

New Year's Day). The market was absolutely frantic and I loved it—even if my aching head (and dodgy stomach) didn't.

I love markets. I make a point of trying to do a bit of aimless wandering through markets in every city I visit. You really get a feel for a city and its culture by walking around watching people buy severed pigs' heads (or whatever tickles the locals' fancy).

A large section of the Hoi An market was ablaze with red and gold decorations on sale for Tet. Competing for attention were stalls selling 'Chúc Mùng Nam Mói' cards, wrapping paper, calendars, banners, plates, cups and, oddly enough, piles of posters of Vietnamese pop bands (all of whom looked like the Vietnamese version of Backstreet Boys). The stalls were also doing a thriving trade in 'lucky money envelopes'. These miniature red envelopes are stuffed with 'lucky money' (*li xi*) and are given out to children and old folk on Tet eve. The colour red brings good luck and new paper money brings prosperity. I bought a pack of ten for my visit to the Vietnamese family in Ho Chi Minh City.

In my half hour of aimless wandering around the market, different stallholders asked me very nicely if I would like to buy a large bag of coriander, a plastic bucket and a machete.

'You want?' asked a man who insisted on waving the machete in front of my face.

'No, thanks,' I said. 'I'm right for dangerous weapons at the moment.'

On my way out I almost got knocked over by a woman on a bicycle with half-a-dozen live chickens hanging from the handlebars. Mind you, for chickens that would inevitably end up boiling in a pot they looked quite happy. Maybe they were just relieved they weren't black chickens at the Market Festival held in Bac Ninh province in February. According to tradition, *everyone* must buy a black chicken and chop off its head. Ducks have a slight advantage in the survival stakes at a similar festival, which is also held in February. It's called the Duck Chasing Festival. The ducks have one up on the black chickens because they get a head start before they're caught and given the chop. For those vegetarians among you who find all this abhorrent, there is always the not-quite-as-cruel Soft Noodle Festival held around the same time. At least the soft noodles would be easy to catch.

I took a bus trip to visit My Son. This is a little known fact, but I sired a child during my tour of duty in the Vietnam War and . . . Sorry, I couldn't help myself there. My Son is actually a collection of ancient ruins that the Americans managed to ruin even more. My Son was the site of one of the most important intellectual and religious centres in Asia and some of the monuments date back to the 4th century. Still, that didn't stop the Americans using it for bombing practice. I spent most of my time there trying in vain to imagine the pile of rubble as a grand monument, but still had quite a pleasant day frolicking around the verdant valley and napping by a cool, clear stream.

I returned refreshed and ready for whatever death-defying stunts Nick had in store for me. Thankfully, on this occasion he didn't try and get me killed. He only tried to do my back in. We went to his apartment on the outskirts of Hoi An so I could help him lug his large kumquat tree (sitting in an even larger ceramic pot) up two flights of stairs. When we finally had the tree in prime position on the top balcony and I stood doubled over, groaning and clutching my back, Nick said, 'I've got another one we have to move at the café. It's . . . a bit bigger.' A bit bigger, all right. It wasn't dissimilar in size to the Christmas tree they erect each year in front of the Rockefeller Center in New York.

What made our arduous task even more, well, arduous was that the Vietnamese staff in the café couldn't stop laughing at us. At first I thought they were chuckling at our pathetic huffing and puffing as we tried to manoeuvre the tree into position. But, no, it was the kumquat tree. It sagged terribly to one side. Nick had bought a dud.

'How much did you pay?' Hai asked Nick.

'I'm not telling.' Nick grunted.

Later on, Nick told me confidentially how much he paid. Later still, Hai told me how much he *should* have paid. Nick was (how can I say this nicely?) ripped off blind. Poor Nick. As an outsider, he was just trying to be a part of the whole Tet thing—even if he did have a terrible sagging problem.

Nick's friend Tí was joining us for dinner. 'G'day, mate!' Tí said as he shook my hand. Tí had studied at Adelaide University for four years, doing Bioeconomics (or something just as impressive). But he missed home, so he came back to Hoi An to work with his dad in the family clothes store—explaining to him, I imagine, how Bioeconomics could do amazing things to his genetically modified fiscal gross yield.

'I'll take you to the best hot pot spot in Hoi An,' Tí told us excitedly.

Except it wasn't in Hoi An. We rode for 30 minutes in the dark to a restaurant seemingly in the middle of nowhere. The waitresses were quite surprised to see a couple of westerners turn up and they all hovered around Nick and I taking it in turns to poke at our hairy arms and giggle. We were the only people eating. There were plenty of people inside, but they were almost all men drinking and gambling.

I ate so much of the hot pot it began to pour out of my ears. But I kept on eating. It was just sensational. A large pot of clear tasty broth, set on a tiny gas stove, bubbled away on our table as we added prawns, tuna, squid, mussels, vegetables and mountains of coriander. Whenever we finished we filled the pot and started again. Tí hardly ate any (so of course Nick and I had to take up the slack).

Tí said he was saving himself. 'I'll be force-fed a 10-course banquet every night for the next four days,' Tí groaned. 'Dad buys a huge pig and we eat the lot. For two days after Tet, I can't get off the bloody couch.' I ended up eating so much hot pot I was lucky to get out of my bloody chair.

Five days before Tet

I didn't need Nick to help kill me. I was more than capable of doing it myself. All I had to do was hire a moped. If you've read my second book, *Planes, Trains & Elephants* (I've heard it's a cracking read), you may remember that after I attempted to tear off my leg on a motorcycle I swore I would never hire one again. Well, I did—even though it wasn't technically a motorbike. It was a Minsk, a machine of dubious pedigree from that motorbike-manufacturing powerhouse Belarus. It was more like a noisy pushbike.

The reason I needed my Minsk was to visit a cemetery. In the week leading up to Tet, family members visit the graves of deceased relatives to invite them home for dinner. Gee, I wonder if they invite the fat aunt that always tried to tongue-kiss everyone . . . Live relatives at Christmas are bad enough, let alone a few smelly old ones. Before they do the actual inviting, though, the family gives the grave a good scrub—you don't want the dead rellies thinking you're neglecting their graves.

I rode out of Hoi An through narrow streets that smelt strongly of fresh paint. Indeed, every street smelt of paint. Out the front of most houses there was someone painting something—a fence, or wall, or door, or gate. One young guy had even painted his little sister. Inside each house there were people on their hands and knees scrubbing the floor while others swept every nook and cranny. One house even had all its furniture laid out in the front yard while they hosed out the rooms inside.

All this fastidious cleaning is part of that whole starting-the-New-Year-afresh thing. It also helped to explain why they were doing a roaring trade in mops at the market. I had just assumed that the Giant Stocktake-Clearance Mop Sale was on. Two boys rode past me on their bicycles. After giving me funny looks because I was going so slow, the youngest of the two asked me where I was going.

'You're going the wrong way,' he said in absolutely perfect English. 'I'll take you to a nice cemetery.' Há was 13 and wanted to be a tour guide when he grew up. 'I want to practise,' he said.

The cemetery *was* nice. Most of the graves had been freshly painted and cleaned. Some were still covered in dirt and grime, though. Either the people in them had no living relatives or they actually *were* those horrible aunts who tongue-kissed everyone.

'So, do your dead relatives visit for Tet dinner?' I asked Há.

'Yes.' He was very matter-of-fact about it.

'Do they eat much?'

'No, not much,' Há said quite seriously.

'What does your family do?'

'They just drink and play cards.'

'Do they eat much?'

'No,' Há shrugged.

'A bit like your dead relatives, then?'

'Yes.'

We left the cemetery and the boys rode along beside me, chatting. Há would make an excellent tour leader. He wouldn't shut up.

His friend didn't get a word in. In fact, he hadn't said a word the entire time. A big part of being a great tour leader, I told Há, is knowing where all the good local restaurants are. My ploy worked and Há took me to a good local restaurant. I followed them down a dirt track to where a small market was in full swing. On the side of the road was a ramshackle restaurant full of happy slurping people. I told the boys I'd buy them lunch. Há took this as a good opportunity to order absolutely everything on the menu. Plates kept coming out. Plates piled high with fried shrimp, boiled eggs, pickled beans, chicken wings, noodles, rice, steamed pork and some squashy brown stuff that tasted like squashy brown stuff. The whole banquet was under 10 dollars. The two cans of Red Bull the boys drank cost more than the entire food bill.

I headed for the beach as I needed to lie down for a bit. Every meal I'd eaten (er . . . gorged myself on) so far in Vietnam had been a gluttonous feast. At least I wouldn't turn into a fat bastard because Vietnamese food makes you poo a lot.

I crashed in one of the hundreds of rented deck chairs on the beach and tried to have a nap. Unfortunately, I was rudely interrupted every few minutes by women trying to sell me mangos or pineapples. That's just what I needed—more food.

·

I met Haí for dinner at his café. Nick was having dinner with his Vietnamese girlfriend.

'Nick's kumquat tree looks better,' I said. It was no longer sagging.

'Yeah, Nick re-potted it,' Haí grunted. He then went on to tell me a long-winded story about moving from your home to another country and how it takes a while to get used to your new home and you might feel tired and sometimes get sick. I had no idea what he was talking about. Then he finally explained, 'The fruit might fall off the tree, and if they do on Tet and hit the ground . . . it is *very* bad luck for our cafe.'

'What can you do?' I asked.

'It's okay. I have told Nick that he has to lie under the tree *all* day to catch any falling fruit.'

Four days before Tet

Why is it that whenever, and wherever, I sit on a bus, the person with the largest arse plops themselves next to me? On the way to My Son I had a six-foot American lady with a bottom that was six feet across sitting on me, and now I was getting crushed by an Englishman who obviously had huge trouble saying no to a second, third and fourth serving of bangers and mash. I had six hours of sandwiched thighs to put up with as the bus chugged its way north to the former imperial city of Hué. To make the journey even more unbearable, I made the terrible mistake of asking the Englishman where he had come from. For the next hour he rabbited on with every tiny detail of his crossing of the something or other border into somewhere or other—I'm not exactly sure what he was talking about, because after about two minutes my eyes glazed over. I'd nod now and again and grunt in agreement while I concentrated on looking out the window.

Not far out of Hoi An, we passed the first of many kumquat farms. Hundreds of ceramic pots, with perfectly pruned trees laden with orange fruit, were neatly lined up in front of each farmhouse ready to be hauled to market. Even though the windows of the bus were closed, I could smell the fragrance of the fruit.

A drizzly rain was falling as we drove into Hué. I checked into the first hotel I stumbled upon as I didn't fancy traipsing around in the rain to save a couple of bucks.

The rain had stopped by the time I left the hotel for a wander into town. Hué in the early evening was a city of lanterns, with cyclos (rickshaws), scooters and bicycles meandering three and four abreast down dimly lit, tree-lined streets. Within the brick walls of the citadel—the old moated city—families gathered under flickering neon lights to watch flickering televisions. And, oddly, people everywhere were lighting little fires in the street, burning piles of paper on the footpath, in gutters and even on doorsteps. Hué was also a city of petty arsonists.

After checking out the Forbidden Purple City (which was neither purple, a city nor forbidden—they allowed me in, after all), I ducked into the labyrinth of narrow lanes inside the citadel. Peeping into people's houses, I saw lots of card games going on and plenty of drinking. Tet celebrations were in full swing here.

I was squeezing down one impossibly narrow lane when I heard loud music and even louder out-of-tune singing. I peered through a small window into a tiny, dark and smoky room. A bunch of 20-somethings were crammed into the corner watching a large-screen TV and belting out a bit of karaoke (another favourite Tet activity). Before I knew it, the door was pulled open and I was dragged inside. A glass of beer was shoved into one hand and a piece of dried squid dipped in hot chilli paste into the other. The lads were well and truly pissed. Two large crates full of empty Huda beer bottles were ample proof of their consumption.

'You drink!' said the only fellow who seemed to speak a little English. I took a sip. 'No, no,' they chorused. They wanted me to skol. As soon as I downed the glass they handed me another. 'Drink!'

they chorused. After skolling three beers, I was handed the microphone. At least that gave me an excuse to put down the squid. It had the consistency of old shoes and tasted only slightly better.

Now I have to admit that I'm never shy when it comes to karaoke, so I was more than happy to sing. The list of songs to choose from was really quite incredible. Particularly for such a back-alley, toilet-sized operation. In fact, the song list was the biggest I'd ever seen in any karaoke bar—and, sadly, I've been in a few. I sang 'I Come From A Land Downunder' while the boys hollered and screamed along with no idea what they were singing. I sang song after song, and skolled beer after beer. I even had a go at a Vietnamese song—which made me sound like a chicken on heat. At one point I had a beer, a chunk of squid, a cigarette, the microphone and a copy of *Playboy* in my hands all at the same time.

Before I couldn't stand up any longer, I made motions to leave. After much protest, I was sent on my way with a handful of dried squid and hugs all round. I was seriously drunk and I'd only been there for just over an hour. I skipped dinner (dried squid tends to put you off other food) and staggered back to my hotel. On the way back, a street vendor tried to sell me some more dried squid.

'No, thanks,' I said. 'I'm right for old shoes at the moment.'

Three days before Tet

They must have funny perfume in Vietnam. At my hotel the previous night I'd booked a dragon boat trip up the Perfume River to visit the royal tombs. The Perfume River smelt like sewage. Thankfully, after leaving the centre of Hué, the river opened up and a pleasant breeze (and smell) drifted over us. The dragon boat was a wide flat-bottomed boat with two brightly painted dragons' heads jutting out from the bow. Our first stop was the splendid and much-photographed Thien Mu Pagoda. I 'oohed' and 'aahed' for a minute, took a photo, then wandered out of the pagoda grounds and into the dusty streets of the adjoining village. A few entrepreneurial barbers had set up makeshift shops (consisting of a mirror nailed to a wall) on the side of the street. Smart idea. *Everyone* gets a new haircut for Tet, so they were doing a brisk trade. As well as getting busy, they were also getting rich: the price of a haircut doubles during the week leading up to Tet. Mind you, by the look of some of the haircuts going around, I don't think the 'barbers' were star pupils at Hairdressing College. Most favoured the Eddie Munster look.

We spent the rest of the day cruising up the river visiting the tombs of the 19th century Nguyen Dynasty. They were all rather impressive. However, what impressed me the most were the quarters Emperor Tu Duc had set aside for his wives. All 104 of them. Astonishingly, despite the devoted attentions of each and every one, he didn't produce a single heir to his throne. But by gosh he would have had a lot of fun trying! The tomb of Minh Mang was the best of the bunch. Marvellously restored, the brilliantly coloured and heavily ornate temples and pavilions now look just as they did when they were built in the 1840s.

Afterwards I went for my usual wander into the nearby village. There was a bit of restoration work going on there as well. People were frantically painting and cleaning in preparation for Tet. Most of the houses still looked quite shabby compared to the wealthy folk's houses in Hoi An, but I was glad to see that some things are universal—like henpecking before a big event. One poor chap was getting an absolute earful from his wife. It seemed that she wasn't happy with his painting technique. She was screaming at him and hitting the poor sod over the head with a broom. His painting looked fine to me. I can't imagine what she'd do to him if he forgot to take out the rubbish.

I returned to Hué in time to visit the Dong Ba Market. The place was sheer madness. And that was just the car park (or scooter park, in this case). You know what it's like doing Christmas shopping. The battle for a car spot cannot only be stressful but can sometimes even be quite nasty. I've been abused many a time (and I've given out some of my best abuse, too) during the 'jolly' season car-park shuffle. But nothing I'd ever seen or done had anything on the Dong Ba Market scooter park. The fun started when two ladies tried to ride into the same spot. They argued for a minute, then one of the petite and sweet creatures calmly got off her bike and whacked the other one hard in the face. The whackee kept arguing even as a stream of blood started pouring out of her nose. In fact, there was yelling and screaming going on throughout the entire scooter park. I did witness one handy little technique for securing a spot that may be worth trying out next Christmas, though. A man was standing in a spot screaming out, I assume, that it was his, so . . . the other fellow simply ran him over with his scooter. That should work a treat at my local shopping centre.

I almost gave up on the market itself. It was a flowing tide of conical hats. Well, sort of flowing. It was so packed that the crowd could move no faster than a snail's pace (and a crippled one at that). In my first five minutes, a bag of live chickens was shoved in my face when someone tried to bowl me over to get past, and a pipsqueak granny abused the hell out of me because I stopped briefly to look at an onion stall. I wasn't actually considering buying onions, I might add, I was merely amazed at the variety. There were at least 20 different types of onion in all shapes, sizes and colours. I wanted to have a closer look, but the granny started jabbing me sharply in the ribs so I moved on. I crawled through an entire section of sweets. Sweets are big during Tet (so are rotting teeth, I imagine), and along the line of sweet stalls there were enormous piles of red and gold lollies, sugar-coated coconuts, roasted melon seeds and what looked like toffee-coated testicles. On that note, I left the market to get something to eat.

I was having dinner with a bunch of backpackers, who I'd met on the dragon boat and had promised to take to a most remarkable restaurant I'd read about. Hué has a tradition of extraordinary cuisine that all began with Emperor Tu Duc, who reigned from 1848 to 1883. At each and every meal, he would order 50 different dishes to be prepared by 50 cooks and served by 50 servants. The cooks had a bugger of a time coming up with new ideas, but soon learned all sorts of methods to turn things like a simple steamed chicken dish into a culinary and visual masterpiece. At Tinh Gia Vien restaurant they carry on that tradition today and do stuff like carve a perfect replica of a chicken out of a pineapple and top it with . . . steamed chicken. A waitress escorted us to a lounge area overlooking an enchanting garden setting where we were given tea and the menu to peruse. The cheapest banquet (which was 11 courses) was $18.

'I'm not paying that,' my fellow dragon boaters whispered in chorus.

'Look at this place!' I said. 'And look at the food. It's amazing!' A couple were sitting below us eating a lobster carved intricately out of a grapefruit (or something similar). But, no. They wouldn't budge. Scummy bloody backpackers. These are the same people who haggle endlessly to save a cent in a market.

'I can get an entire meal for under a dollar,' the tall, skinny American moaned.

'Yeah, but I bet you can't get a pineapple shaped like a chicken,' I replied.

It was four against one, though. I didn't fancy eating by myself, so begrudgingly I followed them out. We wandered down the street dodging spot fires that had been lit every few metres by the city's impressive army of arsonists.

'This place looks nice,' I said, pointing to a little restaurant nearby.

'It's not in Lonely Planet, though,' said the Australian girl. Everyone was standing in the middle of the street reading their Lonely Planet guides.

'This is ridiculous,' I grunted. 'Can't we do anything without Lonely bloody Planet?' I'd just like to add here that I'm a big fan of Lonely Planet guidebooks and rarely travel anywhere without one (even if some of the maps have obviously been drawn by a person who was drunk the whole time).

'Okay, let's all burn our books,' I said. 'Come on, we'll put them all together on the road. Then we can do what everyone else in Hué is doing and set them on fire.'

They all thought I was mad. They'd starve if they didn't have Lonely Planet telling them where to go. So, 10 minutes later we could be found in a restaurant recommended by Lonely Planet. It wasn't too hard to find, either. An enormous sign out the front had a large picture of the *Lonely Planet Vietnam* book and an even larger 'Recommended by Lonely Planet' printed underneath it. Lac Thanh Restaurant was run by a deaf mute cook. It was so popular that another deaf mute cook decided to cash in and opened a restaurant next door called Lac Thien. Not long after that, another deaf mute cook (there must be an abundance of deaf mute cooks in Vietnam) opened Lac Thuan on the other side. By now there's probably seven of them.

We ate a mammoth feast (the food was delicious, I have to admit) and drank an armful of beers all for less than $4 each. The American fellow whined a bit, though, as it was way over his budget.

Two days before Tet

So this was what it's like to be a rock star. I stepped out of Ho Chi Minh City airport to be greeted by thousands of fans all smiling and waving at me. Well, not *exactly* at me. They were waving at all the other arrivees. It looked like entire extended families were at the airport to meet their loved ones. Tet is such a sacred and important time of the year that the Vietnamese people, wherever they are, try to get back to their hometown for a family reunion.

The taxi ride into the city centre was excruciatingly long, hot and dusty. Traffic in Saigon (I'll call it Saigon from now on, because I reckon it sounds more exotic. Oh, and it's a darn sight easier to type than Ho Chi Minh City) was travelling at a hiccupping crawl. It was made up almost entirely of scooters riding up to 10 abreast, many laden down with things for Tet, like presents, flowers, balloons or kumquat trees. According to the *Viet Nam News*, which I'd read on the plane from Hué, a massive road-rules clampdown was in progress in an attempt to stem the Tet traffic jams in Saigon. In the first two days of Tet alone, over 2000 tickets were given out to people driving the wrong way down a one-way street. Then again, that's probably because they couldn't see where they were going. The rider of the scooter next to us had a giant kumquat tree balanced between his knees and had to peer through the branches to have any idea what was ahead of him. Just about every house we passed had the red and gold Vietnamese flag sticking out from a window. The residents of Saigon were also into petty arson and small fires were burning on most street corners. After more than an hour of breathing in scooter fumes, I finally checked into one of countless cheap hotels on Pham Ngu Lao. The one I chose seemed to be almost entirely full of dodgy looking Russians. What is it about Russians that makes them all look as if they are up to no good? The ones in my hotel looked as if they'd just mugged someone.

After throwing my bags in my room (and double-checking that the door was securely locked when I left), I sat in the foyer and waited for my very own personal tour guide to come and pick me up. And, really, I couldn't have found a better tour guide than my friend Matt. Not only had he worked as a tour leader in Vietnam (I'd met him when we worked together as tour leaders in Europe), but he'd also been living in Saigon for six years. He was still in the tour-guiding game, but was now dealing with annoying passengers from behind a desk instead of from the front of a bus. He hadn't planned on staying in Vietnam so long. In fact, he'd even made an attempt to go home to Sydney a couple of years ago but missed Vietnam (and the *very* comfortable ex-pat life) so much that he was back in Saigon before he'd even finished unpacking his bags. He'd now settled into a blissful domestic life with his girlfriend Thi (pronounced Tay). It was Thi's family who I would be spending Tet eve with.

It's always a bit weird seeing Matt (in a nice way, I hasten to add). His identical twin Chris (who appears as my manager in the Country Music Festival chapter) is also a friend of mine, and it takes me a minute to get used to which one I'm actually with.

As we walked to the Tet flower market (an entire park is taken over by merchants selling every flower imaginable for the week leading up to Tet), I asked Matt what the hell the petty-arson thing was all about.

'People set fire to piles of paper at the end of the old moon to burn away old spirits,' Matt said.

'Ah, I would have loved doing that as a kid,' I enthused. 'I used to burn stuff all the time.' We passed a man casually setting fire to the evening paper in a gutter. 'I even set my high school on fire once,' I added. 'I was trying to burn away the bad spirit of maths.'

On our very informative walk I also found out that everyone has a Vietnamese flag at home because it is compulsory to fly the flag on Ho Chi Minh's birthday. And, quite disturbingly, there are government spies in just about every block who will report anyone not flying the flag to the police. Matt also pointed out a few major cultural sights such as the Reunification Palace and what he described as 'a good rub-and-tug place' (this involves a massage and . . . I think you can guess the rest).

The flower market was a kaleidoscope of brilliant colours. There were flowers of every shape, shade and size (I'm sorry flower-lovers, but I know sod-all about flowers so I can't actually give you any names), with stalls spilling out onto the footpath and even onto the road. There was also a rather impressive collection of kumquat trees that had been clipped into the shape of dragons, horses and the animal symbol of the New Year, the goat. The place was jammed with happy families and couples all dressed up in their Sunday best, buying large bouquets of flowers to decorate their homes.

'When you told me a few weeks ago that you wanted to see the flower market,' Matt said, 'I thought, Brian's either turned really boring or become a poof. But I'm actually enjoying it. I've been in Saigon five times for Tet and I'd never seen it.'

'You see,' I beamed. 'This is great.'

'Yeah, but I've seen enough. Let's go drink beer.'

We had dinner at a local beer garden. Work break-up parties were going on all around us (most companies close for a week at Tet), and there was a lot of *Yo*-ing and clinking of glasses going on. As we ate our barbecued chicken wings, we could hear the loud clucking of a chicken in the kitchen. Suddenly there was an extra loud cluck, then silence.

'Well, at least you know the chicken is fresh,' Matt cheerfully remarked as he grabbed another chicken wing.

After dinner we stopped in the street for a *bia hoi* (home-brewed beer). And when I say we stopped in the street, I mean we literally stopped in the street. Someone had set up a few chairs in the middle of the footpath (there are 'bars' like this all over Vietnam). The *bia hoi* was kept in a large plastic container and glasses were hung on the spikes of a metal grille gate next to the footpath. We ordered a beer and watched in amazement as the woman daintily placed a garden hose into the plastic container and sucked the other end to start siphoning the beer out. She gagged for a moment when the beer reached her mouth, then poured the pale frothy beer neatly into a glass. As she placed our glasses down, she smiled—revealing blackened teeth. Matt didn't even flinch as he took a large mouthful of beer. 'Good, isn't it?' he said. I suppose at 10 cents a glass, I couldn't really complain. And anyway, what's a bit of spit between friends?

What followed next was a series of bars that, to be honest, I only vaguely recall. I do remember jumping up on stage and singing 'I Can't Help Falling In Love With You' with a Filipino band in a Spanish Flamenco bar full of Vietnamese. I think I was all right. I didn't fall off the stage, at least. During the course of the evening, and our wanderings from bar to bar, I also remember being accosted and urged to buy postcards, cigarettes, cyclo rides, motorcycle rides, marijuana and some hot sex (not all by the same person, I might add).

Matt dragged me into a girly bar where, after no more than 30 seconds, a girl grabbed my balls and said, 'Nice! You wan' blow job?' Another girl looked at Matt for a moment and said, 'Hello, I know your girlfriend Thi.' We were out of there in less than a minute.

'Shit, I've used all my lucky envelopes,' Matt groaned. Matt had been to the bank before he'd picked me up and had filled a pile of lucky envelopes to give to Thi's relatives. He'd given them *all* out to various pretty girls he'd laid eyes on during the night.

Tet Eve

Why did the bloody bus driver keep blowing his horn? He didn't need to. It was a big fucking bus, for God's sake. Of course people on scooters could see a large and noisy bus bearing down on them. So why wouldn't he shut the fuck up? Okay, maybe I was being a little harsh, but I had a frightful hangover and my head felt as if it was about to explode. I'd woken up early (in retrospect I'm not quite sure how) to take a morning bus tour to the Cu Chi tunnels. These infamous tunnels, from which the Viet Cong mounted surprise attacks on the South Vietnamese and Americans, stretched for over 250 kilometres around and into Saigon. Before we actually saw any tunnels, we were ushered into a room to watch a serious documentary film, made in 1968, about the atrocity of war and the harsh and dangerous life in the tunnels. It was one of the funniest films I've ever seen. Although, the roomful of American tourists didn't seem to find it quite as funny.

The film opened on an sweet-looking local girl standing in a rice field. 'This is Sang. She is an American killer hero.' Sang then casually started shooting an AK47. 'It is *good* to kill Americans,' the commentator added matter-of-factly. It then went on to show lots of Americans being shot, followed by 'The Americans shot our men, our women, our children, our house and . . . even our pots and pans.' And, just in case you didn't believe them, they showed a pile of pots and pans peppered with bullet holes. The tour itself proceeded along similar lines. We were shown, for instance, 'the many ways you can kill and torture Americans.'

The tunnels themselves were incredible. I almost fainted on my short sojourn into one of them, though. Then again, I bet the VC didn't have to crawl through the ridiculously narrow and absurdly hot tunnels with hangovers that would kill a black dog.

At the end of the tour we had the opportunity to play with some very big and dangerous guns. And, for only a couple of dollars, you could shoot some Americans. Well, some Robin Hoodesque targets at least. I'd never shot a real gun before, so I decided to have a go at an M16. You could also shoot an AK47 and other large and noisy guns. I bought five bullets, which was the minimum you could buy. The thing is, I suspected that shooting even one bullet probably wasn't a good idea with my hangover. I was right. The first shot was so loud that my brain shut down for a second and I immediately felt dizzy. I couldn't focus at all for my next four shots. Not only did I miss the target, but I almost followed the suggestion that, 'It is good to kill Americans,' when I spun around wildly and just missed some American tourists. The army fellow couldn't get the gun away from me quickly enough. As we left the shooting range, only metres away from clattering AK47s, I passed two burly soldiers delicately wrapping pretty floral paper around the base of a kumquat tree.

Back on the road to Saigon, we passed through villages of rundown shacks that, despite an obvious lack of wealth, had pots of fresh flowers on their doorsteps and large kumquat trees on display. Most of the shops had closed at midday, but the streets were still full of people rushing about. We drove past the flower market.

It was empty. The park had been totally cleared out and all that remained was a ton of rubbish and a few sleeping drunks. There wasn't a flower or kumquat tree anywhere to be seen.

Matt picked me up on his scooter to take me to that great traditional Tet celebration, an Aussie barbecue. We arrived at a smart-looking house in the suburbs to find a bunch of Aussie blokes standing around a barbecue in the laneway, with Biere Larue beers (now made by Fosters) in hand. Kylie Minogue was blasting out from a stereo inside the house, where the boys' Vietnamese girlfriends were adapting quite well to the Aussie barbie scene—they were making salads. Our host Craig, who shared the house with his girlfriend, was telling us about all the bribes he had to pay to keep living there (it is against the law for foreigners to live with a Vietnamese partner). Just that morning he had given two cops a bottle of whisky each and, as we were standing there, he gave a local police informer half-a-dozen bottles of beer. 'Just so he won't blab,' Craig said.

The house was, in Saigon terms, a palace. It was four storeys high, virtually brand new, and decked out with all the mod cons: reverse-cycle air-conditioning, wide-screen TV with surround sound, DVD, and what I think is the best mod con of all, a full-time live-in maid.

I couldn't face a beer, so I spent the afternoon spread-eagled on the incredibly comfy couch in front of the air-conditioner. By the time we left to go to Thi's grandma's house, I was feeling almost human again.

When I say house, I actually mean dogbox. There were only two tiny rooms—one downstairs and a rickety old ladder leading to the bedroom upstairs. 'I've got no idea how she gets up that ladder,' Matt said. Neither had I. Grandma was almost 80.

'She used to live in a big house in the country surrounded by acres of fruit orchards,' Matt told me. 'But her husband fought for the South Vietnamese during the war, so when the North took control their house was taken from them. He was sent to a re-education camp for three years. One month after he was released he died.'

Grandma motioned for us to sit down and piled two plates with food from pots that were bubbling gently on the stove. Pots of food, I might add, that would have been bubbling away all day—it is tradition that each visiting guest is given a plate of food on arrival no matter what time of the day it is. I wasn't sure I was ready for this. At least, I wasn't sure my stomach was. We were given two dishes: one was called *mang*, which is boiled bamboo shoots and fried pork fat marinated in fish sauce (you don't need a hangover for that one to turn your stomach) and the other was . . . I was too scared to ask. It was some sort of chicken dish with turnips and what looked like ear lobes. Still, it was quite tasty. And at least we weren't offered the Tet staple—*banh chung*. This is fatty pork and bean paste sandwiched between two layers of glutinous rice then wrapped in a banana leaf. I'd seen them everywhere in the markets and the smell wasn't too dissimilar to a fart.

We sat alone in Grandma's house. Everyone else was next door in Miss Hung's flat. Her dogbox was the same size as Grandma's. When we got to Miss Hung's six adults were sitting on the floor, while a bunch of kids were running around the sparsely furnished (two plastic stools!) lounge room. The adults were playing a game that looked like a cross between Chinese chequers and chess. They all had large piles of notes in front of them. Matt had rung Thi earlier in the day and asked if she was gambling. 'No, of course not,' she'd said.

'She's been gambling all day,' sighed Matt. 'She *loves* a gamble.'

'Are you winning?' Matt asked Thi as we sat down on the floor next to her.

'No.' Thi smiled sweetly.

'In Australia we make a New Year's resolution,' Matt said. 'It's a promise that you have to keep. I think maybe you should give up gambling.'

Thi grinned. 'I think maybe I should give up my boyfriend.'

Lying on the ground next to Thi was her Aunty Úc. She was seven months pregnant. She would have to go home before midnight, as it is bad luck to have a pregnant woman in your house on Tet (she's okay in her own house, though).

I was getting excited. It, well, felt like New Year's Eve. I kept glancing at my watch to see how long it was till midnight. The only thing missing from my usual New Year's celebrations was that I wasn't pissed off my head. Oh, and I don't usually eat fried pork fat. It still felt a bit odd celebrating the 'New Year' in February but, if you're into the whole New Year's Eve thing, you could—if you had the inclination and the liver for it—legitimately celebrate it all year. You'd have just enough time to get over your hangover from one New Year's celebration before you moved on to the next one (and if you broke your New Year's resolution you'd only have to wait a few weeks before you got a chance to make a new one!).

Why all the different dates? Before people had a calendar they depended on all sorts of ways to mark the 'New Year', from the changing of the seasons to even the flight of wild geese. Ancient Egyptians celebrated the New Year at the time of the overflowing Nile. Tet is determined by the first new moon of the year. China also celebrates New Year with the new moon. And it's there you could head after Tet to continue partying, because their New Year festivities last 15 days. Your liver would probably only last about 10, though.

You'd need a rest after all that, which is lucky, because there's not much partying going on in the first days of March during the Balinese Saka New Year. The island is used to drunken revelry day and night, but during this 'celebration' the Balinese follow four Nyepi traditions: no light (or fire for cooking); no physical work; no entertainment (including music); and no leaving the home. Woo hoo, get out those party hats.

The wild party continues in Tibet on March 3rd, when locals make the journey to the Jokhang temple in Lhasa to donate yak butter (for beer in return, I hope). After that riotous celebration it's straight to Iran for their New Year—or, as the locals call it, Chahar Shanbeh Suri (try saying that after a few beers). The New Year is the exact moment when the sun passes into the zodiac sign of the ram. This can happen in the middle of the day (so you could end up having the celebration and the hangover on the same day).

April has three big potential hangovers in a row (or one very big one), starting on the 13th when the Sikhs celebrate their New Year in the Punjab. The Bengalis have their shindig the next day, then it's a quick trip to Thailand for Buddhist New Year on the 15th. Known locally as Songkran, the Thai version is basically a giant water fight in which the entire population throws water at each other. A few friends and I celebrated in much the same way a few years back. Oh, except we threw beer at each other.

In May it's off to Baktapur in Nepal for Bisket Jatra. On the final day of the four-day festivities a ceremonial 25-metre tree trunk, roughly carved to resemble a penis, is hoisted into an upright position. Not only can this take hours, but the tree trunk sometimes crashes down on top of people. Now that would really leave you with a sore head in the morning.

Indian Hindus celebrate their New Year at the end of August. And then again in November. And February. And May. They celebrate New Year's Eve four times a year (one for each change of season). Any old excuse for a piss-up, I say.

On September 11th in Ethiopia they should be saying 'Happy Old Year!' In 2004 their calendar will be clicking over to 1997. Does that mean if I go there I will be seven years younger?

Our Jewish friends have a 10-day knees-up in late September or early October. I don't know how much knees-upping goes on, though. In fact, it all sounds a bit serious. They don't even say 'Happy New Year'. They say 'May you be inscribed and sealed for a good year'.

In early December, as part of the New Year's Eve celebrations in Swaziland, the young men walk over 30 kilometres to gather branches from the sacred Lusekwane bush. If any of the men have made love to a married woman or made a young maiden pregnant, the leaves wither on the branch and the rest of the men will beat them.

Finally, you could follow the tradition of any one of over a hundred countries that celebrate the New Year on December 31st and . . . drink a hell of a lot of alcohol.

Back in Saigon, I certainly wasn't in an alcohol-drinking mood. It was ten-thirty and I still hadn't managed to even look at a beer. Matt and I left Miss Hung's Casino and went for a walk to the local pagoda. Locals flock to pagodas all around the country before and after midnight to pray for good luck and happiness in the coming year.

On the way to the pagoda we had to weave through people drinking and partying on the footpath. It was a very warm, humid night and people had set up tables and chairs in front of their homes. We must have screamed out 'Chúc Mùng Nam Mói' a hundred times. I finally drank a beer, though. I had no choice really. Three times we were called over to groups of rowdy drinkers and 'made' to skol a glass of *bia hoi*.

We could smell Vinh Nghiem Pagoda before we even saw it: an overpowering scent of incense hit us two blocks away. On the road leading to the pagoda, hordes of people were selling large bundles of incense sticks. Some of them were over a metre tall (the incense sticks that is, not the people). Lines of beggars tugged at my shirt (well, the ones who had arms did). The beggars almost outnumbered the worshippers. 'This is their biggest day of the year,' Matt told me.

Two enormous ceramic pots in the forecourt of the temple were overflowing with thousands of burning incense sticks. There were so many packed together that half of them were on fire and the flames were over a metre high. The air was thick with smoke and the heady smell was making me feel quite queasy.

Inside, everyone was taking it in turns to rub Buddha's belly and pray for a lucky New Year. The smell of incense indoors was even more pungent.

By the time we got back to Miss Hung's flat I was feeling worse. Not only had the incense made me feel nauseated but my stomach was rumbling like a soon-to-erupt volcano. The fried pork fat was having quite a battle with my digestion. I squeezed into a space in the corner and stretched out on the cool tiled floor.

'Come over here!' Matt hissed.

'No, I'm fine here,' I moaned.

'NO! Come over here!' Matt insisted.

I crawled over. Matt leant over and whispered, 'It's very unlucky for the family to lie or sit in front of the family shrine.' I glanced over to the corner. In my state I hadn't even noticed the elaborate shrine surrounded by flowers and offerings of food and presents. I had been sprawled out right in front of it.

'Miss Hung isn't happy,' Matt said. Miss Hung did look a little pissed off. At least she wouldn't shout at me as it's bad luck to show anger on Tet (it is also bad luck to say the number four, wash your hair, sew, clean, swear, cry, and—the one I like—nag).

Ten minutes before midnight we all stepped outside. Miss Hung set up a small table by the front door with offerings of food (an entire three-course meal) for the deceased ancestors. There were also offerings of liquor, cigarettes, flowers and money. Next door, Grandma was doing the same. I looked down the narrow lane to see more tables, loaded with all sorts of goodies, being placed by front doors. Miss Hung had changed into her new clothes and was now reading her prayers while Thi and her cousins giggled and chatted noisily on the street. 'These city girls are not very traditional,' Matt said. Every house was empty, but inside all the TVs had been left on showing some cheesy New Year variety show.

There was only a minute left till midnight. 'Is there any sort of countdown?' I asked Matt.

'No.'

'Does any, um, snogging go on?'

'Nah. Which is a pity,' Matt sighed. 'Look at all these gorgeous girls everywhere.'

Midnight went off with a bang. And boy, what a bang. The streets were filled with the noise of honking horns, screaming, pots banging and recordings of exploding fireworks (the sale of fireworks was banned in 1995, so people now play tapes of explosions). All this noise is to welcome the Kitchen God back to earth (if he wasn't eaten with the carp, that is) while scaring off any evil spirits that may be hanging around.

Then the real fireworks started. The sky over central Saigon was lit up with a dazzling display of pyrotechnics. At least, that's what it looked like on the TV. We could see the larger ones going off over the rooftops but, like the rest of the people in the street, we crowded around the doorway to watch the TV inside the house.

Not long after midnight, my stomach lost the battle with the fried pork fat. I could feel a good dose of the trots coming on, so I asked Thi if I could use a toilet, like . . . now. 'Use Miss Hung's,' she said. Five minutes later I returned a much happier man. 'Miss Hung is not happy,' Matt said gravely. Oh, no, I should have known better. I'd read up all about Tet and its customs and etiquette before I left and I'd just made the biggest gaffe of all. I was the first person to cross the threshold of Miss Hung's house. It is crucial that the first visitor of the year to each household is deemed suitable. Families take particular care in selecting this visitor. They choose the person they consider the happiest, wealthiest and most influential they know. Not someone, I imagine, with a mild case of the trots. Well, at least I wasn't a single middle-aged woman. They are blacklisted, along with anyone who lost their job or had an accident in the previous year.

Miss Hung was huffing and puffing trying not to show her anger. 'Shall we go?' I whimpered.

'She'll be okay,' Matt said, not very reassuringly. 'I'll explain to her that you have no gambling debts (another blacklister) and, um . . . you're not pregnant.'

'Tell her I'm sort of rich and I'm quite happy.' I was still feeling queasy from the incense and I was verging on delirium. 'I think we'd better go,' I said.

As I jumped on the back of Matt's bike I remembered the lucky envelopes. I had a pile in my pocket for the kids. 'We'll do that tomorrow,' Matt said as we shot out into the crowded street. I thought there was an extraordinary amount of bikes on the road—until we turned the corner. Suddenly there were zillions of them. People were all on their way home from the fireworks in the city. The horns, screaming engines and fumes were overwhelming.

'Bloody hell,' Matt screamed over the deafening noise. 'There's no traffic lights.' The traffic lights of the entire city had gone dead. Oh, great. And just as we came to a huge intersection. There was no way we could cross the sea of slow-moving bikes: they must have been 30 deep. Matt took a deep breath and drove straight in. We were totally surrounded within seconds and were only able to edge a few millimetres forward at a time. The fumes made me feel worse. I was sweating like mad and my head was swimming. I felt like I was either going to faint, throw up or shit my pants.

'I'm going to be sick,' I groaned in Matt's ear.

'What? Can you wait till we get to the other side?' Matt shouted.

'Erghhh!'

Matt put his foot down and barged his way through the wall of bikes. I closed my eyes.

'It's only five minutes to your hotel. Can you make it?'

'Erghhh!'

Matt made it in three. 'Are you okay?'

'Erghhh!' I groaned as I stepped off the bike and staggered towards the door of the hotel.

'I don't suppose you fancy a drink?'

'Erghhh!'

'I guess that's a no, then,' said Matt as I stumbled through the door.

Tet

'Happy birthday, Matt!' I said cheerfully.

'Happy birthday to you too, Brian,' Matt said as he shook my hand. 'You sound all right.'

'Yeah, I feel good,' I beamed. 'Which is nice, seeing that it's my birthday.' The thing is, it was everyone's birthday. On this day in

Vietnam, everyone becomes one year older. Actually, I didn't really want to be a year older. I was old enough thank you. Mind you, I still think I'm 23 (and act that way according to my wife, family, friends and, no doubt, readers).

We were now in the year of the goat. Being born in a goat year is considered terribly bad luck. So much so, in fact, that Saigon's main hospital had been full of pregnant women trying to push their babies out before the New Year. Apparently, Matt told me, there's not much bonking going on in Vietnam during the first three months of the year in case a baby is born in the goat year. I'm okay. I was born in the tough, cool, mighty, powerful year of the tiger. Matt was a snake. 'Well, it's better than being a pig,' I told him.

Matt took me to Chinatown. 'You'll see dragons in the street and stuff,' he said. On the way there we drove past a pagoda. Incense smoke was literally pouring out from the front door. One sniff and I was feeling a bit how's your father again. I wouldn't make a very good Buddhist (or hippy for that matter). All the shops were closed and people everywhere had set up tables and chairs on the streets. Most of them were gambling.

After riding around for a while looking for, but not finding, Chinese dragons, we stopped for lunch.

'What's that?' I asked, pointing to a dish being placed in front of us.

'It's duck eggs with the foetus inside only a few days away from hatching,' Matt said.

'Is it cooked?'

'Nah, it's eaten raw. Do you want to try some?'

My stomach did a little flip. 'Erghh, I'd rather eat Grandma's fried pork fat. In fact, I think I'd rather eat Grandma.' I had a nice safe bowl of noodle soup (minus the cute ducklings).

'Do you want to try and find some of those dragons?' Matt asked.

'Nah, it's our birthday,' I said. 'We should . . . do . . . nothing.' And nothing was what we did. We spent a glorious afternoon lazing by the rooftop pool of a five-star hotel. Matt was a member of the hotel's gym. By the sound of it, though, he didn't see much of the actual gym. For his membership he got a buffet lunch every day, free drinks at the bar between five-thirty and seven-thirty, two massages a week, and unlimited use of the pool. I wasn't surprised when Matt told me he'd put on weight since joining the gym.

We ended our wonderful day with a combined birthday and farewell dinner. We lashed out (it was our birthday, after all) and went to a flash restaurant. So flash that it wasn't in Lonely Planet. The bill came to a little under 20 dollars.

'I can see why you never want to go home,' I said as we waddled out of the restaurant after one of the best meals I'd ever eaten. 'This is a wonderful country.'

'I'm going to Grandma's house to give out my lucky money,' Matt said. 'Do you want to come?'

'Nah, I better not. I'll probably knock something over in Miss Hung's house and it will give her bad luck for the rest of her life.' When Matt dropped me off I handed him my lucky envelopes, 'Give these to the kids.' I had put 2000 dong in each envelope. 'Don't tell Miss Hung they are from me, though. She'll think they're *un*lucky envelopes.'

As I walked to the entrance of my hotel, a prostitute grabbed my arm and whispered into my ear, 'You! Me! Boom Boom!'

'No, thanks,' I said. 'I'm right for Boom Boom at the moment.'

Bean Throwing Festival

Tokyo, Japan
February 3rd

On February 3rd every year the Japanese throw beans at each other. And I'm not talking about nice soft beans, either. These beans are roasted until they are rock-hard. This pelting of each other with the eye-taker-outer beans is accompanied by shouts of 'Fuk-yu!'

None of this is all that strange (oh, besides the 'fuck-you' part) as throwing stuff is actually quite a popular theme for festivals. At La Tomatina in Bunol, Spain (held in late August), they throw—if you haven't guessed already—tomatoes at each other. Which, I imagine, would be a darn sight more enjoyable than getting pelted with rock-hard roasted beans. Over 20 000 revellers take part in La Tomatina and, in the space of two hours, bombard each other with 140 tonnes of large squishy tomatoes. Tomatoes, I might add, that aren't even grown locally (they have to be trucked in). It's actually a good thing that local produce isn't used—Bunol's main industry is cement. Oranges, on the other hand, have gotta hurt. At Il Carnevale di Ivrea in northern Italy they not only throw oranges at each other but on a cold day—the festival is held in January—the oranges have been known to freeze. It wouldn't be too dissimilar to getting a baseball thrown at your head. Still, it could be worse—elsewhere in Italy there is supposed to be a watermelon-throwing festival. I couldn't actually find any info about that festival, though. My guess is that all the people who've taken part over the years now have severe brain damage and can't remember it.

The king of them all, however, must be the pumpkin-throwing festival held every November in Delaware, USA. Quite sensibly, they don't throw the pumpkins at people. The 'Punkin Chunkin' festival involves competitors building elaborate 'chunkin' machines to see who can 'chunk' the 'punkin' the furthest. The record is over a kilometre.

Probably the safest (and softest) throwing happens during the Buddhist New Year celebrations in Laos. Not only is there little chance of getting hurt, but you also end up smelling very nice. They throw talcum powder at each other.

Trying to catch a thrown object is the aim at the Copper's Hill Cheese Roll Festival in Gloucestershire, England. The local vicar throws a massive wheel of double Gloucester cheese down a steep hill and the competitors have to run (read fall) down the hill to catch it.

Catching is the last thing you would want to do at the World Cow Chip (as in poo) Throwing Festival held in Beaver, Oklahoma, every April. The pile of crap that is thrown the furthest is the winner (I bet it's a shit prize). There are only a few rules: the piece of poo must be local (the Texans try to bring their own); they must be more than six inches in diameter; and, if competitors try to 'shape' the shit in any way, there is a 25-foot penalty.

With a similar shape and dimensions (but not quite as smelly), Grandma's Christmas fruitcake is the shotput of choice at the Great Fruitcake Tossing Festival held in Colorado in early January. Or you might prefer the Mullet Toss Festival held in Pensacola, Florida (that's the fish, by the way, not the haircut—although throwing people with mullets would be a heap of fun).

My favourite, however, is the Cat Throwing Festival held in Ypres, Belgium. I would have attended (and participated) for this book, but I found out that they only throw cat *replicas* off the church tower. Pity. If they were real cats, I'd be there every year.

All things considered then, getting a few little roasted beans thrown at me would be a picnic compared to frozen oranges, water-melons, stuffed cats and cow shit.

While La Tomatina is just a good ol' excuse to throw tomatoes at each other, the Bean Throwing Festival (Setsubun in Japanese) is an ancient custom that has been celebrated for centuries. By the old Japanese lunar calender, the end of winter comes on February 3rd, so to ensure that there were no devils or demons lurking around their homes for the start of spring, people threw beans to scare them off. As you do.

Apparently beans are a symbol of the impregnation of the earth (whatever that means) and therefore scare demons. How it works is that the master of the house stands at the front door and throws roasted soybeans inside and outside while shouting '*Fuk-yu wa uchi, Oni wa soto*' ('Fortune in, devils out'). While all this fuk-yu-ing is going on, one member of the household wears a devil's mask so the rest of the family can give them an absolute pelting. The biggest pelting, however, takes place at temples throughout Japan where priests or appointed 'bean-throwers' hurl handfuls of beans onto crowds of people. The largest of all happens at Sensō-ji Temple in the suburb of Asakusa in Tokyo, where the first mass bean shower occurred in 1688 and where I would be spending Setsubun.

It was going to be, I have to admit, very odd indeed. This was my first trip to Japan and I would be spending my first day in the country getting beans tossed at me by a foul-mouthed priest. Actually, I'd contemplated bringing my own beans to throw back, but had second thoughts—a can of baked beans would probably kill someone.

.

The streets of Tokyo were deserted when I stepped out of Asakusa train station. Where the hell were all the people? It was only ten-thirty at night. I thought Tokyo had a population of 50 zillion or some other ludicrous amount. Just two other people had got off the train with me and they'd already shuffled away, leaving me standing alone on the dark and cold street. A street, I might add, that looked like it had only recently been built. I'd never seen such beautiful gutters before. I didn't even want to step on the pedestrian crossing: it looked as if it had only been painted that afternoon.

On the 10-minute walk to my hotel I passed shiny new (or very well scrubbed) offices and shops, and rows and rows of vending machines—there is one vending machine for every 10 people in Japan. One of the machines had 12 different varieties of water on offer. Gee, and I thought there was only one. Besides the vending machines full of beer (what a brilliant idea) and Coke, I had no idea what all the other products with their over-the-top bright packaging were. I did recognise one product, though—it was called God Coffee. (I wonder, does He produce the coffee Himself or is it made by appointment?)

I wanted to stop and check out more, but a bitingly cold breeze was sweeping up the street so I picked up the pace.

I had booked into a 'business' hotel. There are no fancy-schmancy rooms here. They are just your basic, cheap, run-of-the-mill dogboxes. But, hey, that's all you need—a bed, a toilet, a shower and a TV. So what, if they're all on top of the bed?

The first thing I did, after putting my bag down on top of the bedside table (which converted into the bathroom), was switch on the TV (which was sitting on the toilet). I jumped into the lucky-I'm-a-short-arse bed and snuggled up and watched a Japanese version of 'The Johnny Carson Show'—except with a lot more nodding.

·

A crisp clear morning greeted me as I made my way down a now very busy street to the tourist office. I was hungry, but I didn't stop at any of the restaurants on the way. Not that I was afraid of the food, mind you: Japanese is my second favourite food after Italian. I was mostly worried I'd buy something that was beyond my credit card limit. Restaurants were easy to spot. Not only did they all have a red lantern hanging out the front, but they also had all the dishes on the menu set out in the front window—that is, plastic versions of the dishes. More amazing still, among all the plastic raw fish and eels there would be a Daliesque piece, such as a pair of chopsticks hovering over a bowl of *ramen* (noodles), suspended in midair by a single strand of noodle. Which is all very well, but where was the plastic Vegemite on toast or rice bubbles held aloft by a spoon with milk cascading into the bowl? I didn't fancy raw eels (or plastic ones for that matter) for brekky.

Even the McDonald's had a plastic burger and fries in the window. Maccas could save heaps of money on producing expensive plastic versions, though. They could just put one of their real burgers out on display. They'd stay exactly the same for months.

The tourist office was very helpful. Too helpful, in fact. They gave me four maps of Asakusa. They were all just different enough that I had no idea where I was. I'd heard the Japanese were an honest bunch, but maybe they're too honest. A brochure I was given about Asakusa described Hanayashiki Amusement Park as 'one of the tackiest amusement parks in existence' and the Sumida River Cruise 'of dubious value'. These are two of their major tourist attractions. Gosh, imagine if other tourist offices around the world decided to be as honest: 'Don't bother with the Roman Forum. It's just a bunch of old rocks' or, 'The gondola rides in Venice are overpriced and the canals, frankly, stink.'

I spotted the Japanese tourists first. They were all taking photos of the entrance to Sensō-ji Temple. Well, it was either that or the entrance to an outrageously big restaurant. Swinging from a massive gate was an even more massive red lantern. No, it wasn't the home to 1200 different varieties of sushi. This was Kaminari-mon Gate and the world's biggest lantern.

I fought my way through the mass of snap-happy locals and entered the half-kilometre walkway of tiny shops that lead to the temple itself. The tourist brochure described the shops as being 'famous for their small items you'll never find elsewhere'—or indeed ever want to buy. Along with ninja costumes, kimonos, lanterns and cute souvenirs that are soooo cute they make you want to chuck, you could also buy skin cleanser composed of powdered bird drop-pings and seaweed shampoo. One shop, called 'Beauty hair', sold geisha wigs. Women in elegant kimonos bowed at each and every person walking past. I looked in the window and there, sitting on a wooden stand among all these elaborate and very traditional geisha wigs, was an Elvis wig. Not only were the shops tiny, but some of them had up to five staff members—leaving no room at all for customers.

I was getting quite hungry now. All I'd seen so far in the way of food, though, was oh-so-bloody-cute doll-shaped rice crackers and bags and bags of roasted soybeans. As I got closer to the temple, however, there were a lot more food stands. I opted for a fluorescent pink sausage on a stick. Well, it was either that, giant steaming octopus tentacles or a bowl of seaweed.

It was right near the octopus tentacles that I caught my first glimpse of Sensō-ji Temple. It looked like . . . a Japanese temple. With its immense dark wooden beams and vaulted tiled roof it looked like every temple you've ever seen in a samurai movie, the TV show 'Monkey' or on the front cover of menus in Japanese restaurants. It was just bigger. In front of the temple, a cauldron of incense sent puffs of smoke billowing skyward. The cluster of worshippers gathered around the huge cauldron were grabbing at the elusive wisps of vapour, directing it towards their bodies—it is said to be beneficial to your health when rubbed on the body. As proved in Vietnam it certainly wasn't beneficial to my health. After just one whiff of the incense, the sausage in my stomach was contemplating a quick journey north. I took a wide berth and made my way to the steps at the front of the temple.

The first bean throwing was at 10 am. Well, it was either that or the next departure for the train to Kyoto. I wasn't exactly sure. The fellow in the tourist office also wrote down the other bean-throwing times: 12.00, 2.00, 4.00, 4.20, 4.40 and 5.00. Amazing, even bean throwing has a peak hour in Japan!

The first bean-throwers were school kids. They were maybe 6, or 12, or possibly 17 (I can never tell kids' ages). Anyway, they were all very short and wearing matching school uniforms with bright yellow shoes with pictures of oh-so-cute bunny rabbits on them. Each child was clutching a small wooden box full of beans. I tried to move in closer to take a photo but was jostled out of the way by a mass of camera-wielding parents. When I say cameras, by the way, I mean mobile phones. Just about everyone was taking photos with a mobile phone that doubled as a digital camera. They made the models we use in Australia look like something from the Stone Age.

The mobile-phone-wielding parents would all nod and say sorry as they bumped me, then unceremoniously shove me further to the back. On the count of *ichi*, *ni*, *san* the cute little munchkins shouted out 'Fuk yu' in unison and showered the crowd with beans. I tried to catch some but I'd been pushed so far back that the beans didn't reach me. As part of the tradition of Setsubun one must try to catch and then eat the same number of beans as your age to get rid of any bad luck for the coming year. At this rate, I needed to get into some serious jostling. I had quite a few beans to catch.

As soon as the bean throwing finished, a small army of small Japanese men in overalls moved in and began sweeping up the thousands of uncaught beans that were scattered all over the ground. Less than five minutes later the entire area was totally beanless. The Japanese might love throwing beans, but they love cleaning a hell of a lot more.

.

I had an hour to kill before the next bean throwing (or the next train to Kyoto) so I went for one of those aimless wanders I'm so good at. In a street not far from the temple I came across a sign on the pavement advertising (in English) that there was a 'Fun Festival—Now On—Inside'. By the look of the front of the building my guess was that it was an Annoying Flashing Lights Festival. Still, it was a wonderful stroke of luck to stumble upon another festival, no matter what it was. When I stepped inside I almost fell over. Two rather strange festivals seemed to be in full swing. There was the Fucking Noisy Festival and the Chain Smoking Festival. The ear-splitting noise was made by thousands of metal balls crashing against glass in rows and rows of pachinko machines (which are like a cross between a pinball and a pokey machine). I'd heard of pachinko parlours but I sure didn't expect this. Blinding fluorescent lights illuminated billowing clouds of cigarette smoke as rows of mesmerised players sat transfixed by these god-awful noisy machines. Their obsession with the little metal balls was only surpassed by their obsession for smoking. There was an ashtray attached to each pachinko that was almost as big as the machine itself.

I later read that pachinko is now the largest single industry in Japan, outpacing even cars and computers. The richest man in Japan owns the company that produces most of the machines. I bet he lives in a nice *quiet, smokefree* mansion in the country.

I contemplated having a quick go, but the smell of cigarette smoke was making me giddy. I walked out no more than three minutes after I'd stepped into the place and my clothes reeked of smoke. Ah, so that's what the festival was: the Stinky Clothes Festival.

·

The twelve o'clock bean throwing session was performed by another bunch of ankle biters. Again, I was shoved to the back and didn't catch a single bean. I was going to have to get a little bit nasty if I wanted to catch my quota.

I was hungry again and still wasn't quite ready to eat steamed octopus tentacles, so I hit the backstreets to find a restaurant for lunch. Alongside all the Japanese restaurants displaying their plastic food was an Italian restaurant. In the front window sat a plastic bowl of plastic spaghetti bolognese, a slice of plastic pizza, a plastic gelato, a plastic bread roll and a plastic glass of plastic Coke (ahhh, so that's what a glass of Coke looks like!). Mind you, all the Japanese restaurants had a plastic glass of plastic beer in their front windows, which I suppose is quite handy when you've had a skinful and you can't speak. Just drag the waiter outside and point to it.

I settled on a little stall set up on the street selling nori maki (nori rolls to us). Eating nori maki is another Setsubun tradition—although I didn't quite follow it to a tee. The tradition is to eat a 20-centimetre-long nori maki in one mouthful without saying a single word (that wouldn't be too hard!). This will give you freedom from illness (indigestion excluded, I imagine).

I washed down my nori maki with a small can of Asahi beer that cost me $8—20 times the price I'd been paying for a beer in Vietnam two days earlier. I sat drinking my very expensive beer very slowly, and watched the weird and wacky fashion parade of the Japanese youth as they ambled by. The young hip Japanese folk had taken to the US rap look. However, they'd taken it a step further. Make that two steps further. Yes, they were wearing the standard baggy pants, but they were so baggy that you could fit an entire football team into them. Their runners were so grossly oversized that they took up half the footpath. Some of the haircuts were even better. One fellow looked like Tina Turner and one seriously misguided chap had gone for the Michael Bolton look.

.

I rushed back to my hotel to grab my bags as I was moving hotels. I wanted to be closer to the action, so I had booked a night in a 'capsule hotel' close to the temple. Okay, that's not the real reason. A capsule hotel is bloody cheap and I'm a tightarse. I knew what I was in for, though. I would be staying in something akin to a morgue.

Not for those prone to claustrophobia (or suffocation), the average capsule is not much larger than a coffin. Given the way the capsules are piled on top of each other and next to each other, the only person who would feel at home in one would be an undertaker.

The local businessmen (or 'salarymen' as they're called in Japan) generally stay in these cocoons when they miss the last train home to the suburbs. A taxi ride is out of the question because the fare can run into the hundreds of dollars. Literally. The fare from the airport to the centre of Tokyo alone is around $450. You could *buy* a taxi for that price in some Third World countries. But then again, for that price I assume the Tokyo taxi driver takes you home for a 10-course dinner and a foot massage, and lets you have your way with his wife.

The Riverside Capsule Hotel was in quite a dirty area (I saw an empty can in the gutter!) hidden behind the train station. Next door was the Lust Hotel and across the road was the Hotel Passion. These were 'Love Hotels' where guests can not only stay the night, but also stay for a 'rest'. A 'rest' is two hours. However, there generally isn't much 'resting' going on. They're not called 'Love' Hotels for nothing. Gee, if they had Love Hotels in Australia a 'rest' would only need to be five minutes (and two minutes of that would be checking out the bar fridge). These love shacks are not only ideal for illicit affairs (some places have rooms with built-in sound systems that play heavy traffic noise so you can call your wife and tell her you are stuck in traffic), but are also convenient for married couples. Crowded together at home with extended families, in rooms separated by paper-thin walls, couples find that it's not that easy to feel sexy with a mother-in-law on the other side of the partition. They must be popular, though. There are an estimated 35 000 Love Hotels in Japan. Boy, that's a lot of resting!

The reception of the capsule hotel was full of vending machines. There was a couple with cigarettes and beer, but the rest were displaying toothbrushes, business shirts, singlets, socks and underpants. The salarymen can then head straight to the office looking fresh without going home. And if they want some company for the night there is always the vending machine selling porno magazines. You can get all sorts of stuff from vending machines in Japan, including nappies, dried squid, Bibles, boiled eggs, chopsticks, roses and, my favourite, 'schoolgirls' used knickers'. I kid you not. These exist. They even have a picture of the former owner on the front of the vacuum-sealed pack.

I checked in, squeezed my bag into an impossibly small locker in reception and rushed back to the temple for the next bean chuck. Quite a crowd had gathered now and I edged my way slowly into the midst of the throng gathered around the platform. Ah, so this was what it is like to be tall. Looking around all I could see were the tops of heads. The crowd was mostly made up of vertically challenged old people. It should be easy to catch beans now. My elbows were perfectly positioned at head height.

Lines of priests, chanting and carrying white lanterns on sticks, were making their way up onto the stage. They looked uncannily like members of the eighties' pop band Flock of Seagulls. They were all wearing white jackets with overly large shoulder pads and had blow-dried big hair.

The flock of priests shouted out a mass 'Fuk-yu' then let fly with five minutes of frantic bean throwing. I didn't stand a chance. The pushing and shoving I could handle. The elbows to the groin I couldn't. Then out came the umbrellas. As soon as the bean throwing started, the old folk put up their umbrellas in unison and pushed them inside out to form giant bowls (I suppose the oldies did have a heap of beans to catch). When the bean-throwing frenzy had finished I was left clutching one bean in my hand. An old lady was crawling underneath my legs picking up beans. Cheat. You're supposed to catch them. To be fair, though, she had quite a lot to get—she looked about 173.

After getting those few pokes in the groin, I needed the loo. I found a spaceship-like public toilet behind the temple. To fit in with the spaceship theme, the toilet itself looked like Captain Kirk's command post. I was confronted by a complex computerised commode with a long panel attached to the side of the bowl that displayed an array of buttons and green and red blinking lights. There were little simple illustrations next to each button showing what would, or might, happen if you pressed it. One was for a lovely wash spray on your bottom, another for a jet of water straight up your clacker, another for a blow dry and one that looked like it plaited your bottom hairs. It took me five minutes to find the button to flush the toilet.

I made my way back to the stage to get myself into a good catching position for the next chuckin'. I wasn't missing out on beans this time. The four o'clock bean throwing was the first of the celebrity sessions, so a large crowd was already milling about. Three geishas dashed by me as I squeezed my way to the front, but I only caught a glimpse of their stiff beflowered coiffures and powdered faces. As they walked up the stairs I tried to take a photo, but all I got was a shot of arms holding up mobile phones taking photos. Men in dark suits and women in traditional kimonos marched up onto the stage behind them and took their places in a single line facing the crowd. The crowd started cheering. These were the celebrities. I didn't recognise a single one (mind you, the only Japanese celebrities I know are Yoko Ono, Pokémon, the blokes who could jump up into trees backwards from the TV show 'Samurai', and Godzilla). I could hazard a guess what two of them did for a crust, though. The two massive blokes with the funny haircuts were obviously sumo wrestlers. One of them barely made it up the stairs. Girls were screaming so I guessed one or two of the other ones were pop stars or soap stars.

The hurling began in earnest, but I lost track of the beans when one of the sumos got me a beauty smack in the eye. By the time I regained my composure the flinging had finished and I hadn't caught a single bean. The crowd's hubbub faded as the bean throwing stopped and the male and female personalities onstage took turns on the microphone. One celebrity didn't speak. She sang. Well, more like wailed. She may have been a famous singer back in the 1920s but she now sounded more like a dying cat with a bad case of the flu. Another fellow must have been a famous bird impersonator. He spent five minutes doing a rather good impression of what I believe was a silver-headed thrush.

The next two celebrity bean-throwing sessions were much the same. Fat sumos, geisha girls, soap stars and my pathetic attempts to catch beans. My bean count was now a miserly four. I still had another . . . ahem, cough, cough . . . beans to catch in the final session to make up my age.

It was in the fourth and last celebrity chuck that I spotted a celebrity I knew who wasn't Godzilla. Not only knew—he was one of my favourite TV characters when I was a wee lad. It was the original Pigsy from that classic, badly dubbed, Japanese show 'Monkey' (Pigsy's real name is Toshiyuki Nishida and he's now a popular stage actor, in case you're interested). Pigsy looked exactly the same as he did when the show was made in the mid-seventies (but without the pig ears). 'Ahhh, so you wan' to fight me do you, hey Pigsssy?' I screamed out to the bafflement of the people standing next to me. I was so excited. I never imagined I'd see a celebrity I actually knew.

I threw in a few well-placed elbows during the next bean shower and managed to catch a tidy sum of five beans (and two of them, I'm proud to say, came from the hands of Pigsy). I tried to push my way to the front to say hello to Pigsy, but he'd already run off to help save Tripitaka.

For my efforts from seven bean-throwing sessions I'd managed to catch a rather pitiful nine beans. However, it was while I was staring at the deep red sunset that appeared behind the five-tier pagoda that I had a brilliant idea. There was one sure way to get heaps of beans thrown at me. I trooped back to the tiny street of tiny shops and bought myself a devil's mask. It was simple. All I had to do was walk the streets and I'd get beans thrown at me galore.

It was dark by the time I found the residential area of Asakusa and the streets were empty. That was okay. I'd just knock on some doors. There was only one tiny weeny flaw to my plan, though. Everyone seemed to be out. No one answered the first four doors I tried. Of course, that may have been because they were hiding behind the curtains saying something like, 'Honey, there's some dickhead westerner pretending to be a devil outside!'

When I eventually found someone home I was greeted with a 'what-the-fuck-do-you-want' look and had the door slammed in my face. At my 27th house a woman finally threw beans at me. After she laughed at me hysterically for two minutes that is. I did well, though. I caught seven beans. Things were looking up. It was then, however, that I had to make an important decision. Do I keep going and make my bean quota and therefore avoid a year of terrible and irreparable bad luck or go to the pub?

It only took me 10 minutes to find the pub. According to my brochure from the Asakusa tourist office, the Kameya Izakaya (*izakaya* means tavern) was not only 'the oldest bar in Tokyo', but—and this was what I was looking forward to the most—it had 'Fine food expertly served by waitresses in appetising forms'.

I only hoped this restaurant didn't have an ornamental pond. Allow me to explain. Two nights before I left home I had taken my wife to 'The best Japanese restaurant in Melbourne' for our wedding anniversary. As we walked in I looked over at a bunch of people having *teppanyaki* (an entire meal that is cooked on a hot plate in front of you) and was thinking that maybe I should have booked that instead of the less spectacular but much more romantic table for two. While I was gaping at the other diners, I stumbled down a step I hadn't seen and lost my balance. I calmly steadied myself without, I thought, anyone noticing. Well, that was until I looked down at my feet to see that I was standing smack in the middle of the restaurant's large ornamental pond. I only just missed stamping on a little turtle and the nosy fish sniffing at my toes. As I stepped out, the entire restaurant watched (and giggled) as four waiters appeared at my feet to wipe my now sodden shoes.

As we sat down, people kept glancing over and smiling. Just at the point where people had stopped staring at us, I reached for the menu and knocked a more than likely very expensive ceramic pot onto the floor, which duly exploded into a thousand tiny bits. Not surprisingly, the waiter didn't bring over a wine menu.

Even if there was an ornamental pond for me to step into at the Kameya Restaurant Bar, no one would have noticed. The place was full of drunken salarymen. The waitress (with the appetising form) sat me down at a table next to a fellow who didn't even understand 'hello' in English. He stared at me dumbly until I said 'konnichi wa', then he smiled and nodded half-a-dozen times. I ordered a beer (and a beef-stew-soup-type thing) while my new friend ordered one beer and three large glasses of brandy liqueur. He took one sip of the beer then skolled an entire glass of the liqueur, then another sip of beer and skol, followed by another sip and skol.

On that note I went to the loo. The man standing next to me at the urinal was pissing all over his shoes. When he tried to readjust his aim he headbutted the wall. He smiled inanely at me as he staggered out with his fly still undone. While I ate my beef-stew-soup-type thing, my tipsy friend chain-smoked and delicately picked his nose—which sort of spoiled my enjoyment of what turned out to be a delicious meal. It was when his soup arrived that I realised I was sitting opposite someone famous. He was the Japanese Loud Slurper Champion. His slurping was so loud it shook the crockery. I tried my very best to compete, but he wasn't the champion for nothing. I needed some serious slurping practice if I wanted to keep up with the Japanese. On the way out I noticed the plastic version of the beef-stew-soup-type thing in the window. I wouldn't have ordered it if I'd seen it on the way in. It had the appearance of a bowl of nasty looking vomit (minus the carrots).

I headed back to the Riverside Capsule Hotel. I was keen to see what it was like to watch TV in a coffin. Plus I was dead tired (boom boom). My bunch of coffins were on the fifth floor. When I walked into my 'room' I burst into hysterical laughter: it honestly did look like a morgue. The coffins were piled three high and four deep on either side of the small room. I was in coffin number 18 out of 24. A green light by each door showed which capsules had been reserved. There were three lit, but no one was about (dead or alive). I crawled through my tiny hatch (I was on the ground floor) and was surprised to see not only a TV but also a shelf with a radio, alarm clock and night lamp. It was all a bit cramped to say the least, and it was lucky I'm so short. If I stretched right out, my toes could touch the end wall. I settled into bed and switched on the TV (which was mounted up around my knees). After flicking through a few stations I was thrilled to find my favourite show—'Buffy the Vampire Slayer'. It was dubbed into Japanese but it was kinda cool watching Buffy doing a bit of high-kicking karate and speaking Japanese. 'Ahh, so do you wan' to fight me, do you, hey vampire?' I did a bit more flicking and happened upon one of those wacky Japanese game shows. A fat bloke was made to run up and down stairs till he could hardly breathe, then—just before he was about to collapse—headphones were slapped on him and he was handed a microphone. He attempted to sing along to a tape, while trying desperately to catch his breath. Back in the studio, the contestants, who could only hear his singing, had to guess the song. When one of them got it right, the fat bloke got up and started running again.

In the cruelty stakes that's nothing compared to some other shows I'd read about. On one game show a grandma has to answer questions about pop culture correctly to prevent her grandson being catapulted hundreds of feet into the air. The big brother of cruelty shows, however, is a rather extraordinary twist on the show 'Big Brother'. A fellow called Nasubi, who had no idea what he was in for, was stripped naked and shut in an apartment alone with no food, furniture or household goods. He could only leave after he had won over US$10 000 in prizes by sending in postcards to contests. He stayed for over a year. I'm not quite sure what he ate in that time, though. The postcards he didn't send, perhaps.

I wasn't quite as uncomfortable as Nasubi, but my mattress was so thin that my hip was digging into the hard floor underneath. What I needed was another mattress on top. That shouldn't be too difficult, I thought—there were 21 empty capsules with spare mattresses next to me (and above me). I ducked across the narrow passageway between the capsules and started to drag out a mattress from the capsule opposite. It was harder than I thought and I had a difficult time squeezing it out of the tiny door. I was also rushing a bit because I was, well . . . kinda naked (I'd run out of clean underpants and I was planning to wear the same pair two days in a row—I didn't fancy wearing them during the night as well).

Getting the mattress into my capsule proved even more difficult. The whole thing became all twisted and squashed up. In the middle of a complex manoeuvre to straighten it out I passed wind and, um, well . . . sort of followed through. In my defence, I hasten to add, I was still suffering from a bout of a rather nasty liquid trots that I'd picked up in Vietnam. It was only a small bit of, er . . . you know . . . and made a puddle about the size (and colour) of a Hob Nob biscuit. Before I EXPLODED, I bolted—still naked—to the loo. When I returned, I noticed a green light had come on in the capsule I'd nicked the mattress from. That meant that five floors below someone had checked in. Oh, shit. Literally. I tried with what little was left of my might to pull out the mattress, but the damn thing wouldn't budge. It was stuck. I pulled harder. A terrible tearing sound accompanied the mattress coming loose and revealed, funnily enough, a huge tear in the sheet. Oh, shit all right. I somehow managed to throw the mattress back in the capsule okay, but the tear and poo were still on top. I pulled the sheet around and hid the unfortunate mess I'd made underneath the mattress. I was just about to straighten up the quilt and pillow that were all creased and very un-Japanese-like when I heard the elevator. I dived into my capsule and pulled down the screen door just as my soon-to-be-quite-surprised very-near neighbour walked in. My heart was beating so loud I was sure my new capsulemate could hear it. He stayed for less than a minute then left. He hadn't even noticed that his bed was all messed up (and maybe a little smelly). It should be okay, I thought. He'll come back later pissed and won't even notice the difference.

It took me a little while to calm down and when I did I couldn't get comfortable at all on the thin mattress. In fact, I think it was worse than before. There was a nasty bump in the mattress. I reached down under the sheet and pulled out . . . a bean. It must have come from somewhere on my clothes. Oh goodie, that made all of 17 beans that I'd now caught. I didn't fancy eating this one, though. I didn't know where it had been.

Snow Festival

Sapporo, Japan
February 6th

At the 2003 Sapporo Snow Festival a bunch of Japanese fellows with way too much time on their hands built a perfectly detailed, three-storey-high scale model of the British Museum. Out of snow. It took 28 days, 148 truckloads of snow and 1636 men to make it. Yes, wow! Which is exactly what I said over and over again when I stood in front of it. I saved an extra big wow, however, for the moment when I saw a Japanese woman going arse over tit on the icy path. She ended up sprawled on the ice, legs akimbo, with her skirt up around her neck—revealing the most incredibly frilly pink knickers. Then again, this was nothing strange. Everyone in Japan wears frilly pink knickers. (Only kidding.) The thing was, there were people slipping over everywhere. This didn't just happen because it was 10 degrees below zero and the footpaths were dangerously icy, but also because the snow festival was right next door to Japan's largest beer hall. There was so much slipping and sliding going on, in fact, that after a day at the festival I rechristened it the Sapporo Slipping Over Festival.

I was in Sapporo for less than one minute before I slipped over. I marched out of Susukino subway station and immediately slipped (doing an impressive flip with a half twist) on the iced-over tram tracks. With my large backpack on, I finished up like an upside-down turtle and needed the help of a little old man to get me upright again. That wasn't the only thing that gave me a shock when I stepped out of the nice heated subway station. It was bloody freezing. Small flurries of snow were whipping around me and my teeth soon began to chatter ominously. I shouldn't have been cold as I was wearing a huge jacket that made me look like the Michelin Man, ridiculously overpriced ski gloves and a micro-thermal Gore-Tex hat. As I stood there shivering, a line of giggling schoolgirls sauntered past wearing pleated mini-skirts with their bare un-shivering legs showing.

I'd never been in a big city under a deep blanket of fresh *white* snow before (in London, for example, the snow very quickly turns to grey sludge). Sapporo looked like a winter wonderland theme park. Even the rubbish dump I passed in the train from the airport looked like a fantastic frosted fairyland. With its neon-plastered buildings, wall-to-wall bars and sleazy strip clubs, the Susukino area—where I now stood shivering—looked like Times Square. This was the biggest and sleaziest entertainment area outside of Tokyo. Even so, under a sugar-coated cover of snow, Santa in his sleigh wouldn't look out of place dashing down the main street.

In the side streets the snow was piled so high in places that from the footpath I couldn't see the road. A two-metre-high wall of neatly packed snow was heaped either side of the narrow and treacherous path. Mind you, the locals are quite used to an abundance of the white stuff. In winter it snows and snows then snows some more. Storms regularly develop in Siberia, pick up moisture in the Sea of Japan, then just dump snow all over Japan's northern most island, Hokkaidō. Even the southern beaches, with their popular summer resorts, have two metres of snow on them in winter.

I had to clamber over a mammoth mound of snow to enter the street where my hostel was located. According to my guidebook, 'If you plan to visit the snow festival, you should book accommodation *well* in advance or take a course in igloo construction.' I'd booked the Sapporo Inn four months before. The igloo construction course was fully booked up. I felt quite chuffed with myself as I stood in the reception of the hostel nodding repeatedly at the manager. My early booking had not only procured me the cheapest place in town but it also looked quite swanky. The manager, whose name was Subaru (I wonder if he has four-wheel traction on the slippery snow?), showed me the spotless shared bathroom, the cosy lounge area and finally my well-appointed dorm room. Which was, and I couldn't believe this, empty. Where was the, to quote my guidebook again, 'cavalcade of international visitors' staying? Gee, that igloo-building course must have been good. And I mean really good. Besides me, two other Japanese girls were the only guests in the entire hostel.

Subaru nodded at me a few dozen more times on the way out as I headed to the first of the three sites that made up the Sapporo Snow Festival (called Yuki Matsuri in Japanese, by the way). The Makomanai site was a subway trip out of town in the grounds of the Eleventh Division of the Japanese Ground Self-Defence Force (Japan's army is not allowed under UN law to be called a defence force, only a *self*-defence force). This was the children's site where, according to the Snow Festival website, I'd be able to see, among other things, a three-storey-high Mickey Mouse surfing on a wave in Hawaii and a sculpture called 'Delicious Land'. I had no idea what 'Delicious Land' was. The website didn't help either. It offered: 'Welcome to the land of delicious rice! The vegetables, grown under the vast sky, have also been waiting for you'. To be honest, I was really quite excited. Years ago I had seen the Sapporo Snow Festival on the news back in Australia and was totally wowed by the mind-boggingly mammoth and complex snow sculptures. It's amazing to think that it all started in 1950 when a handful of high-school kids built a couple of small snow sculptures in Ōdōri Park. The next year, the Self-Defence Force built a whopping big sculpture of a naked woman (as you would) and ever since then has built the bulk of the large sculptures. I'm not quite sure how it helps in their training to defend the country, though. 'Quick, the enemy is approaching, build a snow sculpture of the Disneyland castle! AND HURRY UP WITH THAT NAKED WOMAN!'

The fellow sitting next to me on the subway train was downloading porn on his mobile phone. What amazed me even more, however, was that he was wearing thongs. I hoped I was on the right train. The announcer said, I believe, that the train was going to Egypt (which might help explain the thongs). A girl sitting opposite me was reading a book, in English, entitled *Teaching English as a Second Language*. I asked her which stop I should get out at for the Snow Festival. She didn't understand me. 'Your course isn't going too well, then?' I said, but she just looked even more bewildered.

As I stepped out of the station, the sun came out. The surrounding hills, which were covered with what looked like icing sugar, were sparkling in the glaring sun. Ski runs snaked their way down into the valley (Sapporo was home to the 1972 Winter Olympics). The main gate into the Makomanai site was right across the road from the station and best of all, particularly for a tightarse like me, this—and in fact, the entire festival—was free.

Just inside the gate was the most wondrous sight. Hundreds and hundreds of half-metre snowmen of identical size and shape were set out in neat lines. Astonishingly, kids had made them all. Even more astonishingly, no one had made his or her snowman bigger than, or different from the rest. A few had put cat's ears or pig's noses on them, but basically they were all identical. There were a couple of kids (and adults) adding new snowmen to the line, so I decided to have a go. I grabbed one of the sleds, filled it up from the allocated snow pile 20 metres away and found myself a spot. I contemplated building mine away from the evenly spaced line, but a couple of fellows from the Eleventh Division were overseeing proceedings. However, even though I adhered to the size guidelines, I decided to put a bit of Aussie into mine and built a kangaroo. When I finished I stood back to admire my work and was quite surprised to see it looked absolutely nothing like a kangaroo. In fact, it looked more like something you'd see in a very scary horror movie. Oh boy, was I in trouble. I noticed a Japanese man next to me staring at it. Then at me. But no, he turned and gave me a big beaming smile. The Japanese really are so polite. I could have built a penis with a massive scrotum and he still would have smiled at me.

I walked past tents selling oh-so-bloody-cute souvenirs and into a vast space full of extravagantly mountainous snow sculptures glistening blindingly brightly in the sun. The first one in a long line of them was called 'The Space Tank'. Ah, so that's the Self-Defence Force's secret weapon. They simply shoot small children down the long icy slides (that were built into the sculpture) onto oncoming armies. There was a long queue of laughing red-cheeked kids waiting for the slide (or upcoming attack). A sign at the front said, written in English as well as Japanese, 'This slide, in the form of a futuristic space tank, can be enjoyed by children of all ages. Perhaps excitingly.' (At least that's what it said in English. The Japanese may have been slightly clearer.) In fact, most of the sculptures had a slide built into them that could be enjoyed excitingly.

A whole bunch of the sculptures were celebrating Japanese cartoon characters. There were enormous cartoon elephants, tigers, rabbits, owls and frogs, and something that looked unnervingly like Hannibal Lecter. The animals were set in elaborate scenes like a castle or a forest. I wasn't quite sure what animals Rekky and Hosshi were supposed to be but they were the mascots of the Yokohama Bay Stars baseball team. Near the elephantine sculptures of them, the mascots themselves were running around. I'd keep my kid well away from them, though. According to the sign, 'Rekky and Hosshi would like to play with your childrens smalls'. They also had quite an odd recruiting policy for the baseball club: 'We will do our best to make our team more attractive.' Members of the Eleventh Division were marching around looking menacing: not only did they have helmets on, but their hands were held firmly on large truncheons just waiting for something to happen. You just never know when one of those kids will try to jump the queue for the slide.

As well as building large snow sculptures, the Japanese Self-Defence Force consider taking happy snaps of tourists part of their military strategic training. Visitors were handing their cameras over to a line of soldiers that were standing in front of the 'Welcome to the 54th Sapporo Snow Festival' sculpture. The soldiers were taking nice smiley family shot after nice smiley family shot because, after all, you want to make sure you know how to take a nice smiley photo of an invading army. I gave my camera to a fellow brandishing a large rifle. I hoped he wasn't going to get confused when I asked him to just aim and shoot.

On the way out I queued with a bunch of five-year-olds to have a go on the Space Tank slide. The man helping the kids onto the slide treated me just like one of the five-year-olds. In fact, no one gave the adult dressed as the Michelin Man squeezing down the narrow slide a sidewards glance. Which was odd, considering I saw a sign near the bottom that read 'For little children (age 0–3)'. In hindsight it probably wasn't a good idea to go down an ice slide on my way out as I spent an uncomfortable train journey back to town sitting on a very wet bottom.

It was almost dark when I alighted from Susukino subway station even though it was only four o'clock. The main street of the entertainment district (read: brothels, sleazy bars and sex shops) was the second site of the festival. What would they have here, I wondered. A giant vagina, perhaps? Close. The first sculpture was called 'Beautiful Angel'. She was a sweet looking angel with voluminous bosoms and outrageously erect nipples (well, I suppose it was quite nippy). She was just one of about 50 three-metre-high sculptures that were arranged in a long line down the middle of the street. They weren't made of snow, though. They were all sculpted out of clear ice. Just like the footpath. As I skated down the street, an inebriated fellow (or someone with a terrible sense of balance) slipped on the perilous pavement and made an impressive thump as his head hit the ice.

Among all the amazingly intricate dragons, animals, cartoon characters and busty angels were sponsored sculptures. Unashamedly so, too. There was a giant Suntory beer can, a pot of noodles and an enormous pack of Kool cigarettes. Girls wearing mini-skirts (with the biggest goose pimples I've ever seen) were handing out cigarette packs galore. The work involved in carving these huge chunks of hard rock ice in such detail must have been enormous. Then again, carving ice would be a picnic compared to the backbreaking work at the Stone Carving Festival held in Bogota, Colombia (also home to the Cocaine Carving Festival). You'd need more than just a few days and an ice pick there. At the Butter Sculpture Festival in Tibet, life would certainly be a lot easier—albeit with, I imagine, even more slipping over than at the Snow Festival. These elaborate sculptures, some of which take months to create, are made from coloured yaks' butter. On the gruesome front, on the other hand, you can't go past the Maryland Wildfowl Carving Festival. I didn't think the RSPCA would be too keen on that one. Particularly if the ducks were being carved while they were alive. Luckily for the ducks, I finally discovered that the entire festival is devoted to carving ducks out of wood—which is nowhere near as much fun.

Well, it looked like the cavalcade of international visitors had finally arrived in town. There was all of one other person in my dorm room. He was leaning out of the open window (turning the room into a fridge in the process) having a cigarette and playing with his mobile phone. His name was Toshiyuki from Tokyo. 'I work with J-phone,' he said holding up his mobile. 'You know . . . David Beckham.' He had a colour picture of David Beckham on his phone screen. Mind you, that wasn't the first time I'd seen David Beckham on a phone screen since my arrival in Japan. I must have seen half-a-dozen people on trains or in shops with a picture of Becks on their phone.

In my short time in Japan I'd figured out that the Japanese, including Toshiyuki, were obsessed with three things: smoking, mobile phones and David Beckham. Everyone, regardless of age, smoked like there was no tomorrow (and the way some people smoked, there probably wouldn't be). If they weren't smoking, they were playing with their mobile phones. Not actually using them, I might add, just playing with them. Well, when they weren't downloading pictures of David Beckham, that is. He was everywhere. I'd seen him on TV and billboards advertising Vodaphone, Castrol, a fashion label and, oddly enough, chocolate-covered almonds. Passing a newsstand in Tokyo, I saw him on the covers of no less than seven magazines. There was even a David Beckham Shop in the Tobu department store where they sold David Beckham clocks, plates, tea towels and underwear. My favourite symptom of the David Beckham obsession, however, occurred during the World Cup Finals in 2002. Women—and I'm talking lots of women here—were modelling their pubic hair on David Beckham's haircut at the time. This involved brushing the hair into a mohican and then dyeing the peak an 'eye-catching colour'. I wonder if Posh had hers done as well.

Toshiyuki showed me his photos—which were naturally on his mobile phone—from a one-week trip through Hokkaidō. The quality was simply remarkable. The shots themselves were more remarkable still. There were shots of his icebreaker trip through a sea of brilliant blue icebergs, a hundred or so majestic brown sea eagles perched on jagged pieces of ice, fishing through ice holes and the subsequent catch of enormous silver fish, steaming hot mineral baths on the beach and ballooning over vast pine forests. Wow, what an extraordinary trip. And, like every good Japanese tourist, Toshiyuki had planned every minute of his jam-packed trip (I met a Japanese fellow on the Trans-Siberian train who, I kid you not, spent the entire four days on the train planning his two days in Moscow). But perhaps the scariest thing was that Toshiyuki's plans for the next 24 hours were absolutely identical to mine. And I mean identical. A dip in an *onsen* (a Japanese open-air mineral hot spring), followed by a Genghis Khan barbecue at the Sapporo Beer Hall. Then to Ōdōri Park to see the main festival site lit up, off to bed, back to Ōdōri Park in the morning (to see the sculptures in the daylight), lunch at Rāmen Alley (a celebrated lane of dwarf-sized noodle restaurants), then aboard the afternoon bus out of town. I found it a little uncanny, to say the least. I'd only been in the country for a week and I'd turned into a Japanese tourist (well, not quite . . . I hadn't taken anywhere near enough photos yet).

The *onsen* was attached to a large hotel on the outskirts of town. We had to scrub ourselves clean in a large shared shower room before we stepped into the *onsen*. I may as well have been naked when I stepped outside. All I had to cover my bits and pieces was a 20-centimetre-square 'modesty' towel (or penis towel as I called it). Well, at least I didn't have much to cover. The temperature gauge outside was hovering around the −15 mark so I'd shrunk somewhat. The spring was actually a collection of smaller pools that were joined together and surrounded by snow-covered boulders.

The water was scalding, but I didn't mind. It was either that or snap-freeze. There were about a dozen other men in the water (although it was a rare unisex *onsen*, there were no women in sight). Toshiyuki and I waded through the waist-deep water to the far end of the spring where we found virtually a whole pool to ourselves. I sat on a submerged rock and did what everyone else was doing. Put my penis towel on my head.

Toshiyuki suddenly gasped with excitement. Two Japanese girls toddled out of a door right next to us (the women's changing room) and shuffled into the pool. They were trying, without much luck, to cover up all their bits and bobs with a 'modesty' towel only fractionally larger than ours. Toshiyuki was staring that much I wouldn't have been surprised if he'd gone and got his mobile phone to take some photos.

After about half an hour of slow cooking, it began to snow with huge fluffy flakes floating out of the night sky. It was the most magical sight. As the snow hit the hot water, clouds of steam filled the air till we could no longer see the other side of the pool (or the girls, Toshiyuki noted). Not long after that Toshiyuki suggested we roll around in the snow naked together. Thankfully, I'd read up about *onsens* and knew he wasn't planning to engage in a bit of kinky sex play with me, but that it was just one of those wacky things that Japanese folk do. It's supposed to invigorate the skin and revitalise the soul. I told Toshiyuki that we'd more than likely just freeze our bollocks off. On the count of three we jumped out together, found our patch of snow and rolled around like dogs. I'm not ashamed to say that I squealed my head off. Particularly when I got a nasty snow rash on my willy. Jumping back in the water was even worse. My entire body stung (my willy felt like it had been dipped in acid) and I squealed some more. Not surprisingly, Toshiyuki thought it was time to go. Not because of the stinging, I might add, but because of my embarrassing squealing. For Japanese people, *onsens* are more than a bath; they are a place for quiet reflection.

·

I felt incredibly relaxed as we tramped our way through the fresh snow to the Sapporo Beer Hall. Well, that was until Toshiyuki slipped over in the middle of the road, grabbed me for support, then dragged me down on top of him in a messy heap. Gee, and we hadn't even had a drink yet.

Sapporo was the first beer brewed in Japan and the cavernous beer hall was built in 1876. Apparently, the interior had beautifully carved beams but I couldn't tell. The entire room was full of smoke.

And not only cigarette smoke, but smoke from the mini barbecue grills that were set up on each of the hundred or so tables. The first staff member who spotted us screamed 'Irasshai mase' into our ears. Then a waiter yelled the same. This freaked me out a little, particularly when the whole staff of 40 or so screamed it at us. I could even hear the cooks and dishwashers in the kitchen yelling it out.

'What's going on?' I nervously asked Toshiyuki.

'Irasshai mase means welcome. They are all welcoming us.'

These sudden outbursts would go on all night as new guests arrived and a noisy 'goodbye' would follow when anyone left. As we were led to our table, I noticed that most people were in the middle of an absolute feeding and drinking frenzy. Which was exactly what Toshiyuki and I had in mind. We were going to have the ¥3500 (about $50) all-you-could-eat-and-drink-in-100-minutes 'Genghis Khan Barbecue'. Less than a minute after we sat down, a hotplate was thrown onto the middle of the table and we were both handed large mugs of cold frothy beer. 'If we drink seven beers,' Toshiyuki enthused, 'then the food will be free!' Plates of marinated mutton, mushrooms, bean shoots, cabbage and onions were spread out on the table and before I could say 'arigato', Toshiyuki had a pile of stuff sizzling away on the grill and had skolled half his beer. For the next 100 minutes we hardly spoke, and when we did it was only to say 'Hmmmm' (the marinated mutton and lamb just melted in your mouth) and 'kampai' (cheers) followed by 'Hmmmm' (the beer just melted in your mouth). Actually, it was hard to get a word out of Toshiyuki. Like a lot of Japanese people I'd met, he was shy when it came to speaking English.

'I don't speak very much good Engrish,' he said.

'No. You speak very much good Engrish,' I said. 'A lot betterer than many other Japanese people I've met,' I added.

There was one other thing I was very impressed with about Toshiyuki. He managed to eat, drink and smoke all at the same time. When our 100 minutes was up we'd succeeded in eating our body-weight in food and downing six half-litre mugs of beer. I sat back groaning and clutching my now heavily bloated stomach. It felt like quite an achievement—albeit a gluttonous one. Well, that was until Toshiyuki pointed out that the group of petite young ladies at the table next to us had drunk eight beers each.

As the staff farewelled us on the way out, I groaned back at them. We weren't the only ones being farewelled either—there was a whole bunch of people staggering out the door. And, like us, they were all making their way to the main festival site, Ōdōri Park. And, again like us, they were all having trouble staying upright. In fact, two people slipped over before we even made it out of the main gate of the brewery. A few more were doing some sort of weird dance by frantically waving their arms around trying to keep their balance. Toshiyuki had quite a sway going, too. Actually, most people were swaying somewhat. But that was probably more to do with the fact that the Japanese are cheap drunks. I'm sorry, but it's true. Apparently, the Japanese are especially susceptible to alcohol because their bodies lack sufficient ALDH enzymes to break it down, so they get pissed quicker. And fall over quicker.

It was now bitterly cold, but at least I was warm. I had a pair of thermal underpants on. They were keeping me deliciously toasty, but the problem was that because they were cheap (that's the quality not the price as I'd bought them in Switzerland) they kept falling down. All night I would get funny looks as I shoved my hands down my pants and fiddled with my crotch.

Ōdōri Park isn't really a park. It's a long strip of land squeezed in between two streets lined with dull grey office buildings. When I stepped into it that night, however, I gasped at one of the most spectacular sights I'd ever seen. Like an opaline dream world, the park was a glittering procession of megalithic monsters, cartoon characters, palaces, castles and temples spotlit in a multitude of colours. The first sculpture, the three-storey-high British Museum, was an extraordinary deep aqua. It was only the sight of the lady's pink frilly knickers as she fell over that dragged my eyes away from it.

We 'oohed' and 'aahed' as we stood in front of the incredibly intricate 'Palace Museum' (from the Forbidden City in Beijing), which was lit in the most amazingly vibrant shades of green and red. I was mightily impressed, even though—according to the diagram at the front showing how it was done—it would have been a doddle to build. There were three photos captioned: *1. Prepare model. 2. Build framework. 3. Snow is put, and it works.* It certainly does.

A lot of snow certainly was *put* on the next sculpture. And it works. It consisted of three massive snow cows. Behind the cows was the site of the International Snow Sculpture Competition, with a remarkable collection of eagles, dragons, elephants, fish and the ubiquitous cartoon characters. Twenty-one teams from 19 countries had taken part. Each three-man team had only four days (working from 9 am till 9 pm and not a minute longer) to complete their sculptures, and were given identical tools to work with: 4 shovels, 2 buckets, 4 pairs of rubber gloves, 2 chisels, 1 axe, 1 ladder and 1 scaffold (and 1 pair of thermal underpants!). The Hawaiian team, which was made up of chefs who usually made ice sculptures for dining room tables, came second to that other powerhouse snow sculpture nation . . . India. Not surprisingly, the Indians made a sculpture of an elephant.

In true Japanese style, each sculpture along Ōdōri Park had a spot marked in front of it from which to take the 'best photo'. The larger sculptures had a 'photo stage' with a steady stream of people rugged up against the cold queuing to get into the prime happy snap position.

'My toes are numb,' I moaned. My thermals weren't quite up to the task.

'Shall we rest at the station?' Toshiyuki said pointing to a 'Smokers' Rest Station'. The large 'heated' caravan with smoke pouring out of the open door had a sign on the front saying 'Smoking here is good for you'.

'Oh, if that's the case,' I said after reading the sign, 'let's go have a few cigarettes then.' The caravan may have been the smokiest place I'd ever been in, but at least my toes were soon thawing out.

I would have had more than cold toes if I'd gone to the Shibare Festival held in Rikubetsu-cho in the north of Hokkaidō. That too is a snow festival, but there are no cute snow sculptures. The only sculptures you'd be likely to find there would be frozen bodies. Participants spend the night lying in a field of snow in a sleeping bag—it's usually around –20. Those who last until the morning are given a certificate. That's it. Gee, I'd want at least a new car for turning into a human icypole.

I found this festival on an incredibly long list of all sorts of festivals on the Japanese National Tourist Organization website. The major ones are described, but in many cases you have only the name to go by. Some sounded very interesting, if not a trifle weird: the Sakai Cutlery Festival, Head of Sparrow Festival, Portable Shrine that is Naked Festival, Kind of Melon Festival, the Aha Festival (the eighties' Norwegian band must be big there), the Ogre Shooting Festival and, my favourite, the Sending God away on a Thing Festival.

The last of the Ōdōri Park sculptures was the largest of all. Celebrating the anniversary of the arrival of 'the black ships' to Japan, it was made up of an almost life-sized sailing ship, a 10-metre-high church and, in the middle of the two, a bust of 'Captain Perry', whose head was as big as my house. It deserved a big 'Wow!'. So did the bloke who, when taking a photo of his wife, did a triple pirouette when he slipped on the ice. He got a lovely photo, though. Right up his wife's skirt.

On the way out of the park we passed a sign which read 'Please wear nice sensible shoes'. At that point I duly slipped over.

•

A crisp clear day greeted us as we made our way back to Ōdōri Park to see the sculptures the next morning. We were going to be just as impressed seeing them in the daylight. And sober. They *were* just as impressive and, better still, we got to witness a spectacular mass slipping over. A Salvation Army type band was setting up in front of the 'Captain Perry' sculpture when the tuba player slipped and fell onto the French horn player, who in turn fell on the flautist, who pulled another six members of the band down with her into a messy heap on the ground. What surprised me the most, however, was that they were all wearing nice sensible shoes.

We left Ōdōri Park, the Amazing Acrobatic Band and the magnificent snow sculptures to have an early lunch. Hokkaidō is famous for its *rāmen* (egg noodle broth) and Rāmen Alley is *the* place to have it. You could smell the miso and soy two blocks away. You could hear the slurping from one block away. The alleyway was merely a metre wide and at least 20 tiny *rāmen* restaurants were jostling for business. And when I say tiny, I mean tiny—most of the them only held eight people. The restaurants were already crammed with diners and we had to wait a few minutes for some people to leave. The kitchen in the place we chose took up most of the restaurant. A bench ran down two sides of it and we had to squeeze past two Slurping

Champions in training to get a seat. It was good and bad having my own personal translator with me—Toshiyuki ordered god-only-knows-what from the menu on my behalf. Toshiyuki set a cracking slurping pace, but in my rush to keep up with him I merely managed to make a fine mess of my lap. The soup was so hot and spicy that my ears, which had been frozen for two days, thawed out.

On the way to the bus stop Toshiyuki said, quite seriously, 'Do you know whose sculpture I would have liked to have see?'

'No. Whose?'

'David Beckham. That would be very good.'

Naked Man Festival

Okayama, Japan
February 15th

It didn't look good. On the evening news they were showing lines of stretchers loaded with men dressed in nappies being rushed into a hospital where even more men in nappies were lying on hospital beds. Some of them were screaming. Some were covered in blood. And some looked like their nappy-wearing days were well and truly over. I couldn't understand a single word the newsreader was saying, but I imagined phrases such as 'buckets of blood', 'crushed heads' and 'what the hell were these people thinking?' were being used. Fear, like a small weed, started to grow in my belly. These men had been participating in a Hadaka Matsuri, or a Naked Man Festival. In 24 hours' time I would be participating in the largest of all the Naked Man Festivals, the Saidai-ji Eyō in the southern city of Okayama.

There are around a dozen Naked Man Festivals, with slight variations in rites, held in different towns around Japan. The one being shown on the news had taken place in Nagoya. I later learnt that one person had died, two were in comas and 36 others were hospitalised.

I should be fine, though. I'd sent a letter to the mayor's office in Okayama asking if I could participate and I received a note back saying, 'We are wishing from the bottom of our heart, for Mr Brian who comes from a distant place, this festival becomes a lovely experience.'

Before I go any further I should probably explain to you what a Naked Man Festival is. First of all, participants aren't actually naked. Each one wears a nappy. Actually, it's worse than a nappy. It's called a *fundoshi*, and it is a bit like the ritual garb of a Sumo: a thin strip of cloth up your crack revealing your bare buttocks to the world. Wearing this *fundoshi,* I was going to squeeze my way into a temple with a horde of other men in nappies and wait until midnight for all the lights to be turned off. What happens after that? Well, I was about to find out. Apparently, what ensues involves trying to catch a holy stick (called a *shingi*), all-in brawls, a dead body or two, and lots and lots of sake.

The Saidai-ji Eyō festival draws about 10 000 Naked Men each year. Some are corporate teams of first-year salarymen attempting to bond (what's wrong with a few pints at the pub?), some are martial arts *dojo* teams looking for prestige, and some, like me, are just there because . . . hang on a sec, why was I there? Every year there is a team fielded by the Yakuza, the Japanese mafia. They are easily identified by their villain's costume, consisting of a jet-black *fundoshi* and long bleached-blond hair. The main reason they attend is so they can beat the crap out of people (especially foreigners) for no particular reason at all. The organisers try to exclude the Yakuza—

who are stereotypically tattooed—by banning people with tattoos, but the mobsters maintain a crack squad of cunningly untattooed Yakuza especially for the occasion.

I was having urgent second thoughts as I stood with my mouth agape watching the news. I just hoped I wasn't going to make the news back home. Not because I might be terribly injured—I just didn't want to be seen wearing a nappy.

I'd decided to lash out for my final night before the festival and had booked into a *ryokan* (an authentic Japanese inn) in the traditional village of Kurashiki, an hour south of Okayama. It certainly didn't look very traditional when I stepped out of the train station. In fact, Kurashiki looked like nearly every other Japanese city, with tons of neon, pachinko parlours, karaoke bars, red-lanterned restaurants and lots of people scurrying about. I wondered for the first 10 minutes whether I was in the right place at all until I walked through an archway on the busy main street and stepped into the Japan of 200 years ago.

Miniature stone bridges arched over a long canal that was lined with willow trees and ancient black-tiled warehouses, which had been converted into shops, restaurants, tearooms and museums. And the cobblestoned streets with no Toyotas zipping about were particularly pleasant. It was really quite delightful. I got to see just about all of it in my first 15 minutes. But that was because I couldn't find the *ryokan* as all the signs were in Japanese. At one point I even wandered into someone's house. It had the traditional sliding door of a *ryokan* but I stepped smack into the middle of a family lunch. As you'd expect, they were quite surprised to see me. I only found the *ryokan* after I asked an old man who escorted me to the door while lugging a giant sack of rice.

The reception of the Naraman *ryokan* was empty. I took off my shoes and donned one of the pairs of plastic slippers that were sitting by the door before stepping inside (I'd read up on my *ryokan* etiquette before I'd arrived). I called out repeatedly without reply, so I went for an exploratory amble down one of the corridors. I wandered into the kitchen, much to the astonishment of the lady washing dishes, who quickly ushered the poor, stupid, lost westerner back to reception.

A maid appeared wearing a classical kimono and wooden sandals. Her hairstyle looked not dissimilar to Marg Simpson's (except that it was black). She looked as if she'd been in the game a long time, too, and had wrinkles on top of her wrinkles. She indicated that I should follow her as she toddled up the steep narrow staircase. Her wooden shoes echoed down the corridor as she led me up and down stairs and through a labyrinth of cramped passageways. There was no way on earth I'd be able to find reception again.

My room, with its sliding screen door made of paper, was a simple square room with a *tatami* (reed mat) floor. I was scolded for wearing my slippers into the room (I got confused—there's a lot of *ryokan* etiquette to take in). They had to be left by the door. In the centre of the room was a low table that was surrounded by cushions. My bed (a futon) would be stored in the cupboard that took up one wall. I was motioned to sit down then she disappeared.

For five minutes I waited uncomfortably on the floor. Just as the pins and needles in my foot started to kick in, she returned with a tray of tea. I was given a registration form to fill out. The entire thing was in Japanese. Because I'd said 'hello' and 'how are you?' in Japanese when I'd arrived, she thought I could speak the language fluently. She waffled on for a few minutes then indicated that I should tick three different times that were set out in a series of boxes. I figured out that the choice of morning times were for when I wanted breakfast and I assumed one of the times in the evening was for dinner. I was a little bit worried about the other time, though. She kept nodding and winking at me so I guessed that was when she was going to have her way with me. An hour before dinner seemed like as good a time as any for sex, so I ticked six pm. She seemed pretty happy with that.

After an hour of traipsing up and down stairs and wandering aimlessly along corridors, I finally found the way out. I ended up having the most marvellous day. A delicious lunch at a quaint little restaurant was followed by a visit to the Ōhara Museum of Art, which was simply amazing. Here was this little gallery in a tiny town way off the tourist track with one of the most impressive collections of paintings and sculptures I'd ever seen. Textile magnate Ōhara Keisaburo had travelled to Europe extensively in the early 1900s and returned with works by Monet, Manet, Rodin, Matisse, Picasso, Renoir, Cézanne, El Greco, Toulouse-Lautrec, Gauguin, Degas and Van Gogh, and set up this museum in his home town. I virtually had the museum to myself. It was so peaceful, in fact, that I fell into a deep sleep in the guard's chair in the Impressionists room. It was lucky someone didn't call an ambulance, actually, as I probably looked dead. I awoke with my head slung backwards and my mouth wide open.

Back in my room I switched on the tiny TV and watched the dead Naked Men on stretchers. While I stood there in shock, the phone rang. 'You. Bath. Now,' said the maid who then promptly hung up. Right, so this was my bath time not sex-with-an-old-Japanese-maid time. There was only one teeny problem: where in the hell was the bath? I dressed in my *yukata* (cotton kimono-like dressing gown thingy) and shuffled around the corridors for 15 minutes before I found the bath. The maid was quite flustered about my lateness and almost shoved me into the *o-furo* (traditional Japanese bathroom).

I scrubbed myself first (you have to be squeaky clean before you can bathe in Japan), then stepped into the deep and scaldingly hot bath. After a good 15-minute soak, I got out and noticed I was almost as wrinkly as my hostess was.

Back in my room the table had been set for dinner. The maid walked in with an enormous tray piled high with bowls and plates of food. Must be doing the rounds, I thought. But, no, it was all for me. She took one glance at me and motioned for me to stand up then casually untied the *obi* (belt) of my *yukata* (I was naked underneath, by the way). Now I was sure she was going to have her way with me. Thankfully, she simply retied the *obi* in the opposite direction. I later read that the only time the *obi* is tied on the left is when a *yukata* is being used to dress the dead.

The dinner was fabulous (even if I couldn't positively identify half the stuff I was eating). There were 12 courses, including miso soup, pickled pickles, sashimi, *yakitori*, tempura prawns and vegetables, good ol' octopus tentacles, a *nabe* stew, a whole baked fish and other odds and ends that may or may not have once belonged to an animal.

I could barely get up off the cushion when I'd finished. The maid returned with another maid and they both gave me a surprised look. I hadn't touched the large bowl of rice. I was surprised too, actually. I hadn't even seen it. With so many bowls of stuff to work through I'd simply overlooked it.

The two maids put on the most elaborate show as they made up my futon bed in the centre of the room. They did some impressive origami moves while folding the sheets, then bowed continuously as they walked out of the room backwards.

I had a bit of a slipper dilemma. In the entrance to the toilet there was a pair of plastic 'toilet' slippers. The etiquette is to change into these slippers when you go to the loo. My dilemma was that they were a bit wet in places on top. Had the last person to use the slippers pissed on them? It didn't really matter in the end. I wore my own slippers in and dribbled on them anyway.

·

I waited in my room for 20 minutes for breakfast to arrive. I stumbled down the stairs to find out where it was and was given another blasting by the maid. Breakfast was being served, naturally, in the 'breakfast' room. I sat down next to two men wearing their *yukatas* who were ploughing into bowls of rice and seaweed. Cornflakes and toast and jam it certainly wasn't, but I had to experience a true Japanese breakfast. Although I drew the line at the dried seaweed. And the raw egg. And the dried fish. And the cold miso soup. I did eat the rice, though.

I checked out (well I think I did, anyway. I filled out another indecipherable Japanese form) to the constant bowing of the maid. She was still bowing when she followed me out into the street.

I caught the train back to Okayama to visit one of the Three Best Gardens in all of Japan. The Japanese have a penchant for rating and numbering things, and besides gardens they have such other top trios as the Three Best Castles, the Three Best Scenic Spots and the Three Best Beaches. Then there are the Three Strangest Festivals, which includes the Naked Man Festival in Okayama. Wow, I would get to do two of the big Threes in one day. I'd already seen two other things from the Three Best lists. In Tokyo I'd visited number two on the list of the Three Best Toilets (although I'd only done number ones) and in Sapporo I'd seen one of the Three Best Drunks.

The gardens of Kōraku-en were immaculate. The lawns looked as if they'd been trimmed with nail scissors. A meandering gravel path weaved its way past ponds, moss-covered boulders, mini temples and even a mini tea plantation and rice paddy. The place was full of Japanese tourists taking photos. To be part of the action I stopped to take a photo of a line of almost-budding cherry blossom trees and waited for eight people to move out of my shot. Every single one of them was crouching down taking a photo of twigs on the ground.

.

I checked into a hotel near Okayama station and, after a little a nap (during which I dreamt that I pooed in my nappy), I had a lovely meal in a *yakitori* restaurant. I couldn't read the menu, so I sat next to the chef and pointed to things cooking on the grill.

I was catching a bus to the festival. Someone from the mayor's office had kindly contacted me and told me that there was a busload of 'Engrish' teachers heading there and I was welcome to join them.

The bus ride was scary. Well, not the ride itself, but the stories I heard. At the front of the bus, a Naked Man veteran took the microphone and gave us new bloods a few words of advice. 'Remember, there are NO rules. They are allowed to do anything short of killing you in order to get the *shingi*. No matter what, hang on to your "buddy" [a buddy is someone you team up with who then stays with you the entire time—and also gets the medics after the Yakuza beat the shit out of you]. Do not strike with your fists—use your elbows if you have to. Stay away from the men in the black *fundoshi* . . . they *will* try to kill you. And, this is the most important one of all, clench your butt cheeks when they pull on your *fundoshi*.' We were then taught the Hadaka Matsuri chant, '*Washoi! Washoi! Washoi!*' No one was quite sure what it actually meant, though. Hopefully not, 'Punch me! Punch me! Punch me!' And we skolled sake. Apparently, one does not dare face the gods of Japan (or other drunken men in nappies) sober.

John, an incredibly tall American who was sitting next to me, then lifted my spirits even further with stories of his exploits at last year's festival. He first told me that his flatmate, who wasn't running this year, called it 'the worst human experience he has ever encountered'.

'Don't get drunk,' he said as he sipped his sake. 'Stay sober.'

Gee, I wished he'd told me that before I'd had three beers, two cans of hot sake and a couple of shots of fermented plum liqueur.

'Whatever you do, don't fall down,' he went on. 'Last year there was an older guy behind me, who was probably in his fifties, who went down. The crowd started moving and it was either trip over him and get dragged down as well or step on him. My friend was holding my wrist screaming, "Don't fall over. Don't fall over!" Meanwhile, this old guy was getting dragged along the ground. We finally pulled him up and his entire back was bleeding. His face was bleeding as well. He was a right mess. The party was over for him.'

I skolled the rest of my sake. I wasn't going to be sober.

'Out of our group of 10 who participated last year,' John said with a grin, 'we had two broken ribs, a broken toe and a couple of black eyes.'

'That's pretty bad,' I whimpered.

'Nah, we did all right,' he said.

The venue for the Naked Man Festival is the Saidai-ji Temple, which is in a typical semi-rural Japanese town on the outskirts of Okayama. Surrounded by mountains and ringed by rice paddies, the small timbered houses with their blue-tiled roofs encircle the main street of shops. At the end of the street stands the temple.

The entire history of Saidai-ji and the festival is not recorded, but it is known that men have gone there every February to participate since the 1600s, and that the ceremony is steeped in Buddhist spirituality. The Hadaka Matsuri was a physical representation of devotion. February is a cold month in Japan so to run about unclothed is meant to be a show of faith. Similar to the running of the bulls in Pamplona, the Hadaka Matsuri is Japan's ultimate test of manliness and bravado, of strength and the ability to take punishment; a crucible from which one emerges stronger. Or with pneumonia.

A test of strength was also the main reason for the world's most famous Naked Man Festival, which in its modern form is the most watched event on Earth. The Olympics, founded in the 8th century BC, was originally a festival of naked men competing in athletic events where the first prize was 'a woman skilled in fair handiwork'. I bet.

I certainly didn't fancy getting naked. It was only a degree above zero and the rain was coming down in sheets as we stepped off the bus. The ground was a sea of mud. I was struggling to keep warm, yet here I was just about to run around in nothing more than a nappy. I was pretty sure it was going to be the silliest thing I'd ever done. Then again, it could have been sillier. I could have gone to the Penis Festival in the town of Komaki where a three-metre, 280-kilogram wooden penis is paraded down the main street. Women pat it, stroke it and even kiss it. And naturally, they get their photo taken in front of it (I've seen photos—it's as if they are standing in front of the Eiffel Tower). That's not all, either: schoolgirls walk around licking foot-long penis lollypops and chefs make penis-shaped meals (I bet they do the old banana and two scoops of ice cream trick). One week after the Penis Festival there is, you guessed it, a Vagina Festival. Held on the other side of the island, the festival celebrates the vanquishing of a demon that lived in a woman's vagina that would bite off the penis of her lovers (I knew a girl like that once). Yes, when it comes to kooky festivals the Japanese certainly excel. Among my favourites is the Jostling Festival held in Yamoto where men in *fundoshis*, well . . . jostle each other till they've all fallen over. There's a similar flavour to the Pinching and Beating Festival in Niigata, the details of which I'll leave to your imagination.

The Japanese don't have a monopoly on painful festivals, though. In Mamala, Indonesia, for example, they have a Broomstick Beating Festival where men beat each other's bare backs with brooms until they bleed. Mind you, in Japan it's not only the adults who are crying with pain. Every February, the small town of Hirado hosts the popular Crying Babies Festival. It's basically a competition, and the rules are fairly simple: two bubs (they must be under one year in age) are placed on a stage facing each other, then—to the delight of the crowd—a large man starts the competition by screaming as loud as he can into their faces. Drawing inspiration from a wise old Japanese saying that 'crying babies grow fast', the first baby to start howling is declared the winner. While we're on the subject of babies, I was just about to buy a nappy. Lining the narrow street, among all the restaurants selling octopus tentacles, were stalls hawking the prerequisite *fundoshi* and *tabi* (socks made of the same wafer-thin material as the *fundoshi* and sporting the split-toed style of the ninja). I stopped to make possibly one of my strangest purchases ever.

John already had a 'buddy', so I latched myself onto the next biggest bloke, Mike from Canada. Like me, he was at his first Naked Man Festival.

'This is fuckin' insane,' he said as a bunch of Naked Men rushed by us.

'No,' I said. 'We're the ones who are fuckin' insane.'

With *fundoshi* and *tabi* in hand, we 10 foreigners who were participating were ushered into a small blue tent, packed tight with naked men (as in *totally* naked men) drinking sake. After a few minutes of staring at Japanese willies I stripped off, only hesitating for a second before bashfully removing my underpants. A tiny, ancient Japanese man looked me over with distinct amusement (which seemed to be aimed mainly at my western willy). This man's sole purpose in life (well, tonight at least) was to gird the loins of naked men. I handed him my long strip of cloth. He unrolled it, then motioned for me to hold one end under my chin. The remainder was passed between my legs and twisted into an ominously-looking cord. With no warning, my dresser pulled. And pulled hard. Fabric snapped up through my legs, splitting my balls in two and pretty much guaranteeing I'll never have any more children. Somehow, it got worse. He turned his back to me, holding the fabric over his shoulder, and then heaved with all of his body weight. I clenched my bum cheeks like I'd never clenched them before. It didn't really help. The tight cord wedged right up my crack. He yanked it so hard, in fact, that my feet left the ground. The remainder of the strip was rolled around my waist, and the last bit that I held under my chin dropped forward, hanging like a loincloth. I slipped my feet into my *tabi* and taped them up. Then I skolled another sake. Without warning, two Japanese fellows put their arms around me and dragged me towards the exit. I just managed to grab hold of Mike on the way out. This was it. Quite amazingly, I could hardly feel the cold. My internal fires were burning brightly on a combustible mix of sake and adrenaline. Mike and I locked arms and began running.

The actual run through town was a frantic blur that cannot be captured by memory. Everything swirls by and you are only aware of the feeling of surging forward. The long path up to the temple gates was lined with police holding back people trying to touch you for good luck. We passed through this gauntlet and, like gladiators racing into an arena, we burst into the temple grounds, which were surrounded by towering grandstands.

A huge cheer exploded when Mike and I, foreign novelties that we were, made our entrance. The roar of the crowd was overwhelming. Suddenly, we were diverted to the right. The temple was directly in front of us, but for some reason everyone was turning, and turning fast. Being stuck in the middle of this, I simply went along with it. I looked across and saw Mike grinning like a madman.

Then I saw the lake. A small lake that everyone was dashing into including—by the look of it—us. I had no choice; it was like being in a runaway train. I was going in with all the rest of these loonies. When I splashed in, I didn't feel a thing—my entire body had now gone numb. In the middle of the lake was a large stone pillar that we had to go around. The chanting of '*Washoi!*' reached fever pitch as we splashed out of the water. It was then, freezing and scared shitless, that I finally figured out what '*Washoi! Washoi! Washoi!*' meant. My guess was that it roughly translated into 'Fuck! Fuck! Fuck!'

We charged for the stairs that led to the dais of the massive temple. Four wide steps lead up to a wooden platform that was now packed with chanting men. Mike and I made it to the middle of the crowd as we squeezed our way right into the centre of the dais floor. The crowd crushed in on all sides and at times we would sway back and forth with the waves of bodies. It took me all of two minutes to lose my 'buddy'. Mike had muscled his way to the front while I got stuck in the middle of the sea of bodies.

The temple platform is designed to hold a few hundred people at best. Thousands of naked men were now attempting to squeeze onto it. The chanting of '*Washoi! Washoi! Washoi!*' was becoming deafening. Men kept pouring up the stairs, yelling, slipping, clambering and slithering their way onto the platform. I could see quite a few unlucky souls who were in the unfortunate position of being right on the edge, ready to be pushed back down the stairs when the crowd surged backwards. When I say that these men were pushed back down the stairs, I think the phrase 'flung back down the stairs' is more apt. Arms were flailing about and where there were once four or five people, suddenly there were none.

Over the next two hours (which seemed like many more) our nightmarish situation got even worse. Just when I thought that no more people could possibly be squeezed onto the platform, the pack got closer and tighter. On the catwalks overhead, a handful of solemn, innocent-looking priests had been looking down solemnly (and innocently) at the crowd below. Now they began ladling cups of ice water onto us. Because there were so many bodies crushed in together, curtains of steam started to rise from the mass like some ghostly fog. The steam suppressed any air and it was getting— though it was hard to believe—very hot. By this stage cascades of icy water were landing everywhere. The steam dissipated for a moment and you could see the army of priests on the catwalks above throwing bucketfuls down onto the crowd.

The whole scene was lent an unearthly dreamlike quality by the steam pouring off our bodies with each cast of water. My throat was sore from the continuous chanting, but I couldn't hear myself scream above the noise. I was getting a good workout, though. I must have trotted 20 kilometres on the one spot.

At one point I'd somehow managed to get pushed towards the front. A skinny fellow shoved me even further forward. When I put my hands out to stop myself falling, I got two handfuls of a large man's wobbly bum cheeks as he tried to clamber up the wall.

The mass of flesh careened drunkenly from side to side. Doing my best to be nimble and stay on my feet, I was carried helplessly left, then right, then backwards, then forwards. A slip would have been lethal. The backwards drift was the most frightening, as the majority of runners are hurt each year by being violently ejected from the platform and sent tumbling down the long wooden staircase of the temple. An elbow collected me in the eye and knocked out my contact lens. Oh good, now I was half-blind.

I had to get off the platform. I was about to burst. I desperately needed a piss. I couldn't hold on any longer. All that sake had taken its toll. I had thought I could hold on till the end, but I was in terrible pain. I managed to squirm through the bodies and—wet as I was—it was easy to slide past. I timed my exit down the steps with the moving mass of people so I didn't get thrown down headfirst and stumbled off the bottom step into the drizzling rain. It was then that I began pissing in my nappy (well, that's what they're for aren't they?). People were standing right next to me with their arms touching mine as the warm wee poured down my legs. I had no choice as my bits and pieces were bundled up so tight I couldn't get them out. While I was in my weeing heaven, a large man crashed down the front steps right in front of me and landed on his head. Two smaller men exited right behind him. I thought they were trying to help him, but realised they probably weren't when they started kicking the hell out of him. Eventually a swarm of white-raincoated police with clubs arrived and laid into the two assailants. The two men actually tried to put up a fight with the police but were beaten into submission. Meanwhile, not one of the hundreds of police bothered to check on the man lying in the mud. He was able to stand up of his own volition, but by that point he must have had absolutely no idea where he was. Somehow he managed to stand and he staggered away, bleeding heavily from cuts and gashes all over his body. One of the police finally noticed and escorted him away. The two men who had attacked him were not taken into custody; instead they were allowed to re-enter the fray. Someone was shouting out something through the enormous loudspeaker. 'What are they saying?' I asked a Japanese man next to me. 'Naked Men! Please don't fight!' he said.

As I stood there shivering (and still weeing) a large Japanese man put his arm around me and started hugging me. This had happened a lot already. The Naked Man Festival is big on camaraderie and everyone is in it together as brothers. Even when you're pissing in your pants. Then again, all this hugging was a trifle worrying. I found a lot of my info on the Naked Man Festival on a gay website called <jboys.com.jp>. This website not only listed all the Naked Man Festivals, but also told you the best way to rub you body against other naked men and how to quickly unravel a *fundoshi*. I should have taken note of that. It would have saved me peeing in my pants.

After relieving myself I moved back closer to the platform. Fights were breaking out everywhere now. A large Yakuza head-butted some poor sod next to me who went down like a sack of potatoes. The Yakuza were roving around the fringes looking like lions stalking a herd of gazelle. They were waiting for the person with the *shingi* to come out, then they'd gang up on him to get hold of it. My toes took a hammering as I tried to squeeze my way in closer. I had to get closer. And it wasn't because I wanted the *shingi*. I didn't want to be beating practice for the Yakuza.

Without warning, the lights went out. This was it. Midnight. I flung my hands up skywards and could feel other arms next to mine. We were grabbing blindly for the soon-to-fall *shingi*. A collective roar went up from everyone.

Everything was now dark except for a zillion camera flashes from both in and outside the temple. From where I was standing, the constant flashes lighting up the darkness seemed to have a magical kinetic effect. The fervour reached its peak. The priest dropped the *shingi*. Or at least I think he did. Because of the darkness I never actually saw it. Mind you, if it had landed in my hand I was going to chuck it away as quick as you can say '*washoi*' because who ever got hold of the *shingi* was going to get hurt. Bad.

After the drop, the lights flooded back on. What followed next was nothing short of pandemonium. Swarms of bodies flowed like a tidal wave and piled on top of whoever had hold of the *shingi*. Simply catching the *shingi* is not enough for Naked Man glory. One must carry the *shingi* through the gates of the temple. You may ask why grown men in nappies beat the hell out of each other to get hold of a stick. Well, not only will the winner be endowed with auspicious powers, increased fertility and manly strengths for the upcoming year, but he also gets quite a nice little cash prize of ¥500 000 (about US$5000).

Someone was making a bolt with the stick down the stairs. He was holding the stick high up in the air. Then I saw who it was. It was Mike! We made eye contact for a second just before a large Japanese man grabbed him in a headlock and threw him to the ground. Then, and I'm not exaggerating here, at least 50 blokes jumped on top of him. Well, that's it for Mike then. Here comes that hospital bed.

I ran over to the pack of bodies. Maybe I could help my 'buddy'. What was I saying? I was going nowhere near that stick. Or the flying fists. I just wanted a better look. The crowd surged as someone else got hold of the stick. Suddenly I was being pushed by the mass of bodies into the wall of the stadium. A wall that was lined two deep with police. Oh, shit. I had nowhere to go. I was getting tightly pressed into the line of police and soon became very closely acquainted with one of the policemen—my face squashed against his face. The crowd surged again and I made a very quick exit from the scene.

A guy staggered past me covered with blood. His entire back was one giant bright red gravel rash. I stood back (and I mean way back) and watched the moving fist fight. Mike tottered over looking a bit worse for wear.

'I had the fuckin' stick!' he bellowed with a wild grin.

'Are you all right?' I asked.

'Yeah. A couple of bruises but I'm fine,' he said sounding a little out of it. In fact, I'm sure he was because he ran back into the rabid pack of Naked Men. I never stayed to see who got the *shingi* over the line (it can take up to an hour to get the *shingi* the 50 metres to the gate). I'd had enough. I staggered back to the tent covered in mud, blood and urine.

There are certain moments in life when it seems as if a beer has never tasted sweeter and this was certainly one of them. John, Mike and I stood around, Asahi cans in hand, recounting the event in its entirety. I was still in a daze. I didn't even know how I had got the can of beer. I certainly wasn't carrying a wallet in my *fundoshi*. Sleet was falling onto our bare shoulders. Amazingly, I didn't even feel the cold anymore.

Mardi Gras

Sydney, Australia
March 3rd

'Let's go find Troughman,' Miss Stephanie whispered into my ear.

'Good idea,' I said.

It was five-thirty in the morning at the Sydney Gay & Lesbian Mardi Gras After-Party and I was about to go poking around the men's toilets with a bloke called Miss Stephanie in search of another bloke called Troughman. Let me just briefly explain who Troughman is: he is a man who likes lying in a trough. And I'm not talking about your common-or-garden trough. Oh, no. I'm talking about a piss-trough. As in your common-or-toilet-block piss-trough. Troughman will lie in a urinal all night wearing nothing but a pair of rubber under-pants while partygoers—how shall I put this?—piss on him. You might think this sounds a trifle weird and you're right, it is. But I'd already witnessed so much weird shit in the past few days and hours that this was just going to be Weird Shit Sighting no. 20-something.

Weird Shit Sighting no. 1 happened a week before I even flew to Sydney. I was doing a spot of research on the internet when I came across a website called the 'Mardi Gras Graffitti Board'. For days leading up to Mardi Gras, people send in messages about such things as what they should they wear to the After-Party or speculation about who might perform there (past 'surprise guests' have included Kylie Minogue, Sheena Easton, The Village People, Boy George and just about every other clichéd gay icon you can think of). It was among all these messages that I found the aforementioned Weird Shit no. 1: 'I have 15 thoroughbred stud gerbils available at competitive rates. These little babies sure know how to squirm. If you wanna buy, just ask around the Men's near the front for Felchman.' I'd be giving Felchman a wide berth, but nowhere near as wide a berth as I'd be giving a fellow called Cumrat: 'I'll be in the middle of the dance floor in my jocks with my cock out at 7 am. When it gets late I get really fucking horny. Does anyone want to meet me there?' People did ask important questions on the Graffiti Board as well, though: 'If you put your drugs in gelatine capsules and then in a little plastic bag and store them up your anus, will the sniffer dogs be able to detect them?'

Weird Shit Sighting no. 2 happened as I was boarding the plane in Melbourne to fly to Sydney. When I opened the overhead locker above my seat, a nun's habit fell on my head. Its owner wasn't even slightly embarrassed. Half of the passengers on the flight looked gay in both senses of the word. Most were buffed, bronzed and waxed up. I felt skinny, pale and hairy (probably because I am but that's not the point). The guy sitting next to me looked like Michelangelo's David (but with a better tan). Apparently, there's a chunk (or hunk!)

of the gay community who spend the months leading up to big event 'preparing' themselves. They double their gym routines, fry themselves silly in the solarium and wax just about everywhere (and everything!). One fellow who wrote in to the 'Mardi Gras Graffiti Board' was worried what sort of impression his nipples were going to make: 'I went to the gym last night and, looking in the mirror after my workout, I decided that my nipples needed to protrude a little more. Has anyone got any suggestions to get that right nipple look? I guess it will have to be clothes pegs on the nipples for a week.'

So what was a skinny, pale, hairy and pegless-nippled fellow like myself doing headed for the Sydney Gay & Lesbian Mardi Gras? A few months earlier I had told Julie, a friend of mine from Sydney, that my new book was going to be about festivals.

'You *have* to do Mardi Gras!' she said. 'I can get you a job as a volunteer Parade Official *plus* tickets to the After-Party.' (This would be Julie's fifth Mardi Gras as a volunteer and she had worked her way up to the rather grand sounding Area Coordinator.)

'What's a Parade Official do?' I asked.

'It's basically crowd control.'

'How am *I* supposed to control a crowd?' (As I mentioned before, I'm not big in the 'buffed' department.)

'You'll have to do a crowd-control course. We run one for all the Parade Officials in Melbourne, as well as Sydney.'

There was one vital question left. 'Do I get a megaphone?' I asked excitedly.

'Maybe.'

'I'd be really good with a megaphone.'

'We'll see.'

'STAND BACK EVERYONE!' I screamed into the phone. 'See.'

A week later I called Julie again. 'I can't make the crowd-control course. I'll be away overseas,' I said.

'Oh . . . that's okay, I can pull a few strings and you won't have to do it.'

'Yeah, but what happens if I, like . . . really have to control the crowd?'

'I'll give you a quick lesson on the techniques to use when you get up here. I've also got a pamphlet called "How to Handle Very Difficult People" that I can give you.'

'But I already know how to do that,' I said. 'You just . . . run away!'

•

This was not the first time I'd been to Mardi Gras. I had attempted to see the parade a couple of years earlier with my friend Chris. We had arrived late and there were over 600 000 people standing on milk crates in our way. All I could see was a lot of coloured lights along with a boisterous rendition of 'It's Raining Men', so we went to the pub instead.

It's amazing to think that the Sydney Mardi Gras started because of a wake for Judy Garland but it's true. On June 24th, 1969, a wake was being held by a bunch of gays in little bar called Stonewall in New York when the police stormed in and demanded that they stop singing 'Follow The Yellow Brick Road'. The homophobic police began harassing, then beating the patrons. The patrons took a stand and fought back. The result was a three-day riot. In 1978, to mark the ninth anniversary of the Stonewall riots, a troupe of Sydney gays marched down Oxford Street. And, wouldn't you know it . . . the police turned up and started kicking and punching them. Fifty-three people were rounded up into police vans and charged with taking part in an 'illegal procession'.

Mardi Gras proper began in 1981 when the original link with Stonewall was broken in favour of celebrating in summer (the gay men didn't like the fact that it was too cold in winter to wear just a G-string and, more importantly, it made their willies shrink). Incidentally, if you've got a thing for small willies look no further than the Reykjavik Gay Days Parade in Iceland held every August. I believe it's also known as the Reykjavik Jellybean Festival.

In 1985, there was a serious attempt to ban the Mardi Gras parade because, as the Reverend Fred Nile put it, 'There will be a Mardi Gras-induced AIDS infestation. The orgy after the parade will spread the disease throughout the entire community.' When rain pelted down on the parade, Reverend Fred Nile announced that God had intervened to drown the debauchery. For outright silliness, though, he had nothing on a Tasmanian Member of Parliament. That chap, who had obviously led a rather sheltered life, claimed—in all sincerity—that there would be no homosexuals in Australia if blokes played more footy at school.

Ironically (well, for the good Reverend at least), the Mardi Gras gets its name from the Christian festival that precedes the fasting of Lent. Mardi Gras is French for 'Fat Tuesday'. Which makes it quite an odd name for the Sydney march, since it's never on a Tuesday and—by the look of all the buffed bodies—there isn't much fat, either. The most famous Mardi Gras in the world is the one in New Orleans, which has been held since 1699. However, Mardi Gras was celebrated long before the Americans claimed it as their own: the Romans celebrated it with orgies. Not unlike Sydney's, then.

By the early 1990s, the Sydney Mardi Gras had been transformed into the current extravaganza: the largest gay parade *and* party in the world. Mind you, the 2003 extravaganza I took part in almost didn't happen at all. In 2002, the Mardi Gras was officially declared bankrupt (they had over-ordered on the sequins). That was easily solved. They just changed their name to the *New* Mardi Gras and the tax department were none the wiser.

By the look of all the solarium tans in the streets the night before, it looked as if the New Mardi Gras was going to be just as big as ever. I met Julie at the pub near her house to do my crowd-control course (she had led the three-hour course in Sydney).

'There are two techniques we use for dealing with Very Difficult People,' Julie began (after our fourth beer). 'There is the Broken Record technique, where you say the same simple message over and over and over again . . .'

'What? Like . . . "There's no place like home, there's no place like home" . . . then tap your shoes together?' I laughed.

'Or,' Julie said sternly, 'there is the Stroking technique . . .' I was going to say I hoped that didn't involve gay men and penises, but Julie (who knows me too well) quickly added, '. . . and no, it's not *that* type of stroking. It's basically just acknowledging the other person by being friendly and concerned. Now, here's the pamphlet on "How to Handle Difficult People". You can read it later.'

I opened it up and the first thing I noticed was a list of the various *types* of Very Difficult People (VDPs in the crowd-control trade) you may encounter as an official. There was:

—*The anxious fear-ridden person*
—*The angry drunk person*
—*The deluded person*
—*The angry frustrated person*

I noticed there was no technique listed for controlling an anxious, fear-ridden, angry, drunk, deluded *and* frustrated person. I imagine you'd need to do a hell of a lot of stroking for that one.

'Well, that's it,' Julie said. We had reduced the three-hour crowd-control course to a tad under three minutes.

'Any questions?'

'Yes.' I'd been dying to ask this all night. 'Is that megaphone mine?' There was a large megaphone poking out of Julie's bag.

'No, that's mine. But I *will* try to get you one.'

When Julie wasn't looking, I grabbed the megaphone to have a go. 'PRICE CHECK ON HUGGIES NAPPIES, PRICE CHECK ON HUGGIES NAPPIES!' I bellowed out (much louder than I had been expecting) across the pub. Every person in the bar looked over. Julie snatched it out of my hand. This probably hadn't helped my chances of getting a megaphone. What happened in the taxi on the way home just about killed off any last remnants of a chance I had left. As we drove down a crowded street, I grabbed the megaphone again and announced loudly to the pedestrians on the street, 'This is the police! Get off the FUCKIN' streets!'

.

The next morning Miss Stephanie picked up Julie and me to go out for 'The Last Supper'—our lunch would be the last meal we'd have until the day after Mardi Gras. I hadn't met Miss Stephanie before and I was half expecting him (as you would with that name) to rock up in a lovely frock, high heels, way too much make-up and a large blonde wig. I couldn't have been more wrong. For a start, he had a shaved head. There was no lovely (or terrible, for that matter) frock either. He was wearing board shorts, runners and a baggy old T-shirt.

We met a few of Julie's gay (and straight) friends at Café Sofia for lunch. At first I couldn't tell who was gay there, either (oh, except that I'd hazard a guess that the blokes I was introduced to as Princess and Janice might have been). Then I noticed that the restaurant was full of men playing with their food. 'I'm too nervous and too excited to eat,' Miss Stephanie told me. To a lot of gay people, the Mardi Gras is like Christmas, New Year's Eve and a Deb Ball all rolled into one. Miss Stephanie had been in the parade four times (once as a gladiator and three times in tiny spandex shorts) and had kicked on at no fewer than 15 Mardi Gras After-Parties.

'It [the After-Party] will be an intimate affair this year,' Miss Stephanie said. 'There will only be 17 000 or so.'

'That's intimate?' I said.

'Oh, yeah. Last year there were 28 000!'

He was also excited that Julie had appointed him the Personal Assistant to the Area Coordinator. 'I get a megaphone!' he said—rather too cockily for my liking.

After lunch we drove to Fox Studios—the venue for the After-Party. We were dropping our bags (with our 'party clothes' in them) off at the cloakroom. And boy, what a cloakroom. It was a massive tent with a 20-metre-long counter.

'Look, there're police sniffer dogs coming here later on this afternoon,' the guy behind the counter told us. 'But they're NOT drug dogs. They are sniffing for explosives and guns.'

Julie told me the organisers would have ensured he told all the volunteers this (the cloakroom was only open early for the volunteers, so they could check in before they had to report for duty). They were worried that if the 700 parade officials thought there were drug dogs they'd down all their pills before the parade. Then there'd be a lot of spaced-out officials staring up into the sky saying, 'Yeah, it's okay, man. Why don't you break down the barricade and join the parade?'

Oxford Street was buzzing. It was only four o'clock and people were already lining the parade route (even though the parade itself wouldn't start for another four hours). People were sitting on the footpath playing Scrabble or cards, or having a picnic. Julie (being the Area Coordinator) had to be at the volunteers' meeting spot early for the arrival of her 80 or so charges. I was introduced to my Team Leader. His name was Barry (Bazza). He was Julie's dad.

'She asked me to help out five years ago and I've been doing it ever since,' he said excitedly. He said everything excitedly, actually. Bazza handed me my T-shirt. It had 'Parade Official' printed on the front and 'We're Here and We're Queer' on the back. I'd had my shirt on for less than two minutes when someone approached me and said, 'Excuse me, can you tell me which way the parade goes?'

'Um . . . I'm sorry, I don't know.'

He looked at my shirt (with 'Parade Official' on it) then gave me a puzzled look as if to say, 'How can you not know that?' I was going to be the worst Parade Official in the history of Parade Officialdom.

Bazza recommended I stock up on some snacks because we would be standing on the parade route for at least five hours. I trotted down to the supermarket just off Oxford Street with my arms crossed over the 'Parade Official' on my shirt. I didn't want to get asked any more questions. As I grabbed an array of energy bars, a woman pushing a trolley laden with, among other things, breakfast cereal, dishwashing liquid and an iceberg lettuce, brushed past me. She was wearing teeny-weeny leopard skin briefs and a matching studded bra. Another fellow walked past wearing pink speedos and Doc Martens. He said to his partner, 'I desperately need some bananas.'

I was asked my second question as I left the supermarket. 'Can you tell me what time the road closes?'

'Five o'clock,' I replied. I had no idea so I made it up. I really should find out something about the Mardi Gras (well, besides how to use the Stroking technique on a VDP).

I met the rest of my team as we made our way to our designated spot on Oxford Street (the road had closed at four-thirty—so I was almost right). There were eight of us in Bazza's team, including a girl with fluorescent orange hair, a guy with shocking blue hair and a bloke called Ozone. My job was to look after a bus shelter. Bazza told me to tell anyone who tried to clamber up on it (for a better view) to get down. If this anyone happens to be a bloke, I thought, and he happens to be six-foot-five and any category of VDP, I ain't telling him nothing.

The crowd was building up and was already four deep. There were still almost three hours to go till the parade started. Standing alongside me (well, 10 metres away on either side) were Rose and Glen. Like me, they looked as if they couldn't fight their way out of a wet paper bag. If any VDPs started giving us grief, we wouldn't stand a chance.

A cross between a comedy act and total chaos was unfolding on the opposite side of the street. There didn't seem to be any Officials doing any officiating (our team only did one side of the street) and the spectators were running amok. The crowd moved en masse (carrying the heavy metal barricades) to the median strip in the middle of the street. Yes, they were supposed to be moved there, but no one had given them the directive to go ahead. A Parade Official (or PO as I shall call them from now on) finally appeared and made them move back two metres. Five minutes later, under the orders of some bozo in the crowd, they all moved forward again. Rose suggested we go over and sort out, in Rose's words, 'the Ferals from the Western Suburbs'. The crowd grunted and groaned when I told them to move. Just up from me, Rose was getting an earful from a menacing looking bloke with about three teeth: 'Make up your FUCKIN' mind! What the FUCK is going on, you FUCKIN' lesbian?' I was just about to go over and help (no, really I was), when the POs for that side of the street finally turned up.

The sun dropped behind the buildings and a cold wind blew up my pants. Glen told me we were standing in one of the windiest spots in the city. Across the street, a VDP jumped (well, technically he fell) over the barricade and started swearing at the crowd and shaking his fists. It took two large POs to drag him back over the barricade. 'He's known as a VDDDD,' I told Rose and Glen.

'What's that?' they chorused.

'A Very Drunk, Deluded, Difficult Dickhead.'

We were lucky we had no VDPs in our section of crowd. In fact, we had VNPs (Very Nice Persons). Back in the early days of Mardi Gras, though, POs didn't have it so easy. They had to fight off police, homophobes and mad lesbians. On one occasion, a PO tried to remove a lesbian who was attempting to jump on a float (to remonstrate that the parade should be about 'military protest' and not 'celebration'). She threw the poor sod to the ground and beat the shit out of him. The POs at the Amsterdam Gay Pride March (the largest in Europe) wouldn't have too many problems with spectators invading the parade route. It's a series of canals where the floats really *do* float.

The parade started a little before eight. The Dykes on Bikes were the first to roll down Oxford Street, creating a cacophony of revs, horns and girls' squealing. Two absolutely stunning girls in leather bikinis roared past on a Harley and, I confess, my mind wandered into a fantasy that involved a motorbike workshop, me, the two girls and a tin of axle grease. The Dykes on Bikes were followed by the Homos on Motos (or Fags on Mags or something like that).

'I can't tell the bloody difference,' Bazza said as he wandered past (throughout the night he would regularly wander by and pass a remark).

'Um . . . most of the Dykes have their tits out!' I pointed out slightly perplexed.

The first float was the St Homo's School (committed to 'Excellence in Deviance'). The float-riders were all dressed as nuns. Naturally they were all men. I tried to spot my neighbour from the flight but—funnily enough—men dressed as nuns all look the same to me. As the floats passed, so did a succession of gay clichés. There was a Shirley Temple float (with a bloke dressed up as the Good Ship Lollipop) followed by an ABBA tribute float, then one dedicated to The Village People (there ended up being *four* of these in the parade). In the middle of all this was a massive vagina on a stick. This was the Ulva Owners and Divers Association accompanied by the Clit-Tickling Dancers. The Giant Vagina was being chased by girls dressed as giant fingers and tongues who would take it in turns to have a good poke at it (or in it!).

The view from inside the barriers was, as my gay friends would say, simply fabulous. The colours, the costumes, the floats and the Luscious Lesbians were a wondrous sight. But being up close did have its disadvantages. First there were the Old Fags. I tell you (and I wish someone would tell them), 70-year-old men wearing nothing but leather G-strings are not a pretty sight. Particularly the close-up view I had of their incredibly wrinkly bums. One of them was dressed in drag. He looked like my grandma. Following the wrinklies were the whales. Or, as they so proudly called themselves, The Large Lesbians. Their blubber in all its glory was out on show. I imagine watching two of them having sex would be like watching the sumo equivalent of all-in wrestling (not that I wanted to imagine it, I might add).

Not far behind them were the bears. More whales—but hairy. One fellow looked like a gorilla (albeit with a beer belly). A 200-kilo fellow dressed in tiny leather shorts and dripping with sweat waddled up to me and gave me a huge hug. 'Happy Mardi Gras, darling!' he said, just before he tried to stick his tongue into my mouth. I quickly swung my head to the side and received a big, wet, sloppy kiss on my cheek. Five minutes later, one of The Village People (well, someone dressed up as the construction worker from The Village People) also gave me a hug and also tried to get his tongue in. This was getting scary, and—more importantly—why weren't two of the Luscious Lesbians trying to kiss me—at the same time?

Just about every religion and nationality was covered: there were the Jewish Gays, Catholic Lesbians, Vietnamese Gay Boys, Lebanese Lesbians and the Transexual North Korean Protestants (or something like that).

'Some of those Asian blokes dressed up as sheilas are not bad sorts,' Bazza said. 'I'd almost have a go at one of them.'

I don't know about that but, I have to admit, some of those fellows really did look, um . . . absolutely gorgeous. A very ungorgeous six-foot-five transvestite hobbled over to me pursing her/his/whatever's lips. 'Would you like a kiss, honey?' she asked. I must have looked utterly terrified (that's probably because I was), because he said, 'It's all right, sweetie . . . maybe later.' She tottered back into the parade as I panicked about the panic attacks I'd be having at the After-Party every time I saw a transvestite.

'Do you reckon that's a bloke?' Bazza asked without a hint of sarcasm. I was getting worried about Bazza (and his choice of optometrist).

My feet were throbbing from almost five hours of standing. They felt like . . . actually they felt like nothing. I couldn't even feel them. I sat down on the curb. Rose sat down next to me.

'Hey, stand up you two!' Julie said as she raced past.

'Gee, she's serious,' I said.

'Yeah, no one is allowed to sit down.'

I immediately sat down again. 'What are they going to do? Sack us?' Rose sat down as well. Five minutes later there were six of us sitting down. Boy, was I going to be in trouble. I did, however, stand up to get a good look at Madam Hussein and her Weapons of Mass Seduction. George Bush, with a massive erect 'rocket' penis was giving John Howard a good serve up the bottom. Little Johnny seemed to be loving it, even when George did 'his load' all over Johnny's back (it was that streamer stuff that comes—or cums!—out of a spray-can). Not long after Madam Hussein came the last of the 140 floats and us. The 700 POs joined the tail of the parade one by one as it snaked its way down Oxford Street. Being near the start of the parade route meant we had the entire four kilometres to walk. Oh, my feet. The crowd were clapping, cheering and throwing streamers at us as we marched by. I felt proud to be gay. 'Hey, Brian! Give me a kiss!' a fellow from the crowd called out to me as he grabbed my arm and tried to drag me in. A few seconds later, a large Maori man said the same thing. I did two things very quickly. I took my name tag off and moved to the centre of the road. It was there that I found Miss Stephanie. He was waving to the crowd (half of whom seemed to know him).

'Hey Brian, can you hold this for a minute?' he said, handing me his megaphone.

I calmly grabbed it and took a step away. 'EVERYONE PLEASE STAND BACK!' I hollered to the crowd. I was just about to say, 'DO NOT PANIC!

I REPEAT, DO NOT PANIC!' when Julie snatched the megaphone out of my hand. She just shook her head.

'Seven hundred volunteers all busting to go to the loo at the end of the parade is going to be very interesting,' I said to Miss Stephanie.

'I'm saving it all up for Troughman,' Miss Stephanie said with a cheeky smile.

We stumbled into the party just after midnight (we had to wait for Julie to pick up our tickets), and made our way straight to the cloakroom tent. I changed my shirt—I didn't fancy the idea of wearing a shirt proclaiming that I was 'queer' around 17 000 gay men. Miss Stephanie and I waited at the cloakroom while the girls (Julie and Rose) scuttled off to the toilets to get changed.

I watched in amazement and amusement as every second bloke walked up to the counter, took off his shirt and pants, checked them in, then swaggered off in tight spandex (or leather) underpants. There may have been a cool breeze blowing around their dangly bits, but these fellows weren't wasting their waxing and weight-work for anything. A guy standing only metres away from us was readjusting his 'tackle' into the most aesthetically pleasing position in his minuscule leather G-string. And oh what tackle he had. And oh what trouble he was going to have preventing it from spilling out of his postage-stamp-sized pants.

'Oh, my giddy aunt,' I whispered to Miss Stephanie.

'That's nothing,' he said. 'One year I was waiting in line out the front and a guy behind me was standing there naked. Well, not exactly naked. He was wearing a cock ring and a Prince Albert!'

'Wow!' I gasped, even though I had no idea what a Prince Albert was—I had heard of it and vaguely knew it was some sort of penis decoration. (When I got home, I looked up 'Prince Albert' on the internet and I was greeted with a picture. A picture that made me grab my groin and grimace. A large metal ring went in through the eye of a penis and came out just below the knob.) What I should have said was 'Ow!'

'On the Mardi Gras Graffiti Board I was telling you about,' I said to Miss Stephanie, 'there was a guy who said "Look for me. I'll be wearing nothing but a tan and my dick dipped in silver glitter".'

'Did he say where he was going to be?' Miss Stephanie asked with a grin.

The girls were taking ages (as they do) to get changed. I'd only changed my shirt and Miss Stephanie was back in his board shorts and baggy T-shirt.

'This is a bit like the Naked Man Festival,' I said (I had told Miss Stephanie about my near-naked exploits earlier). 'Both have men running around in their underpants and both have men desperately trying to get hold of a stick at the end of the night.'

The girls came back all dressed and dolled up. Miss Stephanie and I looked like right scruffs in comparison. We headed off into the party. It was huge. Even bigger than I expected. There were three massive dance venues, plus bars, coffee shops, food stalls, 'chill-out areas' and a large Chupa Chup stand (Chupa Chups being the international standard remedy for people—read almost everyone at the party—with dry mouths caused by the party drug Ecstasy). There were people of absolutely every shape, form, size and colour parading around in costumes that left little to the imagination. We followed a man dressed as a schoolgirl into the RHI (Royal Hall of Industries), which was the largest of the dance venues. As we walked in, Miss Stephanie took his shirt off. The hall was full of men with their shirts off—thousands of them. I left mine on—I didn't want to show them all up. The dance floor was a mass of gyrating men in shorts. We wandered over to the bar. It was twelve-thirty and I hadn't even had my first beer. The party was only just starting. It wouldn't finish until ten in the morning. I'd be lucky to make it to one-thirty. No, make that twelve-forty-five. We squeezed onto the dance floor. It was an immense sauna of bare-torsoed bodies. A speech was made to officially open the party: 'We are here to drink, to party, to fly and to fuck.' The opening 'show' consisted of 96 drag queens strutting around to 'It's Raining YMCAs' or something similar. I was glad to get out of the RHI as it was all a bit hot and stuffy (no wonder most of the blokes had their shirts off). We wandered over to The Dome. 'It's got a costume show,' Julie said. I couldn't tell who was part of the show and who wasn't. On the way in, we passed a gimp (sporting a full leather head mask) crawling on his hands and knees. He was being led by a man in bondage gear brandishing a whip. They both looked very happy.

Amazingly (well, to me at least), there is an entire festival devoted to bondage. The Gorean Bondage Festival in Pennsylvania, USA (where else?), starts with a slave auction, where masters 'buy' slaves which they then own for the entire weekend (you have the choice of being either the master *or* the slave). The slaves are led around in chains and can be put in public stocks, made to wrestle other slaves in mud, or thrown in the dungeon for 'punishment'. Oddly enough, I hadn't added this festival to my itinerary.

On a grander scale (without the dungeons bit) there is Leather Pride Week in San Francisco. It's a celebration of S&M and over 300 000 people turn up dressed in leather (BYO talcum powder, according to their website).

My favourite kinky festival, however, is the Bald Beaver Festival held in New York. It's hugely popular and a doorman checks every person to make sure that they are appropriately shaved. The queue to get in is only surpassed by the queue for applicants to be the doorman.

The Dome was bathed in an indigo light and people were taking turns strutting their stuff on a catwalk in the middle of the room. This was the 'chill-out space' and most people (a six-foot-seven bloke dressed as a ballerina, a couple of leather slaves, some cowboys, a bevy of nuns, and a bunch of Star Trek 'Starfleet' officers among them) were lazing about on couches. We sat on the floor. Miss Stephanie casually offered me an Ecstasy tablet. We'd discussed it earlier and I'd decided that I would take one (well, half of one at least). 'You won't make it to the end of the night if you don't,' Miss Stephanie had said. I've never been into the drug scene. While all the supposedly 'cool' people at art school were smoking bongs and listening to Neil Young, I actually did work and passed. I tried a bong once: it tasted as if I was smoking my dad's socks. I'd done the space cake thing (plus half a joint) in Amsterdam (when in Rome, etc.), but I just ended up sitting in the toilet too scared to come out. I took my half a pill. Miss Stephanie told me I would 'buzz'. I didn't know what to expect. There was always a chance something terrible could happen—I could be seized by a desperate desire to listen to Neil Young songs for example.

'How do you feel?' Miss Stephanie asked 10 minutes later.

'Okay! My feet don't throb any more.' They were feeling quite good actually.

'You might feel a little giddy.'

'No, I'm fine.' I felt awake. A slight 'buzzing'. I felt like a beer. This was good news. Miss Stephanie had told me that the smell of beer might make me feel ill.

My beer tasted just fine. On the way back from the bar I passed a guy giving another guy a head job against the wall. 'That's nothing,'

Miss Stephanie said when I sat down again. 'Back in the old days there would be felching going on in the middle of the dance floor.' (For those of you who know what felching is—yes, yuk! For those that don't, I'm sure not explaining it here—ask your vicar.)

On the way out of The Dome I said hello to a young and over-weight security guard hiding in the shadows near the exit. He almost jumped out of his skin. If there was any trouble involving half-naked men, he'd run a mile.

Julie had managed to secure us tickets to the VIP room. 'You'll see celebrities,' Julie said. This was going to be good. Last year, Julie had sat next to (well, near) Kylie Minogue and Ewan McGregor. The VIP room was upstairs in the RHI building. Tables and chairs sat along a wall of large windows overlooking the dance floor. A dance floor that was heaving with bodies under the most impressive laser light show I'd ever seen.

'How many people do you reckon are on the dance floor?' I asked. 'Five thousand?'

'No, seven thousand,' Miss Stephanie said.

'I reckon at least eight thousand,' Julie said.

'Whatever the actual head count,' I said (for want of a better expression), 'it sure is a hell of a lot of blokes dancing around in their underwear.'

Mind you, all these gyrating bodies had nothing on the Love Parade held every July in Berlin. Over one million people crowd the streets for the world's biggest rave party (the Sydney Mardi Gras party is the world's biggest *topless* rave party).

The pill had made me very thirsty (I had the dry mouth thing I told you about earlier) and I paid a ridiculous amount of money for a ridiculously small bottle of water (they certainly saw me—and my few thousand fellow pill-poppers—coming).

'I can see someone famous,' I whispered. 'Don't turn around too quick.'

'Who, who?' Miss Stephanie said, turning his head straight away and scanning the room.

I leant over and whispered, 'Hiawatha.' Sitting behind us was a six-foot-five man dressed as Hiawatha. He looked very scary. He did have lovely boobs though.

We were on the move again. This time to City Live. This was the lesbian (or as a friend of mine calls them, Vagitarian) nightclub. Men could only enter accompanied by a woman. The place (all three levels of it) was full of more sweaty bodies dancing to thumping techno music.

'Why don't the girls dance with their shirts off as well?' I said to Miss Stephanie as I checked out the action on the dance floor. Miss Stephanie joined the throngs on the floor ('After a few Es he likes staring at the mirror ball,' Julie told me) while the girls and I trudged upstairs.

I was feeling all right. I wasn't freaking out or seeing talking elephants. I had got into the Chupa Chup thing, though, so I looked like a real raver now (oh, except that I'm old, losing all my hair and would rather listen to Frank Sinatra than techno music).

We found a quiet little spot up on the top level to veg out for a bit. Two girls standing next to us had their tops off and were playing with each other's tits. 'People pay good money to see stuff like that,' I whispered to Julie and Rose.

After I'd been hanging out on the top level for almost two hours, a security guard grabbed my arm and bellowed into my ear, 'Hey, what the hell are you doing up here? You're not a woman!' I was in the Women's Space. I couldn't believe it. I couldn't believe it because I hadn't even noticed that I was the only man on a floor packed with uninhibited women. As I was escorted down the stairs, we passed another security guard at the bottom. He must have been on the loo when I'd walked up earlier or, a little bit worryingly, he'd thought I was a woman. He was in the middle of grilling a very butch-looking lesbian. He was interrogating her about whether she was a he. She lifted up her top to show him her tits. 'Okay, up you go,' he grunted.

Time had flown (the pill might have helped there). It was already five-thirty but it only felt like midnight. Miss Stephanie dragged himself away from staring at the mirror ball and joined us for a Chupa Chup. Then the moment came I'd been both dreading and looking forward to (in that watching-the-aftermath-of-a-car-accident type way). 'Let's go find Troughman,' Miss Stephanie said.

On the way to the loos in The Dome, Miss Stephanie told me that Troughman had died two years ago. 'What?' I gasped. A ghastly vision of a corpse pickled in urine flashed before my eyes.

'Oh, it's all right. He franchised it out before he died. This is Troughboy or Son of Troughman.'

Not long before Troughman died he was interviewed on OUT-FM and he said, 'I'm getting a little too old for this type of thing. I think it's time to pass the torch onto someone else.' The interviewer replied, 'It must be hard passing the torch when it is always getting doused.'

As we casually strolled into the toilets I hesitated for a second: I hoped Miss Stephanie wasn't expecting me to wee on Troughboy. During my internet searching, I'd found a quote from someone who had pissed on him (and let me tell you there are plenty—Troughman had been a urinal feature at every major party on the Sydney gay circuit). He said, 'Troughman looked all pale and collected, with piss droplets on his moustache. He gestured for me to piss on his face but I wouldn't—it felt too far for a first date and he had such an unpissable-on face.'

The trough was empty. 'Looks like Troughboy doesn't have the stamina,' Miss Stephanie said. 'Troughman would still be at it.'

'Oh, well,' I said. Actually, I was relieved he wasn't there. I really needed a piss.

I went back to find the girls while Miss Stephanie went in search of another mirror ball. The first signs of a pink dawn (how appropriate) spilt across the sky. Outside, people were wandering around in a daze. There were even more dazed looking policemen trying not to look dazed (this was the fresh morning shift—what a way to start your day). I found the girls and we headed into the only venue we hadn't visited so far.

The Horden Pavilion was another massive dance venue. It was six-thirty in the morning and the dance floor was still heaving. The 'bleachers' (the grandstands around the perimeter) were just as full. On the way up to find a seat I saw a guy licking another guy's bottom. I thought this is just about as weird as it gets.

Then again, if I really want some weird shit (figuratively speaking) I could always go to the Burning Man Festival held in the middle of the Nevada Desert every August. Over 25 000 people spend a week in this temporary town (BYO food, water, shelter and drugs) doing all sorts of weird shit. You can participate in the nude croquet tournament, get up to some public sex and debauchery in Bianca's Smut Shack, or drop in at one of the penis, breast and pubic-hair painting booths. As the website says, 'Come and see nude ravers freak out in the desert.'

I wasn't freaked out but I was starting to feel quite tired now. A lot of people looked tired—there was a lot of lounging about going on. I slumped down in one of the chairs. Milling about on the edge of the dance floor I noticed a large bearded bloke wearing white overalls wandering around. He looked totally lost and bewildered. He looked like a plumber. In fact, he probably was. He had probably come to fix some pipes but had been sent to the wrong address. I was about to go down and ask him if he was all right, when I caught movement in the corner of my eye.

I turned around to see a woman right behind me slouched down in her seat. She was wearing a little titty-top and tiny shorts. Shorts that she had pulled back to reveal her, well, beaver (and one, I might add, that would have gained her immediate entry to the festival in New York I mentioned earlier). It gets worse (or better, depending on which way you look at it)—she was having a good go at her clitoris. This was happening only centimetres away from my face. She didn't even flinch when she saw me looking at her. She looked so out of it. I told Rose and Julie to have a wee look behind them. Not surprisingly, they gasped. 'Do you reckon she needs a hand?' I whispered to Rose. Suddenly, a guy walking up the aisle started calling out to her, 'Oi! Hey you!' She looked up. 'Me . . . you,' he said, then pointed outside. She thought about it for a second, then stood up and followed him down the stairs. Wow. On that note we got up and shuffled out.

There was bright sunshine outside. Like vampires, we scampered off through the shadows to the cloakroom tent. We needed sunglasses. I looked in the mirror in one of the Portaloos—I looked like a vampire: I was pale, drawn and had the most horrifyingly bloodshot eyes. We found Miss Stephanie among the masses of bodies lying about on the ground in the shade of the RHI building. I told Miss Stephanie and two of his friends about the bald beaver girl and the world's quickest pick-up. 'That's the most bizarre thing I've ever heard happen at Mardi Gras,' Miss Stephanie said to the agreement of his friends. What, so Troughman, Prince Alberts, felching on the dance floor and being a Judy Garland fan isn't bizarre? Talking about bizarre, I saw the plumber wandering off hand in hand with a guy in furry leopard-skin underpants. It looked like he was finally going to get his pipes well and truly fixed. By eight-thirty the warm sun hit us. It hurt.

I whispered to Julie, 'I think I'm ready to go.' I wasn't going to make the ten o'clock finish.

'Are you coming?' Julie asked Miss Stephanie.

'Nah, I'll stay a little longer.'

A little longer all right. Miss Stephanie finally got to bed at eight-thirty. Eight-thirty, that is, on Monday morning. He stayed up for 48 hours. In that time he visited 15 bars and nightclubs, didn't eat a single thing and dropped seven Es.

'That's nothing,' he told me later. 'I went out again late on Monday night and met a guy who hadn't been to bed yet.'

Gee, that's a lot of drugs. And a lot of Chupa Chups.

Independence Day

Capitan, New Mexico, USA
July 4th

I decided that Capitan, New Mexico, was a town of God-fearin' folk even before I got there. Five miles out of town a large sign announced 'Jesus is Lord of Capitan'. I saw this sign while listening to a broadcast on the local radio station that went something like this:

> Every believer, every unbeliever, every human being including you and me will bow before Our Lord Jesus Christ. It's only a question of when. Do it now while you have a choice. If not, you will have to pay an eternal death penalty. You need Him NOW. So open your hearts and open your wallets and give to Our Lord Jesus Christ . . .

A bit further down the road I passed the Lone Tree Bible Ranch. It looked like your typical lots-of-cowboys-on-horses-type ranch.

I can't imagine too much wrangling goes on, though. Well, besides a bit of Psalm wrangling perhaps.

I felt like I was driving through an episode of the Lone Ranger (the Christian version). The road rambled past rolling prairies of burnt dry grass and stunted shrubs with a film-set scattering of large boulders (for Tonto to hide behind). I chose to celebrate the Fourth of July in the town of Capitan because I didn't want the anonymity of a large city. I wanted a small town parade followed by a great big small town party. I stumbled upon Capitan by typing in 'July 4th parade' on Google and, on page 37 of my search, found the 'Village of Capitan' website with pictures of their Annual Fourth of July Smokey Bear Parade. The parade seemed to be entirely made up of fat people sitting on the backs of trucks waving American flags. It was absolutely perfect. That was exactly the Independence Day experience I was after.

I did find some other interesting ways to celebrate the Fourth of July on the net, though. In Oatman, Arizona, for example, it gets so hot that they hold a massive egg-frying contest—on the footpath. Back in 1986 in Willimantic, Connecticut, they couldn't afford a band for their parade so they asked everyone to bring their ghetto-blasters along. The local radio station then played band music. Last year over 10 000 people turned up to the Boom Box Parade with their ghetto-blasters. In Lovington, New Mexico, they've utilised their large summer lizard population by running The World's Greatest Lizard Race every July 4th. In 1976 this inaugural event wasn't too successful, though. When a large tub covering the lizards was lifted, the lizards didn't move. They were so petrified by the large crowd that they began to eat each other. The lizard with the largest stomach won the title. Still more horrifying is the Rainbow Gathering held in a different 'forest' every year. On the Fourth of July, a haze of hippies (I believe that's the collective noun) sit in a massive circle in a 'meadow', hold hands and chants 'Om' together for a few hours. I think I'd rather eat the lizards.

Capitan had no lizards, hippies, boom boxes or frying eggs to speak of but, besides the parade, they did have an Old West Ranch Rodeo, a Country Dance, a Chuckwagon Campfire BBQ and free tattoos for the kids. The Mayor of Capitan promised: 'Our sleepy village comes awake with a parade and rodeo that's just *too* much fun. We let our hair down and have a great old time.' I pictured a hootin', hollerin' time with a bunch of rowdy cowboys and cowgirls accompanied by lots of knee slappin', moonshine drinkin' and general yee-haain'. I was still picturing this up until five minutes before I drove into Capitan, when I suddenly imagined everyone in the whole town back home by eight o'clock, beating themselves with sticks and asking the Lord for forgiveness because they'd had 'just too much fun'. Celebrating the Fourth of July in Capitan is so popular that all the accommodation in town had been booked out six months earlier. Yep, every single room at the one and only motel in town had been booked out. I had my mind set on watching fat people sitting in the back of trucks so I decided to go regardless. Besides, I knew of a *real* cheap place to stay. It's called the back seat of my hire car (I figured I'd be too drunk to care by the time I'd downed a couple of buck-etfuls of beers with Chuck and Mary-Lou).

·

As I was scrolling through the Capitan website I noticed a bit of a theme beginning to emerge. The Smokey Bear Motel was next to the Smokey Bear Restaurant, which was next to the Smokey Bear Park. Across the road there was, and I kid you not, the Smokey Bear Chiro-practors. Why this obsession with Smokey Bear? Well, Capitan is the birthplace of the real Smokey Bear. In 1950, when a human-caused fire ravaged acres of forest in the Capitan Mountains, a bear cub who'd been badly burned was rescued and nursed back to life by one of the firefighters. The cub was named Smokey Bear after an advertising poster created five years earlier, and he became the living symbol for forest fire prevention. He became so popular that by 1964 Smokey Bear was receiving so much mail they gave him his own zip code.

I drove down the main street (called—surprise, surprise— Smokey Bear Boulevard) and parked in the Smokey Bear Car Park next to the Smokey Bear Motel. I called in at reception on the off chance that there had been a cancellation. The large pasty lady behind the counter grunted. 'Nope. We all's filled up.' Gee, and I thought my grammar was bad.

The entire population of Capitan was out to watch the parade. All 800 of them. People must have come from surrounding towns as well, because there would have been a couple of thousand people lining Smokey Bear Boulevard. Half of those people were sitting in the back of pick-up trucks that lined the length of the street, glistening brightly in the hot sun. They were all parked with the back facing the street and their tailgates down. A few enterprising folk had thrown couches on the back, while others had barbecues sizzling away. The rest of the townsfolk were sitting on fold-out chairs right on the edge of the road. Everyone, and I mean everyone, was decked out in red, white and blue. I ambled down the main street and it didn't take me long to realise that I was, and I'm not exaggerating here, the only person not wearing red, white and blue. It was incredible. People were wearing T-shirts emblazoned with 'America the free', 'I'm an American girl', 'God bless America', 'God loves America' and 'God is America'. One lady just had 'I'm proud to be' on the front of her shirt. The full message actually read 'I'm proud to be an American', but the bottom line was tucked in between her ample breasts and even ampler stomach. People were dressed up in 'stars and stripes' pants, dresses, shorts, cowboy hats, socks, shoes and knickers (or so I imagined).

As well as street stalls selling American flags, stuffed Smokey Bears and cowboy hats, there was a stand giving away FREE hotdogs. Not shy when it comes to free food, I had three. Even if it was only nine-thirty in the morning. The bubbly lady serving said, 'Happy Fourth, honey!'

'Why, thank you,' I said cheerfully.

'You bet!' she said.

'And so do you!' I chirped.

The parade started with a fat bloke sitting in the back of a truck waving an American flag. Well, he wasn't actually waving the flag because he seemed to be asleep (or dead), slumped in a huge lounge chair. He was Grand Marshall Ben Leslie and looked about 70. The woman who was driving the pick-up truck looked even older. What followed was a succession of pick-up trucks, tractors, cowboys and cowgirls on horses, and lots of red, white and blue. As each entrant (there was a prize for Best Float, Best Tractor, Best Dressed Cowboy, Best Dressed Cowgirl and Best Fat Bloke Sitting in the Back of a Truck) rolled by, the crowd waved their flags and screamed out 'woo-hoo!', 'alllllright!' and 'you go girl!'. First up after the Grand Marshall was Congressman Steve Price who was walking behind his truck (which was full of fat people waving flags) shaking hands with babies. Cowboys and cowgirls were taking their horses through very impressive backwards and spinning around manoeuvres, but I was much more intrigued by the hefty members of the Capitan Hunting Club who were all clutching whopping big guns and straddling an incredibly large dead elk on the back of a truck.

As every truck went past, the occupants would throw handful upon handful of sweets to the crowd. The parade had only been going for 10 minutes and the young boy standing next to me had already filled a plastic bag. No wonder there was an abundance of abundant butts. Of course, not all the people sitting in the backs of trucks were fat. The Lone Tree Bible Ranch truck (well, actually a long trailer being hauled by a tractor) was loaded with gorgeously slim and sweet 20-something year-old girls with the Lord in their hearts (the boys with the Lord in their hearts were all piled on the tractor). All virgins too, I imagine. But then again they all probably went begatting like mad up in the barn loft after the parade (well, that was the vision I had in my head at least).

There were all sorts of things on the back of parading trucks. There was a team of boot-scooters, a pack of dogs, a bunch of folk wearing 'Jesus Loves Us All' T-shirts, a cowboy singing (well, miming) along to his 'Big Hit' and, of course, the star himself, Smokey Bear (who was fat and waving an American flag). The parade ended with a cavalcade of fire trucks blasting out their sirens so loudly I couldn't hear myself think about getting a couple more free hot dogs.

There was still an hour before the rodeo started, so I wandered down to the Smokey Bear Fair in the Capitan High School Gymnasium. It was full of god-awful handicraft crap and awful godly T-shirts like 'Blessed is the nation whose God is the Lord', 'Say YES to Jesus' and one that could easily be misinterpreted—it had a picture of Jesus with 'Come unto Me' written underneath it.

I did a very unChristian thing and snuck under the fence to enter the Annual Smokey Bear Stampede and Smokey Bear Calf Scramble—it saved me six bucks! I'd never been to a rodeo before; only ever caught a glimpse of one on TV. But that was because the cowboys, who must have been a few fiddles short of a hoedown, only lasted long enough to catch a glimpse of before getting thrown from their rather pissed-off bulls and horses.

I squeezed into a space in the grandstand just in time for the Mayor's opening speech: 'Welcome to our Jool-eye Four-eth celebration. I'd like to start with a prayer. Our Lord, we thank you for giving us the greatest nation on earth and we pray that our children grow up to be as patriotic as we are . . .' And so it went on. And on. So much so, in fact, that I was praying he'd hurry up and finish praying.

After the Mayor had thanked the Lord for everything on this planet, all the competitors entered the arena (on their horses naturally) and lined up for the national anthem. As each one of the 80 cowboys entered the arena, the announcer read out his name. It sounded like the roll call from a Hollywood Western. There were, among others, Clint Holt, Twister Furlong, Ace Patterson, Tye Chesser, Cody Hatley Jnr and Stetson Smith. I had to stop myself from yelling out 'Yee-ha' every time he called out a name.

By the first note of 'The Star-Spangled Banner' everyone was up on their feet with hands and hats placed firmly on their hearts. A local girl sang the anthem with an almost orgasmic passion. The lady next to me had tears rolling down her cheeks. In fact, there was hardly a dry eye in the place. I hate to admit it, and I'm a little embarrassed to do so, but I also had a tear in my eye. I was moved. These folk's patriotic fervour may be ridiculously over the top but, golly gee, they love their country. For a second there I wanted to be American, too. I wonder if other countries of the world celebrate their Independence Day with such frightening fervour. It's actually quite amazing how many countries have an Independence Day; most do, in fact. Which means, of course, that most countries were at one time ruled by someone else. There is an Independence Day holiday going on almost every day of the year. In July alone, 23 countries celebrate their independence. Let me quickly bore you with a list:

July 1th—Canada, Rwanda, Belarus and Burundi

July 4th—USA

July 5th—Algeria, Cape Verde and Venezuela

July 6th—Malawi and Comoros

July 7th—Solomon Islands

July 10th—Bahamas

July 11th—Mongolia

July 12th—Kiribati and Sao Tome and Principe

July 20th—Colombia

July 21st—Belgium and Guam

July 25th—Costa Rica

July 26th—Maldives and Liberia

July 28th—Peru and . . . finally

July 30th—Vanuatu.

I did a quick bit of research on the net and found a page of letters written by children about their own country's celebrations—some of which seemed rather odd. A boy from Pakistan, for example, said, 'It's very exciting because the government cleans the roads.' Eulalie Tungu from Zaire said, 'My family celebrates independence by killing animals.'

What astonishes me, and frankly is a bit of a worry, is how much I know about America's Independence. Ask me about any other country's independence and I couldn't tell you diddly-squat. But I can tell you, without looking up any book, that the American Declaration of Independence was signed on July 4th, 1776, by—among others—Thomas Jefferson, John Adams, Benjamin Franklin and John Hancock, and that 13 colonies joined forces to break away from English rule. I can also tell you that all the men who signed the

Declaration wore stockings and wigs. It's frightening how much American history we do know. I mean, I even know such useless shit as some of the amendments from the Bill of Rights (passed a decade after Independence—also by Thomas Jefferson, I believe). Just off the top of my head, there are: freedom of speech; the right to petition the government; the right to bear arms; and the right to a speedy and public trial by an impartial jury. I can't find them in any reference books, but I'm guessing more recent amendments include: the right to have big butts; the right to make trash TV shows; and the right to shoot up fast-food restaurants.

There was no shooting at the rodeo, but there was some Horse Catching going on. This was the first event in which, according to the program, 'No tackleberries or quick cinch equipment are allowed'. Four men each took it in turn to rope their horses before they all bolted out of the arena together. The first couple of teams were interesting to watch. After that it was about as exciting as going to church. What was missing, which would have made it so much more exciting, were tackleberries. I've always said, you can't have a good horse catching without tackleberries.

There were still another 14 teams to do their horse catching thing, so I took a break to get some lunch. To tell you the truth I was loving it. I was at a *real* cowboy rodeo. With *real* cowboys. Sitting in the grandstand watching the horse catching with a backdrop of rolling prairies and the deepest blue sky, I felt as if I was on the set of an archetypal Hollywood Western.

I mosied over (as one does at a rodeo) to check out the Chuckwagon Campfire BBQ. A line of cowboys were sitting down at a long table in a stiflingly hot tent working their way through gigantuous plates of food. For $7.50 you got a plate of Country Style Ribs, Cowboy Beans, Corn on the Cob, Homemade Dutch Oven Cobblers (which is probably what you'll produce after you've eaten the Cowboy Beans) and Cowboy Coffee. It was just perfect. Real Old West American vittles for the Fourth of July. So what did I do? I went to a Mexican restaurant. I was quite looking forward to it, too. According to the reviewer in a travel magazine that I read: 'El Paisano is a restaurant that I plan my vacation around. The Chilli Rellenos is to die for.' I quite fancy a bit of Mexican now and again, but it's virtually impossible to find the real McCoy (or real McGonzalez) in Australia. Most of the time you are served refried sludge. Mind you, you do get a choice—you can have your refried sludge in an enchilada or a taco.

The walls of El Paisano were entirely covered with dried chillies. They certainly love their chillies in New Mexico. Not only are they America's largest producers of the red and green throat-burners, but the chilli is the state's symbol. Chillies are put in just about everything, too. Only in New Mexico will you find a Green Chilli Burger at McDonald's (they also have a McGrittle—whatever the hell that is).

I had the Chilli Rellenos and a Chicken Enchilada. When the reviewer said that the Chilli Rellenos was 'to die for', I think he meant 'to die of'. Boy, were the chillies hot. I could see why they had the air-conditioning set so high. The chilli was making me sweat more than if I'd been sitting with the cowboys and their Cowboy Beans in the tent oven. Still, the food was so good that I not only scoffed down my two platefuls, I also managed to devour the huge bowl of homemade blue-corn tortilla chips and salsa that had been brought out when I sat down.

There was just one more thing my contented belly full of chilli needed. It needed a beer. Except the restaurant didn't have any. In fact, when I thought about it there was nowhere at the rodeo to buy beer either. My fears were confirmed when I asked the waitress. These

God-fearin' folk were teetotallers. There went my vision of a drunken night dancing on the tables with Chuck and Mary-Lou.

The nearest bar was 22 miles away in the town of Ruidoso. What the heck? I thought. A nice drive up into the pleasantly cool mountains would be lovely. Plus, I wouldn't miss too much of the rodeo—there were still eight hours of Horse Catching and Wild Cow Milking to go. And, um . . . okay, I'll be honest. None of that really mattered. I just felt like a beer.

The drive *was* pleasant. As the road snaked its way up into the mountains the grassy plains soon turned into dense pine forests dotted with holiday cabins. It seemed hard to believe that Ruidoso was a ski town in the winter. Hot and bothered people were wandering past ski-hire shops dressed in shorts and singlets.

I stopped at the first bar I stumbled upon. As I sat on the verandah overlooking ski runs sipping my beer, I took out my map of the area and noticed that a Mescalero Apache Indian Reservation was nearby. 'Can you visit the Indian reservation?' I asked the waiter.

'Not normally, but theys is havin' a festival there today so it's open to the public.'

'Do you know what sort of festival it is?' I asked excitedly.

'They're sacrificin' virgins or somethin' like that.'

'Cool.'

Not only would I get to see cowboys *and* Indians on the 4th of July but I might get some good ol' virgin sacrificin' thrown in as well.

Well, the waiter was almost right about the virgin sacrificin'. It was an Apache Maiden's Puberty Ceremony—minus the sacrificin' bit, though. Still, I'd never seen an Indian (sorry, let's be PC here, I mean a Native American) in the flesh before. I'd only ever seen them in movies where they said 'How' a lot and walked around in moccasins (although Hollywood Indians weren't usually real Injuns, anyway).

My first impression of the reservation, however, wasn't in the least bit Indian. In fact, the only way you would be likely to have heard a 'How' would have been in such sentences as, '*How* many gambling chips would you like?' and, '*How* much money did you lose?' It was a massive casino called The Inn of the Mountain Gods. Because reservations are not government land, Native Americans can bypass state laws and build colossal casinos—and in the process make themselves a helluva lot more money than the locals got for New York.

I couldn't find the ceremony grounds so I pulled into a gas station and asked for directions. My first ever sight of a real Native American was a bloke in greasy overalls asking me if I wanted some gas. He did have a ponytail, though. 'It's not far,' he said. 'Just look for the campsite.'

I was looking out for a few tents and maybe an RV or two, but when I rounded a bend I was quite surprised to see a sea of teepees. They each had a jumbo-sized pick-up truck parked next to them (I suppose it would be a tad difficult to pack your teepee into the boot of the family saloon). I drove up the steep road through the middle of the campsite and parked right out the front of the ceremony grounds.

I'm a shocker. I didn't pay to get in. There was a queue to buy tickets, but I noticed no one was actually collecting tickets so I just waltzed straight on in. As soon as I stepped inside I was surrounded by Indians (quick, call the cavalry!). There were Indians wearing headdresses and moccasins, and even a few wearing war paint. It was truly amazing. A couple of Indian policemen with ponytails walked past. They were carrying bows and arrows and had a couple of white-man scalps tied to their belts. (Alright, maybe that's a slight exaggeration.)

To get to the ceremonial area I had to walk through a small market. There were stalls selling traditional Indian stuff like jewellery, clothes, moccasins, tomahawks and inflatable Incredible Hulks. The T-shirt shop didn't have a single 'God Bless America' shirt for sale. Not surprising, really, 'cause they did steal all the Indians' land and kill off most of them. The shop had 'Apache Pride' and 'I'm proud to be a Native American' T-shirts instead. Oh, and LA Lakers basketball singlets.

The food stalls had stuff like 'Beans and Rice', 'Pow-wow Chicken' and 'Mutton Sandwiches with Green Chilli'. A very pale-faced American fellow standing next to me said loudly to his wife, 'I don't like this funny Indian stuff. I want to get some regular food. Let's go to Pizza Hut.' I kid you not. He actually referred to Pizza Hut as 'regular' food.

By golly the Native American women must bloom late. I walked into the small stadium just as one of the Apache Maiden's Puberty Ceremonies was finishing. The maidens looked old enough to be my mother. I crawled up the steep concrete grandstand and sat next to Geronimo. The view over the reservation was stunning: it looked like somewhere in the Austrian Alps, with majestic pine-clad peaks flanking the lush valley below. I came away with the impression that the Native Americans have done a lot better than the Native Australians, who only seem to get given large tracts of barren desert, but I later discovered that the Indian reservation wasn't quite the paradise it seemed—atomic bombs were tested nearby in the 1940s.

I hoped the Indians weren't just about to give us palefaces our comeuppance. After the maidens had finished, an Apache war dance started. It didn't look that threatening, though. In fact, it looked more like my attempts to dance—only I don't usually carry a lethal-looking spear. I asked the Native American fellow next to me if he was a local. Instead of grunting, 'How, paleface! Me Big Bear!' he replied in a cool American accent that he came from a town called (and I'm not making this up) Truth and Consequences, and that he thought Australia was 'bitchin'.

I had to get back to Capitan. I had to tell all those cowboys that there were some Injuns through the pass, and to get on their horses and go git 'em. Just outside Capitan I was held up by a traffic jam. Up ahead, on the side of the road, was a line of police cars. There were so many flashing lights it looked like a mobile disco. I immediately panicked. I always do when I see a police car. I don't know why, but I suddenly feel guilty. Maybe it's because I'm sure that one day I will finally get busted for all the times I shoplifted as a kid.

What happened next took me very much by surprise. A bottle of beer came flying out of the window of the pick-up truck in front of me. Beer sprayed everywhere as the driver in front of him jettisoned his bottle too. The cops must have been breath-testing for booze. Gee, and I thought these good wholesome Christian folk didn't drink. They must have downed a few, too, because the car in front suddenly turned off the main road onto a gravel one and disappeared in a cloud of dust. The other car followed suit.

I thought I'd be all right, though. I'd only drunk two beers and I had one can of 'take-out' beer that I hadn't opened yet. Well, when I say 'can' I mean 'barrel'. I went to buy some beer in Ruidoso, but you could only buy a six-pack of normal cans. The alternatives were gargantuan so I figured one mega-can of beer was enough for me (and five of my mates).

I drove past the police slowly (hoping there wasn't an APB out for the guy who stole an ELO tape from K-mart in 1977), but there was no booze bus after all. There had been an accident. A horse trailer had tipped over and rolled down a gully. It was upside down (with upside-down horsies in it, too, I imagine). The driver stood on the side of the road scratching his head (and his bottom).

I snuck into the rodeo again (yeah, yeah, I know) just as they were having a break. 'Rhinestone Cowboy' by Glen Campbell was blasting out from inside the stadium. The sun was quite low now and the cowboys, all sitting in a neat row along the top of the corral, were silhouetted against the pale yellow sky. I *really* felt like I was in a Western movie now. I was half expecting the credits to start rolling in front of me any second.

I needed some dinner. I had a choice of the Chuckwagon (not a name that conjures up visions of fine dining) or a bunch of vans selling curly fries and shit. I thought I'd be adventurous and bought a 'brisket sandwich'. I'd seen someone eating one in a movie once but I had no idea what it was. After eating one I still had no idea what it was. It was some sort of meat. Maybe horse. Or even Injun.

I was still hungry and in the mood for experimentation so I bought a corn dog. This, too, was a surprise. The biggest surprise was that people actually ate them. It was a (rather dubious) hot dog wrapped in corn batter and deep fried. The lady serving (who looked as if she lived on a diet of corn dogs) said, 'Do ya want any fixins with that?'

'No thanks,' I replied. 'I don't think anything could fix this.'

I needed a beer after the corn dog (to unblock my arteries), so I opened my monster can and, keeping it in its paper bag, took a few guilty sips. I felt like a bum. I'd hidden behind the grandstand, but I spotted Jim and Tammy Bakker (or their lookalikes) in the shadows staring at me. They were whispering to each other (probably saying, 'Dear Jesus, we have a Satan-worshipping, beer-swilling hoodlum amongst us') and scowling with disgust. I slunk back to the corn dog stand and asked for a large milkshake cup, then poured my barrel of beer into the cup. With the frothy top it looked just like a vanilla milkshake. I could now wander around without being cast to the devil and banished to hell.

The rodeo started again with more clutching of hearts during the national anthem and more prayers. This time it was: 'We pray for our troops who are over in Iraq protecting the greatest nation on earth.' Then there was some more roping of animals. This time it was calves and, I have to say, I was very impressed with the skill and agility of Twister, Stetson and the rest of the gang. A calf was let loose at one end of the stadium and it bolted at break-neck speed to the other end. You could understand why when you saw what happened next. A cowboy would gallop out after the little critter twirling a lasso, and—in a matter of seconds—tie its legs with a sudden painful (I imagine) jerk of the rope. The cowboy then jumped off his horse and threw the calf down hard onto its back. The crowd hooted and hollered, but the calves themselves never looked too impressed.

Sadly I missed the Wild Cow Milking. However, I did get to see blokes who must have been a few verses short of a Bible getting thrown like rag dolls off a seemingly endless supply of rabid bulls. The best 'rider' (and I use the term loosely) lasted all of seven seconds.

As the last of the bulls unceremoniously dumped their pesky cowboys, the sun dropped behind the rails of the corral, turning the dusty air orange. The grandstands were full to the rafters now, and most of the people had changed into their Sunday best: freshly ironed jeans, polished cowboy boots and those funny string tie things that cowboys think look really classy. Dolled up cowgirls were strutting around looking very much like entrants to the Miss Texas Pageant. I suppose this would be their biggest social night of the year. I wonder how many lasso themselves a husband and take away his independence on Independence Day each year.

As soon as it turned dark, much to my surprise, the fireworks started. I didn't think I'd get to see any fireworks. Smokey Bear (well, not him personally, of course) had declared the entire area to be in extreme fire danger and had banned all fireworks. I later discovered that, only a few hours before the scheduled blast off, Smokey had given the organisers a one-off exemption from the ban. And, thank our dear Lord, was I happy he did. It was one of the most dazzling pyrotechnics display I'd ever seen. When you consider how small Capitan is, it really was quite amazing. The night sky was lit up with fizzing, spinning and exploding red, white and blue fireworks for over half an hour.

Five minutes into the show the fellow sitting next to me said, 'Excuse me y'all, I have to go check on mah hoss.' Good idea. I could see a line of them tied up to the corral and, boy, were they freaking out. Not that you could hear them. Despite the cacophony of explosions, the folks around me were hootin' and hollerin' and, I kid you not, yee-haain' along to every bang and pop.

When the fireworks finally finished (it was after ten-thirty) and the thick haze of smoke cleared, I joined the rest of the posse as they mosied on over to 'The Dance'. There was quite a queue to get into what looked like a glorified cow shed. I could hear the twangy sounds of the band playing inside. By the sound of it they played two kinds of music: Country *and* Western. I paid my $8 entry fee and headed straight to the bar. Now this was more like it, I thought. I pushed my way to the front and ordered a . . . pop. That's right, a pop. That's all they had. There was lemon pop, raspberry pop and cola pop, but no beer pop. I stood sulking on the side of the dance floor watching people dancing, laughing and generally having a 'great old time'. I couldn't understand it. What was wrong with these people? How could they have such a good time *without alcohol*?

Jim and Tammy Bakker, who'd witnessed my act of depraved debauchery earlier, were staring at me again and whispering to each other (more than likely debating how many people I'd raped and murdered), so I did the very sensible and adult thing and stuck my tongue out at them. I stayed for a little while, but when the lead singer of the band said, 'Let us pray . . .' I took it as a sign to do a bunk.

I drove a couple of miles out of town (looking for the perfect spot to park my mobile-motel) and, after driving down what may or may not have been someone's driveway, found an idyllic little clearing just off the track. I stepped out of the car and was enveloped by complete and utter silence. For all of a minute that is, until I got my box of fireworks out. I hadn't been able to resist buying some. On the way into Capitan, I'd passed through the town of Carrizozo which had tents set up by the side of the highway with large and brightly coloured signs saying 'FIREWORKS FOR BRIAN'. They didn't really, but they might just as well have. Fireworks were banned in Australia when I was 12 so, as soon as I saw fireworks for sale, I instantly regressed to being a boy who wanted nothing more than to blow up a few letterboxes. I did show some restraint, though. I only bought one box. Albeit a large one.

Even though there was a total fire ban, I figured I was too far away from Capitan for anyone to notice a couple of pissy little skyrockets. Although when I say skyrockets, there were actually eight large balls that came with a tubed launching device. I lit one up and bolted behind the car (I was a wuss when I was 12 as well). A pissy little skyrocket it certainly wasn't. The ball whistled as it shot up high into the air then exploded into a mighty shower of green and red sparks that lit up the entire night sky. They would have seen it in Texas, let alone just down the road in Capitan. Before Smokey Bear and the sheriff's posse turned up, I hastily got in the car and drove another five miles down the road.

I squeezed the car into a small pine forest away from the road and climbed over into the back seat. The view from the back seat was heavenly. I lay on my back staring up at a billion zillion stars. It took me a while to drop off to sleep, though. It wasn't just Smokey Bear that I was worried about, there was also the 'considerable' population of *real* bears in the area that would love nothing more than to tear my body into tiny shreds. Jim and Tammy Bakker were probably after me, too. They'd love nothing more than to take the Satan-worshipping, beer-swilling hoodlum under their wings and show him the ways of the Lord. To tell you the truth, I think I'd rather get torn into tiny shreds by the bears.

UFO Festival

Roswell, New Mexico, USA
July 6th

On July 3rd, 1947, a UFO crashed on a ranch northwest of Roswell, New Mexico. The flying saucer, and the aliens inside, were whisked away by the US Government to a secret underground location. The whole episode was promptly covered up and denied. Well, that's what a lot of the wackos who attend the annual UFO Festival believe, anyway. Is it true? I was going to Roswell to find out. And if not, then at least I could buy some good Star Trek memorabilia. Mind you, the 'UFO community' take the Roswell UFO Festival very seriously. The opening event of the festival, for example, is the Alien Rock & Bowl at the Town and Country bowling alley. Now that's serious. I'm just not quite sure whether you had to be an alien to participate or if they actually bowl aliens.

On the drive into Roswell I could see why the aliens chose to land there. The surrounding desert looked like it belonged to another planet. They probably landed because the vast and desolate moonscape of rocky peaks and mesas looked like their own backyard. The Roswell Visitors' Bureau thinks otherwise, though. They suggest that it was Roswell's wide range of cultural activities and climate that attracted the touring aliens. They were right about the climate. That, too, must have made the aliens feel at home. It was as hot as the surface of Venus.

The first sign of advanced civilisation I happened upon was a colossal billboard on the side of the highway announcing that we should 'BELIEVE IN MIRACLES'. Was it about UFOs? Or even Jesus perhaps? Not quite. Written underneath was 'Junior Whopper only 99 cents!'

I was running desperately low on petrol so I stopped at a gas station on the outskirts of Roswell (it had been a three-hour drive from Capitan). The petrol-pumper, who looked like he hadn't had a bath since 1947, asked, 'Hey boy, where is you from?' When I said Australia, he screwed his face up and spat, 'What the goddamn are you doin' *here*? This place is a shithole!'

'I'm here for the UFO Festival,' I said, pointing up into the sky for some reason.

'Stupid goddamn aliens,' he grunted.

Roswell was like most American towns. All the motels were on a busy and noisy highway on the outskirts of the outskirts of town jammed between Wal-Marts, K-marts, Tire-marts, Crappo-Marts and every fast-food chain known to man (and aliens, for that matter— the burger restaurant next door to my motel had a large sign saying 'ALIENS WELCOME').

I decided to leave my car at the motel and take the bus into town. Bad idea. I'd forgotten how scary it is getting on a local bus in America. They are only ever used by recently released mental patients, really really old people and, by the look of a couple of dodgy fellows up the back, escaped convicts. Even the poor in America don't take the bus. Everyone in America, besides those mentioned above, has a car (and cable TV).

A sign above the front door of the bus said 'Carrying a concealed deadly weapon is prohibited on this bus'. Oh, I see. You can carry a deadly weapon as long as it's not concealed. I bet the escaped convicts were happy about that. The guy sitting opposite me, who looked like an extra from *One Flew Over the Cuckoo's Nest*, was wearing an over-sized cap with 'I don't want a relationship, I just want sex' printed on the front of it. He looked like he'd never had sex in his life, let alone a relationship. He was drinking a bucket of Coca-Cola. And I do mean a bucket. It must have held two litres of the stuff. Now apparently there are 10 teaspoons of sugar in one can of Coke, so that meant he was downing approximately 60 teaspoons of sugar. No wonder he was fidgeting.

A large green neon sign, on one of the countless burger restaurants we passed on our way into town, proclaimed that 'If you prove you're an alien, you get your meal for free'. Ah, so that was where the people on the bus were heading. Most of them wouldn't have too much trouble proving it, either. Particularly the fellow with two heads. When I flicked through my festival program, I noticed that this year's slogan was 'Experience the Unknown'. I'd done that already and I hadn't even been to the festival yet.

The town had certainly embraced the whole UFO thing—to the point of silliness. Along the town's main street the 'Crash Down Diner' had a silver spaceship crashed into its roof; a poster in a bookshop window read 'Just say No to Aliens'; and a furniture store was having a 'UFO-Sale' with a line of little cardboard alien creatures waving from the window.

The UFO Festival began in 1994 as a way for Roswell to develop some form of identity to attract more tourism. Well, it sure worked. Mind you, Roswell isn't the only town to turn their 'claim-to-fame' into a festival aimed at tourists. In Clute, Texas, they have a severe mosquito problem in July. Instead of scaring off tourists, they attract them with the three-day Great Texas Mosquito Festival. Last year 25 000 turned up to partake in such things as the Mosquito Legs Competition and the Mosquito-calling contest.

Other towns that have turned their pests into profits by holding a festival include Eatonville, Washington (the Slug Festival), Carlsbad, New Mexico (the Bat Festival) and Brisbane, Australia (the Cockroach Festival). I suppose the one good thing about these festivals is that at least you don't have to eat any of the little beasties. That's not the case at the Testicle Festival held in Clinton, Montana. They've managed to turn the rather dubious local delicacy of deep-fried bull's testicles into the basis of a fully blown festival that last year attracted over 15 000 people who ate, wait for it, over 54 000 pounds of 'Cowboy Caviar'.

Gee, any old excuse will do for a festival. In Ainsworth, Nebraska, they hold a Middle of Nowhere Festival every June. The problem is that, because they are in the middle of nowhere, hardly any people actually turn up. Even tenuous links are a good enough reason to hold a festival (and make a buck). In Metropolis, Illinois, they bank on the fluke of sharing their name with a famous fictitious town by holding an annual Superman Festival. Some towns may have gone a little too far, though: the Robin Hood Festival, for example, isn't held in Nottingham, England, but in Sherwood, Oregon (any old excuse to wear green tights).

The townsfolk of Roswell may have been guilty of going a little too far. Even the streetlights had been turned, by painting a couple of eyes on them, into aliens. I got off the bus at the planetarium (along with the escaped convicts, who probably thought a large dark room full of people was a good hiding spot). As part of the festival, the planetarium was running a special event called 'The Great UFO Mystery'. Well, the organisers were right. It certainly was a mystery. The first mystery was its location. I ran aimlessly around a group of nondescript and almost identical government buildings for 20 minutes trying to find the entrance. The greatest mystery of all, however, was the show itself. To this day I have no idea what happened. But that probably has something to do with the fact that I fell into a deep sleep halfway through. I did catch the start, though. It began with some rather dodgy animation piece about a couple chasing flying saucers. I didn't see too much else after that. The lights were turned off and the whole domed ceiling became a spectacular moving night sky of a thousand sparkling stars. The in-house astronomer then went about naming every single one of those stars. Using a red laser pointer she pointed to a star and said, 'This is Airyanus Microscrotum . . . and this is Orrofus Rectumus . . . and this one here is . . .' 'zzzzzzzzzz'. I awoke to rapturous applause and the lights coming on. On the way out, the old-timer ticket seller who'd rushed me in so I wouldn't miss the start asked, 'So was it worth it?'

'It was fantastic,' I said.

'Oh, good.'

'Yeah, it was the best sleep I've had in ages.'

I caught the scary bus back to the motel and picked up my car. Not only was the Alien Rock & Bowl 15 minutes out of town in the middle of the desert, but I didn't fancy catching the bus at night (even the escaped convicts would be too scared to catch a bus at night). The car park of the bowling alley was virtually empty. The flying saucers must have parked around the back. According to my festival program, the alien bowling was starting in 15 minutes. Inside was just as empty as the car park. There were only two families bowling. Either there was going to be an incredible last minute rush, or—don't laugh it could be true—the aliens had abducted everyone. 'Is the Alien Rock & Bowl on tonight?' I asked the girl serving behind the bar.

'Yeah,' she said, waving her arms towards the two families bowling as if to say 'Can't you see how busy we are?'

I decided to hang around for a bit (I wanted to see how they'd handle the rush when a third family turned up). I ordered a beer from the bar. 'Can I see your ID please?' the barmaid asked.

'That's very sweet,' I said with a sheepish smile. 'I'll have a Coors, please.'

'No. I need ID, I'm sorry.' She looked serious.

'Look at me,' I said. 'I'm old enough to be your father . . . or even your grandfather.' (They breed 'em young down south.)

'Oh, okay, I'll let you go,' she said sternly. 'But only this once.'

As she handed me my beer, I noticed a couple playing pool and drinking beer. They looked about 14.

I couldn't handle the excitement of waiting for another family to turn up, so after downing my beer I headed back into town. It was only nine-thirty, though, and I wasn't quite ready for bed yet (I'm not *that* old). On the way back to my motel I stopped for a drink at a neon-lit shed called Bud's Bar. I pulled into the car park at the same time as a bunch of good ol' boys in a pick-up truck that was only one step down from one of those 'Monster Trucks'. In fact, the entire car park, and I do mean the *entire* car park, was full of these trucks with their ridiculous and totally unnecessary oversized wheels. My lime-green Hyundai stood out like iridescent dog balls. The good ol' boys were eyeing my car off as I attempted to find a dark corner to park it in. I figured they were probably agreeing that the Hyundai was just the perfect size to drive over and crush into the ground.

Bud's Bar was quiet. There were only a few tables of red-faced pick-up truck drivers wearing baseball caps. Even though the entire bar was wall-to-wall neon signs, posters, coasters and bar towels advertising Bud (Budweiser), I ordered a Corona. Budweiser may be the biggest selling beer in the world, but it tastes like goat's piss—and weak goat's piss at that. I sat at the bar next to a fellow named Bud who was drinking a Bud. He was in his fifties and hadn't worked in 10 years. 'I look after my mum,' he said shyly. He'd never been to the UFO Festival, but he did show me his driver's licence. It had a picture of an alien on it. He was licensed to drive 'ALL flying saucers'. When Bud left I sat and did such sitting-by-yourself-in-a-bar things as reading the coaster (over and over again), slowly peeling off the beer label and methodically eating my way through every bowl of bar snacks within reach.

As I polished off my third bowl of mixed nuts, a guy walked into the bar who attracted even more attention than I had. He was everything the other blokes in the bar weren't. He wasn't wearing a baseball cap for a start. He was young, clean-cut, handsome and didn't have a red face. He was also dressed in a military uniform. With the addition, oddly enough, of a bow tie. He grabbed a beer and sat in the far corner at a table by himself.

When I'm doing the solo traveller thing, I quite often just walk up to people and ask if I can join them for a drink. I get a little bit nervous introducing myself to strangers, but I figure it's better than peeling off beer labels all night. The first minute or so is always very uncomfortable. They are naturally wary that I am either trying to pick them up, a fruitcake, or just your run-of-the-mill axe-wielding psychopath.

Jackson was in the US Marines and had snuck out from his best buddy's wedding reception (which explained the bow tie) so he could have a quick smoke and a quiet beer. 'It's only for 10 minutes,' he said. He stayed for an hour and a half and the quiet beer turned into six noisy ones. Jackson was a 22-year-old from Kansas. In less than two months he would be saying, 'We're not in Kansas anymore,' because he was off to Iraq. In our ensuing drunken conversation we came to the following conclusions: President Bush doesn't mind a war; Saddam Hussein was a nutter; everyone in New Mexico drives a 'truck'; Americans like guns and shooting each other; Australians don't like guns but shoot each other anyway; and the barmaid had incredibly nice tits. We left two hours later as the best of mates.

Back in my motel room I flicked through the 742 TV stations and found the sci-fi channel. An old episode of 'Star Trek' was on. I've never been a big 'Star Trek' fan—I always found Doctor Spock and his very serious ears annoying. And anyway, 'Star Trek' was nothing compared to 'Lost in Space'. As a kid I was obsessed with the Robinson family's exploits (I wanted to be an astronaut until I was 10—then I wanted to be Doctor Dolittle). I even cried once when Mum and Dad took us out for a rare restaurant meal and I missed an episode. Seeing the show now, I still can't help being impressed. Especially by the interchangeable aliens. One week the alien was Robby the Robot (from that classic sci-fi movie *The Forbidden Planet*), then the next week's alien was wearing a gorilla outfit with Robby the Robot's head. Next the alien was in a boiler suit with the gorilla head, and finally the alien donned the gorilla outfit, the boiler suit *and* Robby the Robot's head. What a brilliant show.

·

By nine in the morning it was already nudging 100 degrees. I was in the motel pool before breakfast. I'd missed the Alien Chase Fun Run, but if the Alien Rock & Bowl was any indication then the alien probably had no one to chase him anyway. After another long soak in the pool I drove to the main festival site in the Eastern New Mexico State Fairgrounds. Or, as I dubbed it, the Eastern New Mexico State Dustbowl. It was a vast space comprised of large sheds, corrals for horses and a rodeo staging area (or whatever you call it). The organisers of the UFO Festival had spread all the events right out to make it look bigger than it really was. I had to walk 400 metres through a dusty hot field before I came to the first attraction—the Alien Food Court. Apparently, and I found this quite surprising, aliens eat hot dogs, chilli dogs, corn dogs, fried cheese on a stick and curly fries.

Signs with little green men pointing to the different venues were spaced out (no pun intended) around the grounds. They were written in English, Spanish and Alien. Here's a little known, and frightening, fact for you. Aliens speak Wingdings. It's true. That collection of shapes in the fonts section of your computer is actually an alien language. 'Toilet' for example was '◆□●⌘♏◆'. So, should you be lucky enough to be abducted by aliens, that's one for the phrase book. If only I knew how to pronounce it . . .

Among a bunch of stands near the entrance to the main hall was one called 'Team Encounter'. A large poster explained it this way: 'Sci-fi? No, it's Sci-Reality. Join thousands of people around the world and launch your photo and message to the stars for only $24.95!'

'How does it work?' I asked the fellow who looked suspiciously like a used-car salesman.

'We press a button here in Roswell and your "cosmic call" goes to our scientists in the Ukraine who send it to outer space using a deep space radio transmitter.' He said this with an amazingly straight face.

'Oh, really!' I said, without even the slightest hint of sarcasm.

'You better get in early, though,' he said. 'The next transmission is at four o'clock.' He handed me a folder full of sample messages people had sent. Unlike him, I had trouble keeping a straight face. Here are some examples of the messages: a photo of an obviously inbred family from Alabama was accompanied by the pitiful plea, 'Please clone us'; a Star Trekker had written a long-winded message in the Klingon language; an Indiana family issued an invitation to their farm—'Please call 24 hours in advance so that we may make your visit one to remember'; and my personal favourite from Toronto, Canada, read 'Please send money. Any kind of money. Alien currency is OK. Meteorites are good. Gold, moon rocks, space junk also good. Send to: Maura, Planet Earth'.

I made it inside the main hall (read: giant tin shed) just in time for the start of the Out of this World Costume Competition. The only problem was that I couldn't figure out who was from this world and who wasn't. Contestants and spectators were all milling about together waiting for the start. Some were obvious contestants, like the cute kid who'd been painted entirely green and the two people wearing cumbrous alien masks and robes. But others, well, it was hard to tell. One fellow, who was dressed as Hans Solo of *Star Wars* fame, was watching from the sidelines. He had a great outfit, though; his uniform, boots, gun belt *and* haircut made him look like the real Hans Solo. The only thing that wasn't quite authentic was the massive beer gut hanging over his gun belt.

Among the other competitors were a couple in nightgowns with shower caps on their heads, an alien dog (a dog wearing a helmet and a green suit), and a hippy with long hair and a beard, wearing a tie-dyed shirt and leading his 'alien' around on a lead. The 'alien' was his dreadlocked friend, who was wearing a red plastic raincoat and crawling around on his hands and knees barking like a dog. The hippy kept hitting his thing from another planet hard with a stick as it tried to mount girls' legs.

All the sci-fi nerds, however, were gawking at (and drooling over) Kelly Ostendorf from Long Beach, California. She had a fantastic outfit—its most appealing feature being there was so little of it. She was (barely) wearing a silver pointy bra (without much of the bra part), a tiny silver mini-skirt, silver thigh-length boots and an all-over tan. When one weedy fellow finally plucked up the courage to get his photo taken with her, there was a rush of blokes in glasses and polyester shirts wanting a photo of themselves leering at Kelly's breasts.

The competitors were lined up and marched out of the building to a stage that was set up waaayyyy over on the other side of the festival grounds. I noticed Hans Solo didn't join the line. He'd just come to the festival, as you would, dressed that way. Every step made in the heat sapped energy from you, so imagine how the fellow in the heavy robe and enormous rubber mask must have felt. He would have lost 10 kilos just in the walk to the stage.

I squeezed into a spot in the shade next to a family of Mexicans (who may not have been able to enter because they were *illegal* aliens). The competitors had to stand in the full sun for 15 minutes while the judges tallied their votes. It was really starting to get to them, too. Both contestants in the under-five category were howling their heads off (sounding very much like aliens) and the dog alien attacked the dreadlocked alien, who'd been eating gravel from the ground.

Third place went to the dreadlocked alien, who celebrated by trying to mount Kelly. Second place went to the dog and first place went to the disappearing man in the big rubber mask. There was an audible sigh of disappointment from the sci-fi nerds when Kelly wasn't announced the winner. A fellow next to me said to his friend, 'Kelly should have won!' 'Hmmmmmm,' his friend said while ogling her breasts.

The main building housed the Alien Market Place and the Classic Sci-fi Film Festival. I remembered reading on the Roswell UFO Festival website that every stall in the Alien Market Place had to be related somehow to aliens. The first stall was the Misty Mountain Gourmet Shop, which was selling salsa. I wasn't quite sure what aliens had to do with that, until I saw their sign: 'The taste of our salsa is out of this world'.

A series of collectibles stalls were surrounded by Trekkers salivating over original Dr Spock dolls still in their boxes. I must admit that I got a wee bit excited, though, when I spotted a model of the Robot from Lost in Space and a signed photo of Judy Robinson. I quite fancied her.

Next up in the totally alien-unrelated stall stakes was the Picture Framing Shop. They had a sign up saying 'Aliens Love our Frames'. I can just imagine ⚇☐🗁↗●〰 from the planet ⊠♍❖♌■○, saying, 'Hey honey, we need to frame those photos of baby ☌☐♌, can you pop down to the Picture Framing Shop in Roswell?' On the other hand, that's probably what happened in 1947. The aliens were just dropping in to pick up some frames.

At the end of the first line of stalls was the entrance to the Classic Sci-fi Film Festival. Well, a big black curtain at least. The UFO Festival DJ announced that the next film was just about to start, so I stumbled in and joined the 40 or so other people in the makeshift grandstand. The film, which I'd never heard of before, was called *Inframan* or, as it's called in the original Chinese, *Jung-Gwok Chiu-yan*—which can only mean, 'CrappyCheapMan'.

The opening scene was set in the 'Communications Headquarters' of the 'The World Space Centre'. The camera work was so bad it made my dad's home videos look like Oscar-winning material. A fellow in a painfully tight silver uniform ran up to a bloke in a silver lab coat and yelled (in badly dubbed English), 'Something is wrong with the communications system, professor!' Something was wrong all right. The communications system was made of cardboard boxes and Christmas lights.

From what little I could figure out of the story, Earth had been taken over by 'Princess Dragon Mom' who looked pretty well identical to Kelly with her silver pointy boobs and mini-skirt. Her sidekicks included Cousin It, a robot made of cardboard boxes and—my favourite—a giant turd wearing boxing gloves. None of them, I might add, would even have got third prize in the alien costume competition.

A meeting of World Leaders (who, for some reason, were all Chinese and chain-smoked like crazy) called on the professor to 'get Inframan'. Getting Inframan involved injecting some normal-looking bloke with red cordial. The red cordial scene went on for 10 minutes. It was around then that I thought I'd go and check out some more stalls. I was intrigued to see what else the 'alien-related' stalls were selling. There would have to be one of those dodgy salesmen selling some revolutionary juice extractor (as used on Mars) and, the old favourite, an over-made-up woman selling anti-ageing cream (works a treat on Venusians).

There weren't any juice extractors but there was a woman selling tie-dyed shirts and other hippy stuff—which, when you think about it, is actually relevant. Hippies are pretty bloody alien. One stall had a rather stunned looking fellow sitting next to a pile of videos with a sign that read 'UFOs over Phoenix—Real UFO footage—Only $20'. He'd shot the video himself, but it must have done some damage to his eyes as he was wearing very dark sunglasses.

After completing another aisle of stalls I went back to see how Inframan was doing. He was in the middle of a 10-minute kung fu fight scene with Cousin It (there was a lot of that 'haa! hee! ho!' stuff going on). Inframan was wearing an orange boiler suit (from the prop department of 'Lost in Space' perhaps?) and had tin foil wrapped around his ankles and wrists. He finally blew up Cousin It using the old sparklers in the boots trick. Princess Dragon Mom then brought out her big gun: the Turdman with boxing gloves. When the Princess told Turdman to kill Inframan, he jumped up and down shouting 'Kill Inframan! Kill Inframan'. It was at this point that I almost fell off the grandstand laughing. Turdman sounded exactly like the Cookie Monster from Sesame Street.

Before I actually did fall off the grandstand laughing I went to check out more of the festival. Just inside the entrance to the main hall was an office and a sign saying 'Sighting Reports'. They didn't have much business. The lady manning the desk looked totally bored. I contemplated going over and telling her that if she wanted a good place for a 'sighting' she should just catch the local bus.

It was unbearably hot outside. I could feel the heat of the ground coming up through my sandals. Before I scampered back inside, I spotted Hans Solo again. He was the leader of a Sci-fi Club. There were 10 of them in matching yellow T-shirts (with the '17th Chapter of the sci-fi.org Club' printed on them) and matching yellow floral board shorts. One girl's bottom was so big it looked like she had two of the moons of Jupiter shoved up her pants.

Inframan was almost over when I sat down again. The crowd of 40-odd at the start of the film had diminished somewhat. There were only two people left, and I think one of them was asleep. Inframan had a girlfriend (the Professor's daughter naturally) who was abducted by Turdman ('Give me cookies, give me cookies'). This was followed by a 10-minute kung fu fight to the accompaniment of seventies' porn music. Inframan zapped Turdman with his sparkling boots then turned his attention to Princess Dragon Mom. Another 10-minute badly choreographed kung fu fight scene ensued with more sparkly boots. The film ended with the Professor's daughter saying, 'As long as we have Inframan the world will be safe.' While she was saying this, Inframan was having a good grope at her tits. Fantastic. It was probably the worst film I'd ever seen and definitely one of the funniest.

I escaped the heat of the fairgrounds (after eating some of that well-known alien food—curly fries) and headed back into town to the *air-conditioned* International UFO Museum and Research Center. In the car park of the Crash Down Diner next door was a sign saying 'UFO Parking Only'. If that was the case, then aliens drive Chevrolets.

The UFO Museum was housed in an old picture theatre and a large banner at the front read 'What really happened? You decide'. I decided I liked the museum. It didn't try to 'sell' you the Roswell UFO story, but presented all the facts from both sides (which included witness testimonies, photographs, maps and copies of all the newspaper reports). What is certainly true is that something went on. Whether it was a UFO or a weather balloon that landed in the desert, the government sure were hasty in getting rid of the evidence.

Briefly, this is what happened (apparently): on July 3rd, 1947, after a heavy thunderstorm, a farm rancher named Mac Brazel went to check on his sheep. What he discovered, though, was a considerable amount of unusual debris. It had gouged out a shallow trench several hundred feet long and was scattered over a large area. Some of the debris had strange physical properties; for example, when it was crumpled it returned to its normal size. After taking a few pieces to show his neighbours, Floyd and Loretta Proctor, Brazel drove into Roswell and contacted the sheriff, George Wilcox. In turn, Wilcox reported it to 'Intelligence Officer' Major Jesse Marcel (from the 509th Bomb Squadron) who cordoned off the crash site.

The commander of the 509th Bomb Squadron, Commander Colonel William Blanchard, released a statement on July 8th, 1947, saying that 'a crashed UFO has been removed from the Roswell Area'. In mere hours that very same press release was taken back and replaced by a new one. The 509th Bomb Squadron had mistakenly identified a weather balloon as a flying saucer.

In Roswell a young undertaker named Glenn Davis, who worked at Ballard Funeral Home, got a suspicious call from the 'morgue' at the air field asking for some small airtight coffins and some information on how to preserve bodies that had been exposed to the elements for a few days without contaminating the tissue.

Davis went to the hospital that night and saw the metal from the crash site. He saw some strange signs on one of the pieces that happened to be sticking out of a military ambulance. He was threatened, so he left the premises. A nurse later told him she saw the bodies and she even drew them for him. During the next few days, she was sent to England where she died under suspicious circumstances soon afterwards.

It certainly was compelling evidence. Even if the set of witness photos looked like they came from the Happy Acres Loony Farm Yearbook. As I was checking out one of the exhibits, I caught the end of a conversation that Dennis Balthaser, the resident UFO investigator, was having with a group of visitors. He was telling them that one of the aliens out of the four recovered from the wreckage had stayed alive for six months to a year. 'I've had guns pointed at me trying to get more information,' he said (he didn't say whether it was aliens or humans pointing the guns, though).

At the front of the main exhibition room a few tables had been set up where four 'authors' were selling and signing their books. The first in line was Gloria Ann Hawker. She had written a best-selling true-life account entitled *Morning Glory: Diary of an alien abductee*. She was talking to another woman (who was telling Gloria about the alien she met with big black almond eyes), so I picked up one of her books and read the back cover. Gloria had been abducted by aliens over 50 times. She now worked as a 'hypnotherapist' for people who had been abducted by aliens. I flicked through the book and soon made some fascinating discoveries. For example, did you know that some political leaders are actually alien reproductions? Well, that would certainly help explain John Howard and George Bush.

She also claimed that one in ten people have been abducted by aliens. Ahh, that would also explain why my 44-year-old brother spends most of his time trying to kill aliens in one of those computer games.

One thing I did find very interesting, though, was that the aliens have a pretty good weight watchers' program on their planet. In the book jacket photo Gloria was huge; she was now quite slim. When the lady with the black almond-eyed alien friend walked away I introduced myself and told her I was writing a story about the UFO Festival. After the initial small talk, the following is a verbatim record of how our conversation went (I taped it on my dictophone):

Me: 'So, Gloria, how and where were you abducted?'

Gloria: 'The "Greys" [the name of the aliens] would appear from a bright light that emanated from my bedroom wall.'

Me: 'Oh, right. Um . . . are you still, er . . . being abducted?'

Gloria: 'Not anymore. It stopped for a while when I strangled one of the Greys in my bedroom, then it stopped completely when I told them I was Christian and that I loved God. One time I was in the spacecraft and I asked Raytheon—who was a friendly Grey—and the evil Doctor Grey if they had a creator that they worshipped. He said yes and that when they die they see the most wondrous light and are taken by their creator. After that talk with Doctor Grey I saw a difference in attitude. He began to respect me like a human being. Before that we were like lab rats used for experimentation and our bodies were used for hybrid babies and perverted medical experiments.'

Me (after pausing for a second—the hybrid babies part threw me): 'Do you think the aliens will reveal themselves to us one day?'

Gloria: 'I've been told yes and that in a certain year they're going to let the human populace know that, yes, this species—and not just the Greys either, there are other species like the Nordics, the Reptilians and the Praying Mantises—will let us know they are here. There is a federation of these species but human beings have not been asked to be in that federation. Once we can all get along with each other on Earth and not be cruel to one another then, yes, we will be included and that's when they will make themselves available to us.'

Me: 'Um . . . thanks for that Gloria. Err . . . have a nice day.'

Do you know what the most amazing thing was from all that? Not once did I smirk or giggle.

Sitting next to Gloria was Charles James Hall. He had three alien abduction books for sale (plus one on his theories on the inner physics and structure of the photon). He told me the books were G-rated and that there was no sex in them. 'It's lucky that I'm ugly,' he said, 'because the aliens didn't want to have sex with me.' At the bottom of the back cover of his book it said 'Charles James Hall is not an alien'. I wasn't too sure about that.

I checked out the wall of UFO photos (which seemed to be mostly made up of photos of frisbees taken by Belgian postmen), then wandered into the souvenir shop, which was bigger than the museum itself. They sold everything from Roswell frisbees (so you could make your own UFO photos), to alien Christmas stockings, alien ties and braces and—my favourite—alien firecrackers.

I headed back to the fairgrounds for the UFO Independent Music Festival. It was now so hot even aliens would be complaining. There were only a few hundred folk wandering around in the silly heat (there had been maybe a couple of thousand in the morning). The music stage was out in the middle of another dusty field—they might as well have set it up in the middle of a giant oven. There were only about 50 people in the audience and they were all crammed in tightly under an open tent. It was the only bit of shade. The Little Green Men were playing. Except they weren't little green men—they were just a thrash band from Albuquerque.

The only place that was air-conditioned in the fairgrounds was the Chaves County Farm and Livestock Pavilion where the Speaker Series was being held without a cow or pig in sight. The speaker was another fellow who'd been abducted by aliens. 'They have no genitals,' he told us. 'So, you may well ask, how do they propagate?' (I wasn't but go on) 'Well, I've seen them have sex.' He didn't actually explain how but I guessed he was saving it for when he released his porn video *Hot Alien Sex I*.

I'd almost had enough of 'speakers', but I couldn't miss the 'All Star' discussion at the UFO Museum. Participants in a recent archeological dig at the supposed site of the landing were going to talk about their discoveries. The auditorium was packed with bearded men in polyester shirts. The 'All Star' cast were certainly qualified: there were plenty of BAs, MAs and PhDs among them. There was even someone called Dr Chuck who said things like: 'A chemical analysis of iridium was effectuated and an anomalous forensic blah blah blah blah . . .' All this waffling was accompanied by a slide show. It went something like this: slide of people digging a hole in the ground; slide of people pointing at a hole in the ground; slide of people in deep thought about the hole in the ground; and finally, slide of close-up of hole in the ground.

I never did find out what they discovered, but that was because there was something a lot more important happening—my stomach was rumbling. I snuck out and popped across the road to the El Toro Bravo Mexican restaurant to get some dinner. For a Saturday night in the middle of a festival the restaurant was pretty quiet. Well, when I say 'quiet', I mean there weren't many customers. It was actually quite noisy. A two-piece band, made up of a keyboard player and a saxophonist, were blasting out Barry Manilow songs.

Towards the end of my marvellous meal I had an alien experience. A hip-looking 20-something guy walked up to the saxophonist and asked him if he would play some Kenny G. Now that's fucking alien.

I paid my bill (sorry, my check) and rushed out before I was tortured by Kenny G. I spent my last night at the UFO Festival lying in bed watching 'Star Trek' and thinking that after all these years I still couldn't understand a word the Scottish engineer was saying.

So, did I leave the Roswell UFO Festival as a believer? No. I still think Kelly should have won the Costume Competition.

Tomato Festival

Ripley, Tennessee, USA
July 10th

There was something missing from the 20th annual Ripley Tomato Festival. I walked around the entire Tomato Festival site in Ripley Park and couldn't find one single tomato. There were tomato T-shirts for sale and people fanning themselves with 'tomato fans' (cardboard tomatoes on sticks) but there wasn't a common-or-garden-eating-variety tomato anywhere. I had envisaged hoeing into a big juicy Roma tomato pie or at least a nice simple chargrilled Beefsteak tomato, but the only food options were roasted corn, French fries (and holy ones at that—they were from the Church of Jesus Christ caravan), barbecued pork shoulder sandwiches and the ubiquitous hot dog.

I love my tomatoes. In fact, rarely a day goes by that I don't eat a tomato in some form or other. If I'm not eating a tomato-based pasta sauce (which I do just about every second night), I'm adding tomatoes to a sandwich or salad, snacking on cherry tomatoes or confirming my reputation as one of those strange people who pour tomato sauce on just about everything.

On the drive into Ripley (which is two hours north of Memphis, Tennessee, along the Mississippi River), I could have stopped at any one of the numerous tomato stands set up on the side of the highway to get my tomato fix. You could spot them a mile off. They all had big signs saying things like 'It's Ripley Tomato Time!', 'Eat BIG Ripley Tomatoes Here Now!' and 'Happy People Eat Ripley Tomatoes'. Did that mean there weren't many happy people at the Ripley Tomato Festival? Not at all. In fact, I'd never seen such happy people before in my life. Everyone I'd seen so far had been oh-so-cheerful and oh-so-pleasant.

I asked the sweet-as-pie wholesome country lass working at the barbecued pork shoulder sandwich stand if I could have some tomatoes on my sandwich and she said, 'Sorry, sweetie, we's got no tomatoes.'

'But isn't this a tomato festival?' I asked.

'Sure is, honey,' she said oh-so-sweetly.

Well, I wanted to say, where the hell are the tomatoes? But I didn't, of course. I smiled at her happily, took my barbecued pork shoulder sandwich (without tomato) with glee and merrily skipped off. I just couldn't be even a tiny bit nasty. She was just so, well . . . nice. In fact, the whole population was nice. Even the town itself was oh-so-perfectly-nice. It was like driving into a Doris Day film. And it was not just because everyone was so saccharine sweet either. The town was frozen in a perpetual 1955. I drove into Ripley, past perfect white clapboard houses with perfect flowerbeds and perfectly clipped lawns that looked like carpet. Most houses had an American flag flying from the roof and just about every front porch had one of those two-seater swinging chairs on it. I passed the perfect family having a barbecue in the front yard of what looked like a Hollywood set. Dad was in a crisp white apron cooking and laughing while the perfectly behaved children played happily on the movie-set tyre swing. Doris Day, whoops, I mean Mom came bounding out of the house and, I promise you, waved at me. This was scary.

I'd actually got hopelessly lost trying to find the town, then, when I was about to give up, just stumbled upon it. It was like one of those episodes of 'The Twilight Zone' where a door-to-door salesman takes the wrong turn and ends up in an idyllic little town full of idyllic townsfolk who end up sucking his internal organs out with a straw.

The town was another world compared to the place where I was staying only a few miles away. There was nowhere to stay in Ripley itself, so I was camped out at the Days Inn Motel on the main highway. Right next to a McDonald's and John Deere tractor show-room. When I asked the fellow behind the counter if he had a map of Ripley, he just grunted at me. Now that was what I was used to.

The centre of Ripley was even more 1955 than the residential area—some of the stores looked as if they hadn't changed their stock since then. I parked in the main square, which had a cosy, leafy, time-less air to it, and went for an aimless wander. It was like being in a time warp. I walked past Shear Creations Hair Salon where you could get 'Hairstyles for the Entire Family' (the photos in the front window looked like the cast from 'Happy Days'); Aunt Laura's Jewelry (with a 'Just Arrived' display case of necklaces covered in dust); The Bank of Ripley (with no queues and, even more amazingly, smiling bank tellers); the New Life Fellowship Church (with a sign saying 'God bless the tillers of the land'); and Town and Country Fashions (it looked like tweed slacks were the 'in thing' in Ripley this summer).

People on the sidewalk smiled at me as I passed. They looked like the sort of people who'd say, 'Gee whizz' and, 'Aw shucks' a lot. It was all a bit disconcerting to be honest. Someone said good afternoon to me and I almost jumped out of my skin.

Ripley Park was the main site for the Tomato Festival (pronounced *toe-mate-oh*—when I said *to-mart-oh,* the locals gave me funny looks). As well as the hot dog stands, the festival site also had a petting zoo, jumping castle, arts and crafts fair, a few fairground rides and a stage with an accompanying mini-grandstand for the 'entertainment'. There were only about 20 people wandering around the 'attractions' as the opening ceremony was still two hours away. After my fruitless search for the red fruit, and after I'd devoured my barbecued pork shoulder sandwich, there wasn't much else to do (I'd already petted the llama at the petting zoo). It was time for a beer. I found the one and only bar in town, called—appropriately although a little unimaginatively—'Bar'. It was on the road out of town. There was one pick-up truck in the car park belonging to the one and only patron in the bar.

The bar hadn't been renovated (or dusted) since 1955. It smelt old and musty. I wasn't complaining, though. Not when the beers were at 1955 prices. A bottle of Bud in Memphis was $3.50. Here, it was only $1.25. Sheila, the barmaid, looked like she'd overcooked herself in the sun—she was as red as a tomato. When I told her I was from Australia she said, 'What is you doin' here? Is you lost?' The bar had two small rooms. Sheila was in one room while the sole patron was in the other playing one of those tediously repetitive fruit machine games. I sauntered over and said hello. His name was Jim Bob and he was (surprise, surprise) a tomato farmer. He was wearing overalls and had a Richie Cunningham haircut. He also had his two front teeth missing (they must grow darn hard tomatoes in these parts). 'Where's you from?' he mumbled, without looking up from his machine.

'Australia,' I said.

'That's on the other side of the farm, innit?' he said dryly.

He didn't even bat an eyelid at the fact that an Australian tourist was in town—and it's not like Ripley gets a lot of tourists. In fact, I was probably the first. Ever.

'Have you had a Ripley tomato yet?' Jim Bob asked.

'No, not yet.'

'They's the sweetest, juiciest, tastiest toe-mate-ohs in the whole USA,' he said licking his lips through the gap in his teeth.

'I can't find any,' I whimpered.

'They's everywhere,' he said looking at me as if I was stoopid.

I got lost driving back to the park. Trying to be clever, I took what I thought was a shortcut. I ended up back with Doris Day and Rock Hudson in the suburbs so I asked an old-timer, who was sitting on a rocking chair on his porch, for directions to Ripley Park.

'Wha' sort a' pawk? Lark barb-ah-cue pawk?'

'No, the *park*,' I said slowly.

'Oh, ya mean tha' *Pawk!* It's thataways.'

Ripley Park was abuzz. Everyone was out in their Sunday best (or Friday best in this case). It wasn't hard to spot the tomato farmers. They were wearing freshly pressed overalls and freshly washed checked shirts. They must have been pretty warm, though. Although the sun was low on the horizon, it was still hot and muggy. The cardboard tomato fans were working overtime in the grandstand as I squeezed into a spot next to Ralph Mouth for the opening ceremony.

Some bloke in a suit opened proceedings with a speech: 'Welcum t' tha Rip-leee Toe-mate-oh Festi-vol . . .' I couldn't understand much else after that. All I could make out was 'toe-mate-oh', which he said every fifth word. He ended his drawled out speech with the crowning of Miss Tomato Queen 2003.

I couldn't really tell you what Her Royal Ripeness Rachel Jayne Hammond looked like. All I could see was hair and teeth and a big red shiny dress. There was an article about her in the *Lauderdale Voice* (special Tomato Festival edition) and she said, 'The glitz and glamor associated with being Miss Tomato Queen is a girl's dream come true.' Don't laugh. It's quite a prestigious title. Miss Tomato Queen would now go on to compete for the state title against—and I swear I'm not making any of these up—Miss Strawberry, Miss Okra, Miss Peanut, Miss Peach and Miss Apple. I wonder if the winner then goes on to the national titles against Miss Turnip, Miss Prickly Pear and Miss Brussels Sprout. Hey, it could happen.

Every fruit or vegetable you can possibly think of has a festival devoted to it. There's even a Garlic Queen (beautiful but smelly) crowned every year at the Garlic Festival in Gilroy, California (she wouldn't be the only smelly one, either—in 2003 over 130 000 people attended and ate nearly four tons of garlic). Maybe they could hold a 'World Greengrocery Queen' title with contestants from the Prune Festival in Agen, France; the Gooseberry Festival in Yorkshire, England; the Yam Festival in Accra, Ghana; the Leek Festival in Beamish, England; and the Mumbai Mango Madness Festival in Mumbai, India. Actually, there are all sorts of festivals of foodstuffs. There's the Eel Festival in Åhus, Sweden; the Black Pudding Festival in Mortagne-au-Perche, France; the Sauerkraut Festival in Waynesville, Ohio; and, my favourite, the Spam Festival in Austin, Texas (called Spamarama, its feature events include a Spam Toss and the Spam-Tug-of-War where the losing team gets pulled into a pool of Spam jelly).

The Eel Festival sounds positively delightful compared to some other festivals where the food of honour is so gross you'd need to bring along a bucket. I don't know about you, but I certainly wouldn't be able to stomach the Offal Festival in Cape Town, South Africa. Then again, the Offal Festival would seem like a picnic compared to the Turkey Testicle Festival in Byron, Illinois, where over 300 pounds of 'nuts' are eaten every year (apparently they hang under the turkey's left wing and are about the same size as human testicles). I'd save my biggest big bucket, however, for the Chitlin' Festival in Salley, South Carolina. So what's a Chitlin' you ask? I'm not sure you want to know. It's three feet of hog intestines that are boiled then deep-fried. The smell of this culinary delight, according to a newspaper story I found, is 'similar to a maggot-infested possum that's been sitting on the side of the highway for about six days' (I'd dread to see what Miss Chitlin' Queen looked—and smelt—like). Still, that doesn't stop the hordes of people who turn up to the festival devouring 10 000 pounds of the shit every year. Not surprisingly, I skipped that one.

Instead, I opted for the world's only Tomato Festival without any tomatoes. I bet the Sampiei Tomato Festival in Sicily, the Montlouis Tomato Festival in France, the Leamington Tomato Festival in Canada, the Zeddiani Tomato Festival in Italy and the New Orleans Tomato Festival let the odd tomato in.

Even though I hadn't actually seen a tomato in the flesh yet, I could tell that the folks of Ripley sure do love their tomatoes. That week's edition of the *Lauderdale Voice* was devoted *entirely* to tomatoes. There were tomato stories, tomato recipes, tomato puzzles, tomato quizzes, tomato poems ('Come to the Festival, gonna be a lot of fun. Put on your gingham gown, be sure to tell everyone') and all sorts of trivia about tomatoes. Did you know that tomatoes are the world's most popular fruit (bananas are second) and that their scientific name is *lycopersicon lycopersicum* ('Can I have some lycopersicon lycopersicum sauce on my burger please')? There was even a list and detailed descriptions of 78 different tomato varieties—including the Glamour, Terrific, Fabulous, Beefmaster, Tiny Tim, Big Steven and the Burping Golden Boy. I also discovered, to my amazement, that there are 25 producers of tomatoes in Ripley and four of them use a mulch and trickle irrigation system.

More amazing still was that *every* single advertisement, whether it was for 'Dr Brooks Optometry' or 'Yarbrough Funeral Home', had a picture of a tomato in it. Some had also quite obviously employed the talents of the same very witty copywriter: State Farm Insurance—We *insure* that you will have a great time at the Ripley Tomato Festival; Ward's Accounting—You can *count* on a good time at the Tomato Festival; The Bank of Ripley—You can *bank* on a good time with us at the Tomato Festival; and, best of all, Willie's Discount Tobacco—Have a *smokin'* time at the Tomato Festival!

On the front of the newspaper was a large photo of brothers Russell and Glenn Kiestler, 'The 2003 Tomato Farmers of the Year'. They were both wearing those outrageously large baseball caps that sit high on top of the head. It made them look like Dumb and Dumber (I don't understand how they or the other few million Americans who wear these caps fail to see how darn stoopid they make them look).

I got to see Russell and Glenn in person (minus the Dumb and Dumber caps) at the Opening Ceremony when they were called up on stage to collect their award. The announcer introduced them as, 'fine am-bass-adoors of our country in the pro-motin' of Sunbeam toe-mate-ohs.' Russell looked as if he'd been sampling quite a few over the years as he was twice the size of his brother. Russell said,

'We's so proud t' grow Rip-leee Toe-mate-ohs. They's is, without a doubt, th' best toe-mate-ohs in th' whole Ewe Ess of Ay.'

The entertainment for the evening was from a barber's shop quartet. Except that there were 20 of them. They were so nice, so pleasant, so cheerful, and oh-so-bloody happy it made me feel sick. Everyone was clapping and singing along having a grand old time. I tried to join in, but I felt as if I was at Band Camp. I decided to leave before they started sucking my internal organs out with a straw.

I couldn't leave though. I couldn't find my hire car in the car park. Not only couldn't I remember where I'd parked it, I hadn't actually bothered to take note of what model it was. I just knew it was red and American. The problem was that the car park was full of red American cars—many of the folks in Ripley had opted for rather apt tomato-red cars. I walked around with the remote-locking-thingy pointing it at every red Chevrolet, Ford, Dodge, Chrysler, Buick or Oldsmobile in the car park waiting for the 'beep beep'. When I found it 15 minutes later, I actually whooped with delight (it was a Dodge by the way).

•

For breakfast in the motel the next morning I had a choice of donuts covered in thick icing or toasted muffins with sausage, ham, cheese, egg and pickles. I didn't even bother asking if they had any toma-toes. Anyway, I was fairly confident I'd see and eat some tomatoes on the second day of the festival. After all, there was a Best Tomato Contest, Tomato Eating Competition and Tomato Tasting on the agenda. The first scheduled event wasn't until ten o'clock, so I decided to jump in my toe-mate-oh car and go see me some toe-mate-oh farms.

It was a perfect Doris Day morning with blue skies and a couple of perfectly art-directed fluffy clouds on the horizon. I drove out towards the Mississippi River, where apparently the Ripley tomatoes were grown (I was yet to see one, so I wasn't taking anything for granted). Even the farms looked like Hollywood sets. Long driveways flanked by 100-year-old birch and oak trees led to picture-perfect farmhouses and freshly painted red barns. Everything else was green. Coming from Australia, I'm used to summer draining every ounce of colour from the countryside, but here everything was vibrant green. Including all the tomatoes (there went my plan of jumping a fence to get me some). The road was only wide enough for one car and twice I pulled onto the gravel to let tractors go past. Both drivers were wearing those big baseball caps. And both drivers waved and smiled at me with just a bit too much enthusiasm. Before I entered another episode of 'The Twilight Zone' I turned back to Ripley.

The first Tomato Festival 'event' for the day had lots of tomatoes. You just couldn't eat any. That was because they were paintings of tomatoes. The Fourth Annual Tomato Festival Art Exhibition & Competition was being held in a beautiful old building off the main square. A large sign inside said 'You be the judge. Vote for your favourite tomato'. There were two entire walls full of paintings, including a Van Goghesque tomato, a Monetesque tomato and even an Andy Warholesque tin of tomato soup. When it came to voting I was torn between my two favourites: a really bad sci-fi fantasy in which the planets were replaced with tomatoes; or a post-abstract-modernist concoction that looked as if someone had thrown up on a piece of canvas after eating too many tomatoes. On the voting form I said I couldn't decide because they were both works of genius.

I believe I may have mentioned that I wanted some tomatoes to eat. Well, gee whizz, I sure as hell got some. In the space of half an hour at the Tomato Tasting, I ate 25 different tomato dishes. When I arrived, however, it didn't look that promising. For a start, the venue didn't quite lend itself to a tomato feast. The Tomato Tasting was being held in the First Baptist Church Family Life Center. The only feast I imagined going on there would be of the loaves and fishes variety.

The reality couldn't have been more different. The Life Center was really full of life; people were hoeing into whopping plates of food along trestle tables. Around the perimeter of the room, ladies (of the blue rinse variety) were dishing up portions of tomato-inspired delights to a neverending queue of hungry diners. There was a $4 entry fee, but no one was collecting money and, before I knew it, an oversized plate was shoved in my hand and I was in the tomato conga line.

Among the 25 assorted dishes that somehow managed to get packed onto my plate were three different types of Tomato Soup in tiny bowls, Fried Green Tomatoes, Pigs-in-a-Tomato-Field, Black-eyed Pea Tomato Salad, Beefy Tomato Casserole, Cheese Tomato Quesodillas, The World's Tastiest Salsa, Impossible Green Tomato Pie and, for dessert, Amazing Tomato Spice Cake and Tomato-Soup Cake. I was in heaven. I squeezed in next to a large family and got straight into it. When I stopped for a little rest halfway through, a lady who was cleaning up crockery said, 'Can I take your plate or is you still working on it?'

When I finished working on my delicious meal I immediately felt guilty. It was possibly the best meal I'd ever eaten in the US and I hadn't paid for it. I asked Jean, one of the tomato chefs (she was responsible for the Tennessee Tomato Cornbread Salad) where I could pay and she said, 'Oh my gosh, is you Australian?'

'I sure is,' I said.

'Hey, Mary Lou. This boy here has come all the ways from Australia.'

Within seconds I was surrounded by a group of ladies.

'He cycled here,' Jean told the group.

'No, I drove here,' I said over the 'oohs' and 'aahs' of the women.

'Really! You cycled here? Oh my gosh.'

'All the way from Australia too?' Jean added.

The women 'oohed' and 'aahed' some more, then—when I tried to pay for lunch—Jean said, 'No siree, you is our special guest.'

I certainly was. When I got back to Australia. I did a search on the internet for the Ripley Tomato Festival and found a story in the *Tennessee Tribune* that announced, in the lead paragraph, 'The Ripley Tomato Festival is more popular than ever. One visitor rode all the way from Australia.'

The tomato drought was definitely over. Back at Ripley Park there were tomatoes galore. There were incredibly large ones, perfectly round ones, juicy plump ones and even one shaped like an erect penis. The Tomato Contest included categories for the biggest, tastiest, best coloured and oddest shaped tomato. The sweet wholesome folk of Ripley didn't even notice that one of the entrants in the 'Odd Shape' division looked like something you might put batteries in to make it vibrate. I went to the Official Ripley Tomato Festival tent to buy an Official Ripley Tomato Festival T-shirt and one of the women from the Tomato Tasting almost jumped over the counter to give me a hug. 'This here is the Australian!' she said to everyone within earshot. Another lady turned to her husband and said, 'Hey, Bob. It's the Australian!'

I waved to my fans and headed over to the main stage for the Tomato Eating Contest. They didn't have much trouble finding contestants for that. There is no shortage of Americans who like to eat as much as is humanly possible. The 15 contestants had two minutes in which to shove as many tomatoes down their gullets as possible. Within the first 10 seconds it looked like a scene from *The Texas Chainsaw Massacre*. Blood-red tomato juice and tomato flesh splashed onto their shirts and the table and covered their faces. By the end of the two minutes it looked like the aftermath of a terrible car accident. A 13-year-old chubby black kid won (the first African-American I'd seen in Ripley, by the way). He ate 24 large tomatoes. Astonishingly, and I mean *really* astonishingly, I spotted him less than an hour later devouring a family-size meat-lover's Domino's Pizza. His sister tried to take a slice and he pushed her away. They better watch him at next year's Tomato Eating Contest. He might try to eat the other contestants.

The mid-afternoon heat was now unbearable and I decided to make a huge sacrifice. I was going to miss the Cheerleading Exhibition that was being put on by the local college to go for a swim at the town pool—where, as it happened, the festival theme had been adopted by several local sunbathers. They were doing their very best to turn *into* tomatoes. I splashed around in the pool with an army of children until it was beer o'clock.

There was no one in the Bar. Oh, except Sheila. She was so excited to see me she welcomed me back like a regular and plonked a Coors (which was what I'd been drinking the night before) down on the bar before I'd even had a chance to order.

'Are there any restaurants in town?' I asked.

'Yup, we's got McDonald's, KFC . . .'

'No, I mean like *real* restaurants with *real* food,' I said.

While I was researching Ripley on the internet I came across a 'Ripley Restaurant Guide'. That will be handy, I thought. I opened up the link to find the following list of 'restaurants': Burger King, McDonald's, Pizza Hut, KFC, Taco Bell, Wendy's and, the very healthy sounding, Fatburger. None of them were in Ripley itself, mind you. They were all clustered around my motel on the highway.

'Oh, there is one place,' Sheila said after thinking for a minute. 'Molly's Restaurant has nice food.'

'Sounds perfect. Where is it?'

'It's in between KFC and Wendy's.'

Molly's looked like one of those workers' lunch sheds they have on construction sites. I had to drive through the KFC car park to get to it.

I ordered me some 'Fine Tennessee Beef Steak' and sat back and watched the other diners try to eat their own body weight in food. The size of servings in America is just plain silly. There was enough food on my plate to feed a small army (or one fat American). I remember reading about a restaurant in Texas where anyone who finished a meal got it for free. So naturally the restaurant made the meal the size of Texas. It included a 'bucket' of fries, a 'side salad' which takes up a whole side of the table and a 72-ounce steak (for those of you who don't know imperial measurements, that's about half a cow). Only a handful of people had ever finished it although thousands had tried. It's such a waste of food it's frightening. 'Think of the starving children in Ethiopia,' as my mum used to say if we didn't finish our dinner.

Back at Ripley Park the evening's entertainment had fired up with the 'Web Dalton & the Dalton Gang'. They looked like Jehovah's Witnesses in cowboy hats. People everywhere were nodding and smiling at me. My jaw started hurting from smiling so much. The band was (how do I put this nicely?) fucking terrible. They were playing sort of country-folk, oh-so-pleasant give-me-a-bucket, type music. A policeman walked past me, waved and smiled and said,

'Welcum t'Rip-leee.' Okay, this was getting weird. I just couldn't take so much niceness any more.

I looked at my watch—it was seven-thirty. I figured I could be back in Beale Street, Memphis, in less than two hours listening to some down-and-dirty blues, drinking some down-and-dirty beer and enjoying the down-and-dirty ambience of the sort of place where the police only smiled at you when they are beating you up. I snuck out behind the hot dog stand—in case I was dragged up on stage for an official welcome and a sing-along with the band.

By just after ten I was on to my third beer, dancing to a down-and-dirty blues band at the Rum Boogie Café and not having to smile and wave at a single person. By two o'clock I was verging on a blithering mess when a local lad I'd befriended leant over and said, 'Hey Byron, would ya lark t'see sum fine Memphus black pussy?' He wanted to take me to strip club. 'I don't think Doris Day would approve,' I said as I drained my glass and began to follow him out.

Vodou Festival

Saut d'Eau, Haiti
July 15th

During the two days of the Saut d'Eau Vodou Festival, thousands of Vodouists strip and bathe nude under the Saut d'Eau waterfall to purify themselves. Many shake and cry when they become possessed by Erzulie, the Vodou Goddess of Love. Drums beat incessantly the entire time while regular sacrifices of chickens and oxen are made to Erzulie. Yeah, that's all fine, but where do I learn to make one of those Vodou dolls you stick pins in? I'd already got my photo of Australia's Prime Minister John Howard for reference . . .

I wish I'd known some Vodou (which is the Haitian spelling of Voodoo, by the way) on my first day in Port-au-Prince, the capital of Haiti. I could have had our unofficial and annoyingly persistent wannabe-guide possessed by an evil chicken. Less than two minutes after we'd walked out of our hotel a 'guide' had latched onto us and, no matter what we said or did, we couldn't shake him off. When I say we, I mean me and a Swiss guy called Roger—the one and only tourist in Haiti. Roger was the only westerner I met in Haiti who wasn't a writer, journalist, photographer, Peace Corp volunteer or dodgy businessman. I met him among the utter chaos that surrounded the baggage carousel at Port-au-Prince airport (a one-hour flight, but a world away, from Miami). He had the same 'I don't think I'm ever going to see my bag again' look on his face that I'm sure I was wearing. I asked him if he'd like to share a taxi into town and then, in the taxi, I asked him if he'd like to come to a Vodou Festival with me (not something, I imagine, he'd often been asked back home). I was happy and, to be frank, relieved when he said yes.

Although I generally never get too worried about travelling anywhere, from what I'd read about Haiti, it sounded worse than going on holidays with your in-laws. The US State Department Travel Advisory website said this:

Haiti is one of the most dangerous countries in the Western Hemisphere. In recent years, Haiti has experienced an alarming rise in civil and political unrest. Protests and demonstrations occur frequently throughout the country, and can become violent with little or no warning. Activists often establish unofficial, temporary roadblocks throughout the country, cutting off major thoroughfares using flaming barricades, bonfires and firearms. Assistance from Haitian officials, such as the police, is often non-existent. There are no "safe areas" in Haiti. Crime, already a problem, has mushroomed in recent years. Reports of death threats, murders, drug-related shootouts, kidnappings, armed robberies, break-ins or carjackings occur almost daily. Random stabbings are frequent. The Department of State warns US citizens against any travel to Haiti due to the unstable security situation throughout the country.

Disneyland it certainly isn't. Now you might reasonably wonder why, then, I was going to Haiti.

I'd read an article on the Saut d'Eau Vodou Festival and, beside the fact that the photos looked out-of-this-world, two words stuck out: 'no tourists'. I'd never really been anywhere truly off the beaten track before. Sure, I'd been to exotic places like Mongolia, Morocco and Tasmania, but I would always bump into a backpacker somewhere haggling over a can of Coke. Also, I found the whole Vodou thing utterly fascinating. My and, let's be honest, most people's idea of Vodou owes a lot to Hollywood: groaning zombies, evil possessions, human sacrifices, Voodoo doll curses and scantily attired voodoo priestesses (well, they're in my version at least. I once saw this dodgy but brilliant film called *Voodoo Academy* in which a schoolful of hunky blond boys ran around in bulgy boxer shorts while their scantily attired Voodoo priestess headmistress slowly turned them all into flesh-eating zombies). I wanted to see some real Vodou. Oh, and maybe some scantily clad Vodou priestesses.

The first thing our unofficial guide asked us was if we wanted to buy a woman. Actually, you almost needed a guide (or a woman) in Port-au-Prince just to navigate the footpath. Uncovered manholes and open sewage pits dotted what was already a minefield of broken-up concrete. It was like a treacherous game of hopscotch.

The streets around Champs de Mars (the main square) were packed with men standing around doing nothing. This didn't surprise me. Not after I'd read that a staggering 80 per cent of the population is unemployed. Because of all this standing around, Haiti claims the unenviable title of the poorest nation in the Western Hemisphere. Throw in some political unrest, flaming barricades, murders, drug-related shootouts, kidnappings, armed robberies, break-ins, carjackings and a few stabbings and the country is, to be perfectly frank, fucked up. As it has been for almost 200 years.

Only 500 years ago Haiti was an untouched Caribbean paradise. Christopher Cólumbus soon put an end to that, though. He and his Spanish mates in tights landed there in 1492 and proclaimed it the 'New World' (he thought he had 'discovered' America when in fact he had actually discovered Haiti). When the prospective invaders finally realised that the island of Hispaniola wasn't continental America (the lack of McDonald's gave it away), they lost interest and allowed pirates to vie for control until French men in tights turned up. By the middle of the 17th century, the Haitian third of the island had become a French colony. The French administrators needed someone to wash their tights so, over the next 100 years, they imported over 200 000 slaves from the west coast of Africa. By 1780, Haiti was one of the wealthiest regions in the world. A class system arose, however, with the light-skinned, Catholic, French-speaking minority bossing around the dark-skinned, Vodou-worshipping, Creole-speaking masses. In 1791, the French Revolution inspired a successful slave revolt and, by 1804, Haiti became the world's first post-colonial independent black nation. In 1844, another revolt threw Haiti into a state of anarchy. It stayed there for most of the time until 1957 when François 'Papa Doc' Duvalier declared himself 'President for life'. There was no anarchy now, just fear as Duvalier used his armed thugs, called the Tontons Macoutes, to help him keep control. Terror, torture, murder and all those fun things were very much the order of the day. When Papa Doc died, his son Jean Claude—'Baby Doc'—came to power. Life under Baby Doc wasn't much better. After he was exiled to France, the country endured a succession of massacres and rigged elections. Today, sadly, not much has changed. There are just more holes in the footpaths.

As Roger and I hopped, skipped and jumped around the square, our very informative guide pointed out the sights: 'This is a building'; 'These are people'; and, more specifically, 'These are people selling food'. One side of the square was lined with makeshift barbecues fashioned out of old metal drums. The delicious smell of char-grilled chicken and char-grilled banana filled the hot muggy air. We waltzed straight past all these inviting smells, though. We were going to have dinner with the 'élite crowd'. Only a few uncovered manholes away from our hotel was La Table Ronde restaurant where, according to the Lonely Planet guidebook, an 'elegant marble-tiled terrace' awaited us with 'high-quality Creole food' including the 'not-to-be-missed house speciality of *écrevisse créole* (Creole prawns)'.

The élite crowd must arrive late. The place was empty. We startled a couple of waiters sitting inside who led us back out onto the dusty marble-tiled terrace and sat us down at a dusty table. The élite crowd weren't late; they'd left a few years earlier. The *écrevisse créole* was on the menu, though. When we pointed to it, however, the waiter shook his head. In fact, he shook his head at every single thing on the menu except the char-grilled chicken. When we nodded yes to the char-grilled chicken (he only spoke Creole), he gestured as if to say 'Good choice!' We sipped our bottles of Prestige (the local brew) and watched people standing about in the square. Our guide was waiting for us at the entrance even though I'd told him, in no uncertain terms, that I wasn't giving him any money.

'I guide you back to your hotel,' he said.

'It's across the road!' I said, pointing to the hotel sign down the street.

'It's much better if I wait for you.'

'No. It's much better if you go away,' I said.

Our char-grilled chicken was quite tasty. It came with char-grilled banana and rice. Roger suggested, probably correctly, that they just went and bought our meal at one of the street-stall barbecues. Halfway through our meal we lost sight of it; it was getting dark and the restaurant had no lights. We ended up finishing off our food by the gloom of a sad excuse for a candle that the waiter put on the table. After dinner we sat downing beers talking about travel and commenting on how dark it was. Roger was at the end of an 18-month around-the-world trip. He chose Haiti because he heard it was crazy.

Our guide was still 'waiting' when we got up to leave almost two hours later. 'So now you pay me!' he grunted.

'What for?' I said.

'I waited for you a very long time. It is very difficult to wait.'

I gave him a dollar and told him to go wait in another country. Our walk back to our hotel wasn't as easy as I thought it would be. The streets of Port-au-Prince were so poorly lit that everyone had given up on the footpaths and were walking on the road. That way you only had to negotiate speeding cars without headlights. We dodged the traffic all the way across a street that was so dark even zombies would be too scared to wander down it.

I didn't sleep very well. The word had got out that a couple of foreigners were in town and, before I knew it, the room had been taken over by mosquitoes. The power had gone off during the night, so the air-conditioner wasn't a lot of use. I alternated between covering myself and sweating away a few kilos, and throwing off the sheets to get eaten by the mosquito welcoming party.

.

A wartime evacuation was taking place at the main bus station, or at least that's what it looked like. The departing buses were all packed tightly with people, suitcases, boxes and the odd chicken. There were old American school buses, clapped-out vans and taptaps (big and small trucks with bench seats in the back). Each and every one of them looked as if they had been painted by the Partridge Family. Bright colours and patterns covered every square centimetre. Large signs above every front window carried messages like 'Merci Jesus' (even though I'm not quite sure what they had to thank him for). Almost every sign was addressed to either God or Jesus.

There's an old saying in Haiti that the country is 90 per cent Catholic and 100 per cent Vodou. That's because both religions are practised together. So does that mean Jesus came back as a flesh-eating zombie and Satan made Vodou-dolls of God? Actually, the two religions are closely intertwined. Vodou was outlawed by the colonial rulers, so the local slave population learnt to conceal their practices behind the veil of Catholicism. They would attend Sunday mass, but they would identify Catholic saints with African spirits. Saint Patrick, for example, who is depicted surrounded by snakes, became the Vodou Iwa (spirit) Damballah who, handily enough, is also associated with snakes. These two images fused together in the minds of the followers of Vodou.

Vodouism and Catholicism aren't the only religions to have the whole fusion thing happening. La Fiesta de la Virgen de la Candelaria in Copacabana, Bolivia, is a mix of Christianity and the Inca religion. On February 2nd every year, the locals not only pray to Mary (the Virgin Mary appeared in the town a few years back—she's always popping up somewhere), but also do things like bury llama foetuses under their homes to bring good luck.

I thought we would need God's help (or some llama foetuses) to help us find the taptap to our first destination, Jacmel, but the first driver we asked said, 'Get in now QUICKLY!' He unceremoniously ejected the passenger sitting next to him and we scrambled up into the cabin (we paid the 'First Class' price to sit in the front—all of $3). As we pulled out, I gave Roger an 'Aren't we clever travellers for getting a taptap just as it was leaving?' look. We drove about 10 metres then stopped—for half an hour.

We sat there watching all sorts of people, young and old, standing around the bus station. The Haitians were very good at standing about (they'd make great cricketers). Women walked up to our window with immense baskets balanced on their heads selling warm soft drinks, fruit, sweets, cassette tapes and spare tyres (were we supposed to supply our own?), while handsome children peered at us inside the cabin and giggled uncontrollably when we said hello to them. Well, shouted hello. Loud distorted music was blasting out to the passengers who were packed into the back of the taptap like sardines in a particularly unhygienic can.

We were heading three hours south to the coastal town of Jacmel, where a strong traditional association with Vodou would make it a good place to warm up before throwing ourselves headfirst into the Vodou Festival and its thousands of devotees possessed by chickens.

Once we eventually set out, we were on the road for only 15 minutes before joining the worst traffic jam I'd ever seen. It would have been quicker to walk—with one leg missing. Just to prove my point, a man with one leg hobbled past us on crutches. We'd passed him five minutes earlier. He had been kissing the front of each and every vehicle as it stopped, then asking the occupants for money.

We crawled through the outer suburbs at a one-legged snail's pace. It was so stiflingly hot in the cabin that sweat was pouring down my legs. At least it was washing away the dust. The streets were filthy. I had never in all my travels seen so much squalor. I'm not sure what day 'rubbish day' was and, by the looks of it, neither did the garbos. The garbage looked as if it hadn't been picked up since 1982. It was piled so high in places that cars had to drive over giant mounds of it just to turn into one of the side streets. And this wasn't even one of the 'slum' suburbs.

Stalls had been set up on the footpath by people selling all sorts of odd things, including empty bottles, broken chairs, old pots without handles and more bald tyres. One fellow was selling what looked like a pile of rocks (they were nice rocks though). On the outskirts of the city we passed some buildings under construction, but they were being made from such shabby materials it was hard to tell if the buildings were going up or coming down.

Finally, mercifully, we left the suburbs behind and were soon up in the cool air of the mountains. I stuck my head out the window looking very much like a dog with its tongue out in the breeze. The mountain sides were stripped bare. The peasant population had plundered all the trees, leaving a scarred moonscape of dust and rocks.

Jacmel, in comparison, looked like a tropical paradise. Palm trees and banana trees surrounded the wide, sleepy streets of the small town, which were lined with once magnificent but now faded and decaying townhouses. We made our way to the once magnificent, then decayed, but now magnificent once more Hotel Florita. I'd stumbled upon the Hotel Florita website and instantly fallen in love with the place. There was no helpful information (like room prices) on the site, just the most amazing photos of sweeping staircases, massive white shutters opening out onto large tiled balconies, and grand airy rooms filled with incredible four-poster beds and brightly coloured Haitian art (check it out at <www.hotelflorita.com>). I didn't want to miss out getting one of the few rooms, so I'd made a booking two months earlier. I just hoped my room had twin beds; Roger looked like the sort of bloke who would hog the blankets.

That turned out not to be much of a problem. We were the only guests. In fact, as I was filling out the guest register I noticed that the last guests had checked out five weeks before. No wonder the hotel manager was so happy to see us. The hotel register dated back to 1956 when the original three-storey mansion had been converted into a hotel. The hotel closed in 1974 (mass terror tends to scare off tourists) and opened again, after being restored, in late 2000. While we waited for one of the staff to find the key to our room, I flipped through the entire book and noticed that I was the first Australian ever to stay at the Florita.

The hotel was a labyrinth of corridors, with doors leading to more corridors with more doors. We had to go through four different doors to get to our room. The bedrooms were on the top floor; the second floor held a lounge, formal dining room, study and a library; while on the ground floor there was a grandiose reception area and a restaurant overlooking a large tropical garden. We had the entire hotel to ourselves.

I was planning to search out some Vodou, but that could wait. I had a lifelong fantasy to fulfil first. I wanted to laze about on a Caribbean beach. I asked our smiling hotel manager where the best beach was and he said, 'I will take you there.' Fifteen minutes later, Roger and I were sitting on brilliantly white sand in a small half-moon-shaped cove flanked by rocky cliffs and nodding palms, with sparkling clear water in front of us and the warm sun shining on our sickly white, glow-in-the-dark bodies. Well, at least that's what we would have looked like to the dozen or so dark-skinned locals swimming there. It was just as I had always hoped a Caribbean beach would be like. All I needed was a pina colada with a novelty straw and it would have been perfect.

As arranged, François, our smiling hotel manager, picked us up at five-thirty on the dot. When I told François I was interested in Vodou, he smiled even more widely and said, 'Tomorrow, I will take you to a *houngan* [Vodou priest].' Now that's what I call service— even if he was only taking us there so we could be sacrificed and turned into zombies.

I was looking forward to dinner. I was about to fulfil my other Caribbean fantasy, which involved devouring a giant lobster at a beachside restaurant surrounded by scantily clad Caribbean ladies who constantly wiggle their bottoms. Okay, there may have been a bit of wishful thinking at the end there, but according to my guidebook Le Crevette restaurant fitted the first two criteria. Not only did it overlook the sea, but lobster was the specialty of the house.

The restaurant looked closed. We wandered in through the empty 'Busy Bar' and into a dark and deserted restaurant. We were just about to leave when we spotted the waiting staff sitting at a table in the corner playing cards. 'Do you have any lobster?' Roger asked in French. They all shook their heads. 'Prawns?' I said in something that resembled French. Another collective no. 'But the restaurant is called The PRAWN!' I said in English to a rather bemused response. One of them pointed to something on the menu and jabbered in French to Roger. I didn't need much French to figure out what she was saying. The only thing on the menu that was actually available was chargrilled chicken with char-grilled banana.

I was on a mission now. I had to find some lobster. Yaquimo Restaurant was 'the place to be seen' in Jacmel according to my guidebook. As we trudged up the road I was just hoping it was 'the place to be seen eating lobster'. The outdoor terrace restaurant was lit up with fairy lights, and 20 or so tables were dotted among the palm trees surrounding a large pool. We didn't have much trouble getting a table. We were—surprise, surprise—the only customers.

I did get to fulfil my fantasy, though. I got my lobster. And, as a bonus, our waitress had a bottom and wasn't afraid to wiggle it. There was even some entertainment. While we dug into our lobster, a pack of snarling, rabid stray dogs chased each other around our table.

After dinner we decided to take an aprés-lobster stroll around town. No sooner had we stepped back into the street, a 'guide' appeared at our side. 'I walk for you,' he said. Although that seemed like a novel idea we doubted he could live up to his promise so we told him to go away. Naturally, that only seemed to encourage him. As it turned out, he'd gone to the same school of guiding as our friend in Port-au-Prince: 'This is a church', 'This is a road', and—while we were standing in front of a building with flashing lights, loud music and a sign saying 'DISCO'—'This is a disco'.

We decided to join the crowd of 20-somethings who were queuing up to get into the Disco Concorde. Our guide insisted on getting us our tickets. 'It is five dollars entry fee,' he said. We got our own tickets. The entry fee was one dollar. It is not an exaggeration to say that every single person in the disco looked at us as we walked in. We were, not surprisingly, the only whiteys in the place. The dance floor was so dimly lit I could barely make out the heaving mass of girls wiggling their bottoms to a cross between reggae and dance music (I later discovered it's called 'meringue' music and originated in the Dominican Republic).

We couldn't shake off our wannabe guide. He followed us to the bar, the outdoor terrace and he even followed me into the loo. If I hadn't gone into one of the cubicles, I was sure he would have tried to hold my willy for me. We finally thought we had escaped him when we squeezed onto the dance floor—only for him to turn up with two girls. 'I have two girls for you to dance with,' he said. Both girls were tall with large bottoms and pointy breasts. 'They look like pieces of Toblerone,' Roger said when I commented on their pointy breasts. They didn't speak a word of English. We danced while our guide—turned pimp—stood next to us raising his thumb and winking. My dance partner was so tall that my nose was level with her Toblerone breasts. When our pimp grabbed my hand and tried to put it on the girl's bottom I took it as a sign to sit down. The girls—and our pimp, of course—sat down with us.

We had another beer while the girls sat there smiling at us. When the girls got up again for a dance we headed straight for the exit. Our guide was certainly persistent. He followed us back, and into, the hotel, hassling us for money all the way. While I searched for a member of the extremely elusive staff to get the key, Roger finally got rid of him. 'I told him that we needed a guide tomorrow night and to come back at seven,' Roger said.

'Clever!' I said. We were leaving straight after lunch.

·

Our guide was waiting for us in reception when we came down for breakfast. The two dancing girls from the disco were sitting on the couch next to him. The girls looked as if they were dressed up to go to a wedding. We rushed past them on our way to the dining room. It was there that I hatched the plan for the Great Escape. In a neglected corner of the rear garden I noticed a large metal gate with a large metal padlock. The maid gave us an odd look when we asked if she had a key to the padlock and an even odder look when we asked if she could sneak around the perimeter of the garden to open it. I couldn't help whistling the theme tune from *The Great Escape* as we snuck out the gate into the back lane.

Jacmel looked as if it was in the middle of a war. So many buildings, which had obviously once been grand and beautiful, were in such disrepair that they looked as if they'd borne the full brunt of a recent bombing raid. The town was full of gingerbread mansions with wrought-iron balconies and three-metre-high doors painted in bright greens and blues (well, formerly bright, at least). I know who could fix the place up—get the 'Backyard Blitz' team in for a few weeks; it's amazing what a couple of water features can do to a place. Anywhere else in the world, a town like Jacmel would be a UNESCO heritage site. I just hope this charming town gets saved (or the 'Backyard Blitz' team turns up) before the entire place simply falls down.

It took our guide 20 minutes to realise we'd done a bunk and then find us again. 'I told you I walk for you,' he said. He walked with us as we wandered down to the town's beach. 'This is the beach,' our guide told us. Actually, there wasn't much of a beach to see. That was because, and I'm seriously not exaggerating here, nearly the entire beach was covered in rubbish. In some places it was almost a metre high. The latest 'Keep Jacmel Beautiful' advertising campaign obviously wasn't working too well. It was only ten o'clock and already stinking hot, so we decided to have a rest in the only place that had air-conditioning—the local branch of the Banque de la République d'Haiti. The security guard inside the bank stopped us as we tried to enter and said something in Creole. I said, in English, 'I'm here to apply for a home loan.' He gave me a puzzled look and waved us in. Our guide—who'd probably had his home loan application rejected already—couldn't come in. It was delightfully cool and we were more than happy to lounge about in the waiting chairs until someone threw us out. 'Maybe we should send our guide to get us a couple of beers,' Roger said. By the time we left the bank our guide had finally given up on us.

François was looking dapper in his pressed slacks and business shirt when he picked us up from the front of the hotel. François would dress like this every day, I imagine, whether he had guests or not. As he drove us to the edge of town to visit the *houngan*, he told us how hard it was to keep the hotel running. He was happy if he could just manage to pay his staff every week. François also told us he was a Vodouist and had taken the pilgrimage to Saut d'Eau. 'It is much like Mecca is to the Muslims,' he said. 'No matter how much that it cost or how long that it takes, if you serve the spirits you need to go at least once in your life.'

The *houngan*'s name was Lionel. He had a ludicrously long formal name, but I didn't get much after the Lionel part. As an example of the scale of ludicrousness and nonsensicality we're talking about, I found a website belonging to a *mambo* (a Vodou priestess) whose name was Bon Mambo Racine Sans Bout Sa Te La Daginen. In English it apparently means Roots Without End, Who Was Already There, of Guinea. Indeed.

Lionel lived in a one-room shack. Tacked on the back was a workshop where he made Vodou drums and two 'altar' rooms which were, in François words, a 'good' room and a 'bad' room. 'The good room is used to call the good spirits to bring good fortune and healing, and the bad room is used to call evil spirits to bring vengeance.' The rooms were tiny. Not much bigger than a toilet. They both had shelves piled high with offerings to the spirits. 'It's to keep the spirits happy so they don't turn on him,' François whispered.

The 'bad' room had a black life-sized coffin painted on the wall, with a large white Christian cross painted in the middle. Next to it was a rather scary drawing of a skeleton. The offerings included bottles of rum, four pairs of sunglasses, a small tombstone and vases with skeletons painted on them. Sadly, there were no Vodou dolls (apparently they only appear in New Orleans—and Hollywood). So much for my photo of John Howard.

The 'good' room had even more rum, gin, whisky (it looked as if the good spirit didn't mind the odd spirit or two), wine, beer, vases of flowers, a painting of Mary, sea shells and a Barbie doll in a small velvet coffin. What I found particularly funny was that the 'good' room had offerings of bottles of Pepsi while the 'bad' room had bottles of Coke.

Lionel, who was in his seventies, was incredibly skinny and frail. He could hardly walk, but he happily waddled into the good room for us and posed for a photo with one of his drums. In the photo he is smiling. He only has about three teeth.

After picking up our bags at the hotel, François dropped us off at the bus station. As we said goodbye, he gave us both a huge hug. He really was quite excited to have guests in his hotel.

We went 'First Class DELUXE' on the way back to Port-au-Prince. The driver's cabin had air-conditioning. The only other passenger in the cabin was a sweet teenage girl in a pretty frock who sat behind our seats, squished in beside our bags, reading a romance novel. It was so pleasant with the warm sun on my face that I soon dozed off on the comfortable ride back to the capital. I woke up just as we pulled into the central bus station in Port-au-Prince.

'Oh, fuck!'

'What's the matter?' Roger asked, as he stepped out of the taxi we'd caught from the bus station.

'I've been robbed!' The sweet innocent-looking teenager in the pretty frock had ransacked my bag while I was asleep and had got her sweet little hands into my money belt (yeah, yeah, I know, why wasn't I wearing it?). She had taken about $150 in US dollars and Haitian gourdes, and my one remaining traveller's cheque. Mind you, when I got over the initial shock I was actually quite happy. Thankfully, she hadn't taken my passport, plane tickets, credit card or—my most prized possession—my Buffy the Vampire Slayer pen. There was only one little thing that pissed me off. 'What the hell's wrong with Australian money?' I said to Roger. She'd taken all the other money, but had left the 100 good ol' Aussie dollars in cash.

The robbery did put a bit of a dampener on our arrival at the Hotel Oloffson, though. I had been really looking forward to staying there and I was still cursing (mostly at myself for being so stupid) as we walked up the long driveway. On every trip I take, I generally stay in cheap dives, but I always have at least one big splurge and stay a night or two at somewhere 'flash'. The Hotel Oloffson was certainly that. Set on top of a hill overlooking the city, the elegant white gingerbread building looked flash indeed with its turrets, decorative wrought iron and wide verandahs. To get to reception we had to walk through a lower level verandah that served as the dining room, with views over the pool and lush tropical gardens. My mood soon brightened when I saw that they had cash advance facilities at reception. Finding an ATM in Port-au-Prince would be like trying to find a street without rubbish. The interior of the hotel was just as impressive as the outside. Next to reception was a bar that had been hewn out of the red rock hill which backed onto the hotel. The mahogany bar was surrounded by white rattan furniture and the walls were draped with sequined Vodou flags and Haitian art. On the door of each room, a colourful hand-painted plaque named the 'famous' guest who had stayed in that room. We didn't stay in the main building (there's a limit to my splurging), where names like Mick Jagger, Jimmy Buffett, Jean-Claude Van Damme, Graham Greene, Richard Burton and John Gielgud adorned the doors. We stayed in one of the 'standard' rooms in the 'hospital wing' (the hotel was used as a military hospital during America's occupation). The vast wood verandah with rocking chairs and a stunning view over the city and bay easily compensated for the small room. We stayed in the Ann Margret room. She can't have done too well out her film career, then— the basic room was all of US$68.

We still needed to find a guide/driver to take us to Saut d'Eau, so I dumped my bags in the room and rushed back to reception. I just hoped I wasn't leaving it too late. We wanted to leave the next morning. On the way to reception I passed another guest sitting at a small table on the verandah surrounded by piles of notes and scribbling on a notepad. 'How ya doin'?' he said as I shuffled past. Mike, from Arizona, was writing a thesis on Catholicism's role in Vodou (or the other way around, I can't remember). He was also going to Saut d'Eau and had already organised a guide/driver to take him there.

'Is it all right if we go with you?' I asked.

'I can't see why not,' he said. 'We can share the costs.'

How easy was that? I didn't even make it to reception. And when I found out how much the guide was going to cost I was so happy I hadn't attempted the trip to Saut d'Eau by myself. The guide was US$60 a day and the hire of a four-wheel drive was US$125 a day. Two days at the festival would have cost me US$370 (that's a hell of a lot of beer money). Best of all, though, we would have our very own Vodou expert with us (which would come in very handy when he explained *why* I was getting turned into a zombie).

We had dinner on the verandah under large cooling fans then retired to the bar for a nightcap. Sitting at the bar was another fellow going to Saut d'Eau. He was English and a photographer for the *Sun* newspaper. I don't know if you are at all familiar with the the *Sun*, but it's the sort of newspaper that has lots of photos of Essex girls with ginormous jugs and stories about the love child Princess Diana had with Michael Jackson—accompanied by a headline like: 'Wacko Jacko dips into Di'. What anthropologically insightful, culturally sensitive headline would the sub-editor use for the Vodou festival pics I wonder? Perhaps: 'Zombies go Cuckoo for Voodoo'.

Our ridiculously expensive $125-a-day four-wheel drive looked suspiciously like a $20-a-day four-wheel drive. Our guide, Jean-Robert, had hired the vehicle from a *friend* of his. Still, I was happy to have a car (and a guide). Everything I had read about Saut d'Eau strongly recommended that you hire a guide to take you there (and also to bring lots of toilet paper). We drove past the rubbish piles that were the suburbs of Port-au-Prince as we headed east up into the mountains. As soon as we left the suburbs behind, we entered the American wild west. The desert landscape of sand, shrubs and cacti looked like New Mexico. Oh, except for all the burnt-out cars lying on the side of the road. With his shaved head and John Lennon glasses, Jean-Robert looked like the actor Lou Gossett Junior. He even overacted. As the road turned into a dirt track pocked with one-metre-deep craters, he kept screaming out: 'Terribull! Terribull!' The mountain road *was* terribull. It was like riding on a pneumatic drill. The roads are so terribull, in fact, that even in an all-terrain vehicle the 70-kilometre trip from Port-au-Prince took us over four hours.

It was also terribull because it was so uncomfortably hot in the car ($125 a day doesn't get you air-conditioning—or suspension for that matter). We couldn't even open the windows. If we had done, we would have been covered in white dust in seconds. The mountain looked as if it belonged on the moon. Stripped of trees, it had turned into a massive dust pile. As we climbed the rutted road we drove past what I dubbed the dust children. These sad-looking children were standing on the side of the road with their hands out, begging for food. They were white. Not white folk, mind you, just black kids entirely cloaked in white dust.

The normally quiet streets of the village of Ville-Bonheur were packed with cars, buses, taptaps, horses, donkeys and pilgrims on foot (it would have taken them a couple of days of walking just to get this far). Not much further down the road there was a massive car park in the form of a large muddy field. People were unloading bags, bottles of rum, palm-thatch mats and chickens (for some good ol' sacrificing later on) as they began the final four-hour trek to Saut d'Eau. Jean-Robert ignored the small inconvenience that the road was full of people and drove straight through the middle of them, forcing donkeys as well as people to dive into the surrounding cornfields.

If it was at all possible, the new road was worse than the one across the mountain. It had holes so big that cars could disappear into them. And one had done just that. The rear end of a car was poking up out of a crater-sized hole in the middle of the road. Jean-Robert just drove around it, scattering a few more people and donkeys in the process.

When we finally reached the tiny village of Saut d'Eau, it felt as if I'd just completed 12 rounds with a couple of WWF wrestlers. My back had taken quite a beating, but I soon forgot the pain as we watched the sea of colour as pilgrims trudged up the narrow dirt track leading to the sacred waterfalls on foot, mules, donkeys, horses and oxen. The *mambos* stood out from the flock in their bright red silk scarves and cobalt blue dresses. Jean-Robert stood out even more. He was wearing his 'guiding uniform' of slacks, dress shoes and a business shirt.

Our first task was to find a room for the night (most pilgrims sleep in the open, while some dance to the drumming all night long). This involved walking up to people's houses and asking if they had a spare room. The first 'spare room' we were shown was no bigger than a bathroom and had a dirt floor. They wanted $40 for it. 'Are you possessed?' Mike said to the owner. A few houses later we were shown another tiny room, but this one was a step up in the luxury stakes: it had a concrete floor, but no beds. The owner asked for US$60.

'Have you got cable?' Mike asked.

'No, but they've got cockroaches,' Roger said pointing to our potential roomies scuttling across the floor.

We took the room. We could have wandered around for hours and not found anything better. And besides, the house had a nice verandah overlooking the track up to the waterfall. Plus, it wouldn't be too hard to find if we got lost: it was painted a rather garish pink and green. Jean-Robert told us we could *buy* our beds at the market.

Most pilgrims complete the final five or so kilometres on foot, climbing up a steep stony path, crossing caverns by wading through waist-deep brackish water and crawling up cliffs. But not Jean-Robert. Oh, no. He decided that we should drive up. As the crowd snaked its way along the path through the thick vegetation, the shouts of laughter mingled with prayers were soon replaced with shouts that I imagine translated as something like, 'What the fuck?!' as we barged through them all. I had thought the previous stretch of road was bad. This was so bad that I couldn't stop laughing. Well, when I wasn't getting thrown around in the back like a rag doll. Jean-Robert was trying to drive with one hand. The other one was fixed to the horn. When we crossed a fast-moving river and the water was rushing by just below the windows I almost wet myself with laughter. The whole time Jean-Robert was screaming out 'Terribull! Terribull!' while sweat literally poured off his face. When we finally stopped at the gate to the waterfall and fell out of the car, Mike said, in between hysterical fits of laughter, 'You're a FUCKIN' lunatic Jean-Robert!'

We stopped for a well-deserved drink before we tackled the final stretch of track. For only a few cents a fellow slashed the end off a coconut and we drank the sweet cool juice straight from the gaping hole. Mike had trouble drinking his as he was still laughing his head off. Troops of chanting people banging on drums passed us as we tramped up the final 500 metres to the falls. According to Mike, our resident Vodou expert, the different troops represented different Vodou sects. If that was the case, then they had some rather odd ones. The group that were all wearing LA Lakers tops must have been the LA Lakers sect. I wonder if they play the Chicago Bulls sect, which danced past after them, in a game of basketball later on. My favourite, however, was the condom-mobile-phone sect. A local health agency was handing out silver packets of condoms (three joined together) and this whole sect was walking along pretending they were mobile phones and having pretend conversations.

On the way down the narrow, steep and slippery path to the water-fall I stood on someone. The someone was a man in deep prayer sitting under a tree among burning white candles and calabash bowls filled with rum and sugar water. I knocked over one candle and stood on his hand. Oh well, here comes my first Vodou curse . . .

We rounded the final bend and there it was—Saut d'Eau. For minutes I was lost in awe at the sight in front of me. Three gleaming waterfalls cascaded down a rock wall onto thousands of people wearing only their underwear. They were singing, laughing and chanting as they bathed and scrubbed their feet, arms, legs and everything else under the pounding, 40-metre-high waterfalls in the tree-ringed ravine. The bathing in the waterfall, Mike told us, is the most important ritual at Saut d'Eau, which is considered a place of healing of both physical and spiritual ailments. From time to time, bathers would shout, suddenly possessed by Erzulie (the Goddess of Love—and Vodou's equivalent of the Virgin Mary). Singing, rolling their eyes, collapsing into the water or onto the rocks, they were seemingly oblivious to the swift current and jagged edges. Fellow worshippers rushed over, taking advantage of Erzulie's presence to whisper direct requests in their ears (they ask for everything from good crops to a visa so they can get the hell out of Haiti). Smack in the middle of all this was the *Sun* photographer. Now I could see why he was here. Most of the women were topless. He was taking photos of ginormous jugs. I can see the headline now: 'Voodoo DOLLS!' and with the addition of maybe '. . . with Nice Pins!'

Mike and Roger scrambled down the mossy bank into the water so they could get a closer look at the largest of the waterfalls, which was hidden from view further up the ravine. I didn't fancy getting hepatitis, so I stayed out of the water. I'm not normally so worried about such things, but only a week earlier I'd fallen off a mountain bike and torn my knees to shreds. The sores hadn't healed properly and were still sort of leaking goo everywhere. Water that thousands of people had been scrubbing themselves in probably wasn't the right stuff to start splashing over my dodgy knees—and the worshippers could probably do without my pus. Instead I traipsed down to the bottom of the large pool to see if I could get a view of the big waterfall from there.

I did find a view, but not of what I expected. At the far edge of the pool there was an incredible collection of underwear. There were hundreds of discarded underpants and bras, with more shooting down in the water and adding to the pile. As part of the whole Vodou cleansing ritual, old knickers must be discarded and left behind in the water. I stood there for quite a while surrounded by old knickers because it was so deliciously cool. The spray from the waterfall was a wonderful respite from the suffocatingly hot and humid morning.

As I clambered back up the bank, I stood on a large and rather worn pair of Y-fronts. I couldn't see the main waterfall from the bottom of the falls, so instead I decided to try to get to the top of them. This involved climbing a precipitous track up the steep cliff face. It was quite hairy and at times the only thing that stopped me from falling was clutching the exposed roots of trees.

As I squeezed around a tight corner, a woman staggered down the cliff track towards me. She was trembling from head to toe and her eyes were rolling around in her head. She was possessed by one of the Vodou spirits. Three strapping fellows were holding her, trying to stop her from falling over. It looked just like a scene from closing time on a Saturday night at the local pub.

At length I reached the top and the view was simply breathtaking. Looking back across the valley I had a long, sensational, unobstructed view across green rolling hills of palms and corn. It was particularly amazing when you considered that the other side of the mountain was nothing but desert.

The view down into the ravine was even more amazing. The scale and density of the crowd under the waterfall was extraordinary. It wasn't quite the same mass of crowd that the Hajj in Mecca gets, but then again the Muslim faith's largest and most important festival, with over two million people attending every year, is like a Sunday school picnic compared to Maha Kumbh Mela in Allahabad, India. Simply put, Maha Kumbh Mela is the largest gathering of humanity on earth. Held every 12 years (the next one is 2013), the Hindu festival attracts, give or take a few thousand, around 18 million pilgrims. At least they wouldn't have to queue for the loo. All 18 million people bathe (and wee I imagine) in the Ganges River. Hundreds drown every year in the urine—I mean river.

Some of the Vodouists looked as if they were about to drown. Hundreds of them were standing under the massive torrents of the waterfall with arms stretched wide asking Erzulie for favours, while others were bathing themselves with soap and leaves. I spotted Mike in the midst of it all. He was taking close-up photos of ginormous jugs. By the look of his research, his thesis was actually about the role of ginormous jugs in Vodou. At the bottom of the path a lady was selling bars of Cussons soap. If you're going to cleanse away evil spirits, you may as well do it in style.

On the way back up the track to meet Jean-Robert we passed a bunch of well-dressed folk about to sacrifice a chicken. Six people stood in a circle around a design that had been drawn in white ash on the ground to summon one of the Vodou spirits. The chicken was clucking happily as they passed it around the circle.

By the way, Vodou isn't the only religion which encourages the sacrificing thing. The Islamic world celebrates Aid el Kabir every March by sacrificing sheep. The sheep's head is turned towards Mecca before slitting its throat, then every bit is eaten. Except a few small pieces of the heart and liver which are cast into the corners of each room of the house (no wonder Muslim women wear cloth covering their noses). In some religions it's not just animals that are sacrificed either; Mormons, for example, sacrifice good fashion sense in the pursuit of their religion.

Mike got out his video camera and started filming the chicken sacrifice. Although my guidebook warned that 'violent incidents have followed unwelcome photography' and Mike had already been abused a few times, he kept filming. Even when one of the sacrificers sneered at him and waved his arms angrily in his face. 'I'll keep filming until they physically stop me,' he said. Stop him all right. They looked like they were going to sacrifice Mike instead of the chicken.

Which, when we saw what happened next, would have been rather messy. The *houngan* put the chicken's head in his mouth and crunched it clean off. He then casually squeezed the neck like a tube of toothpaste and put the blood on the ground around the pattern. Mike almost jumped in the middle of the circle so he could get a close-up shot. I walked away. Watching Vodou priests biting the heads off Americans tends to put me off my lunch.

·

The comedy routine of bouncing passengers while chanting 'Terribull! Terribull!' continued on the drive back to the village. We were all quite hungry by the time we got back to what I'd dubbed the Ritz-Carlton. We wandered into the village and stopped at someone else's house for lunch. The owners had converted their home into a restaurant/bar for the festival. Put a few tables out the front, hang up a hand-drawn sign saying 'Restaurant' and *voila!* you have your very own restaurant. They had something different on the menu, too. They had char-grilled chicken with char-grilled banana *and* beans. I wasn't complaining, though. I love my char-grilled chicken. The owners of the house were incredibly friendly, too, and even shouted us a couple of beers. When I asked for the toilet I was led down the main corridor of the house.

'Here!' the man said. There were two doors on either side of the dark corridor.

'Which one?' I said.

'No, here!' he said pointing to the concrete wall and floor.

'Right here?' I stammered. After I'd said 'You mean HERE!' a few more times, I shrugged, dropped my pants and peed in the middle of someone's house.

'Don't ask to use the toilet,' I told Mike and Roger when I returned. 'They'll probably ask you to piss on their bed!'

Jean-Robert went back to the Ritz-Carlton while we went to buy a bed. The small village market had spread out onto the streets and into the front yards of people's houses. Everything from food to bottles of rum, hats, drums, Vodou scarves and flags were on sale, but there wasn't a bed in sight.

'We'll get the concierge to find us some beds,' Mike said.

On the way back, the sound of incessant drums could be heard all around us. We followed the sound of the closest drums and, after negotiating a narrow path through a cornfield, stumbled across a Vodou ceremony in full swing. A crowd of around 40 people all dressed in white was standing in a circle around a *houngan* who was leading a small group of chanting drummers and dancers. It was a joyful uplifting beat and everyone was smiling and laughing.

Mike explained it to us: 'This is known as a *Rada* ceremony,' he whispered. 'The *houngan* uses different rituals to conjure up different Vodou *loa* or spirits. They're trying to conjure up either St Jacque or Ogou.'

'What's that all about?' I asked Mike, subtly pointing towards the six-foot-three man wearing a white crocheted dress on the other side of the circle.

'He's dressed as a woman.'

'Oh, that explains it!'

Mike got out his camera. Oh no, I thought, here comes the human sacrifice. One snap later a very large man sidled up next to us. He smiled and flashed a badge that said 'Vodou Without Frontiers'. He was a Vodou PR man. His job was to spread the good word about Vodou to foreigners. 'Take many photos,' he said. We started snapping away only to get screamed at by a handful of worshippers. 'It's okay,' he said. 'Take many photos.' There was a slight possibility that he had made the badge up himself and liked nothing more than watching a few westerners get sacrificed and cooked in a pot (although, maybe I'm getting my religious stereotypes a little mixed up here).

Just to get myself even more confused on the religious front, we stopped at the small Catholic church. A large assembly of people was slowly trying to force its way into the church. Many were holding up copies of an American passport. Mike told us that the main thing people prayed for was an American passport. Actually, the whole Saut d'Eau thing started when a vision of the Virgin Mary appeared (here she goes again) in 1884 in the foliage of a palm tree near the waterfall. Because Mary is also Erzulie, the Vodou spirit of love, pilgrims pay homage to both. I'm not sure how the whole waterfall thing fits into it, though. I told you I was confused. Mind you, it's possible to be confused every day of the year. Not only are there many confusing religions in the world, there are absolutely thousands of confusing religious festivals. At Paro Tsechu in Bhutan, for example, Buddhist monks dress up as monkeys and dance around the town hitting people over the head with drumsticks. In Konya, Turkey, the real-life Whirling Dervishes (from the Sufi Dervish Order) spin around on the spot for a few hours to have a closer union with God. Or throw up, whichever comes first. In Phuket, Thailand, the Buddhists appease the gods by holding the Chinese Vegetarian Festival. Although there is no meat eaten, there is plenty of skewered, sliced and tenderised flesh. It just happens to be human flesh. Volunteers get two-metre rods pierced through their cheeks, self-flagellate themselves with axes and climb ladders of razor blades.

The Grand Poo-bah of confusing festivals (and religions for that matter), however, belongs to the Zoroastrians. Their Festival of Chahar Shanbeh Suri, held in Iran, celebrates the seven aspects of creation, and the six immortals that were created to watch over them by the Lord of Creation, Ahura Mazda. The age-old battle between the dual principles of good and evil, wise Lord Ahura Mazda and his enemy, the evil Ahriman, is re-enacted during Mukhtad—along with the sixth element of creation, the hermaphrodite ur-human, Gayo-Maretan, who was sacrificed when the world was set in motion on the first Noruz. Gee, and I thought Vodouism was confusing.

We got back to the Ritz-Carlton just as dinner was being served. Jean-Robert had talked us into paying $10 to have a home-cooked meal. We reluctantly agreed only because we thought it would be fun eating with the family and at $10 each we were expecting an absolute feast. So you may imagine my surprise when we were served char-grilled chicken and rice in our three-by-three-metre bedroom with no family in sight. It was just the three of us and Jean-Robert.

'This chicken must have starved to death,' Roger said. I think he was right. Our 'feast' was anorexic chicken, beans and rice. We'd had the same meal (with a better-fed chicken) for lunch in the village for just under $2.

In the middle of dissecting our dinner, Mike casually turned to Jean-Robert and said, 'So Jean-Robert, where do I go for a shit? In the banana tree?'

'What do you mean?' Jean-Robert responded.

'Are the family going to come out in the morning and see an American white ass shitting in the banana tree?'

Jean-Robert, quitely finished eating his meal then said, 'So, now I go find where you shit.'

While we sat on the verandah having a beer during a brief torrential downpour, the owner of the house turned up with our beds. Well, when I say beds, they were actually incredibly thin palm-thatch mats.

'We may as well just sleep on the concrete,' I said.

Roger had the more sensible approach. 'At least the cockroaches will have something to eat before they get to us.' The 'beds' cost us $2 each.

'Would you like a girl for the night?' the owner asked casually. He was a real entrepreneur, this fellow.

'How much?' Mike asked.

'Three dollars.'

'We should have got a girl to sleep on!' Mike said. 'It only cost a dollar more and she would be a damn sight more comfortable than the mats.' He was right. But we'd already bought the mats. Mind you, the prices of lots of things in Haiti didn't make any sense. Like a concrete-floor room with a banana tree as an ensuite costing not much less than a room at one of the best hotels in Port-au-Prince, or a girl for the night for a third of the price of a rather dodgy chicken meal. Even the money itself made no sense. The gourde is the official currency in Haiti, but prices can be in gourdes, Haitian dollars (which are still gourdes, but five gourdes equals one Haitian dollar— which doesn't exist as a note) or US dollars. Throw in the Vodou/ Catholicism thing and it's no wonder I was confused the whole time.

When the rain stopped, we headed back into the village. It was lucky Mike had a torch. It was dark and the potholes in the road were now filled with water. On the way to the village we were twice asked if we wanted a girl.

'Heaps of sex goes on here,' Mike said with a sly grin. 'Women have got sexual licence during Saut d'Eau. It's some sort of fertility thing.'

One girl I read about afterwards sure made good use of her licence. A few years back a *houngan* named Dieu Bon took a young woman to Saut d'Eau. She then astonished him by bonking every man in sight. Dieu Bon said, 'If she had gone and had fun with one or two, I wouldn't have said anything. Let her have her fun, it's Saut d'Eau. But so MANY.' The whole episode is now immortalised in a famous song *Dyebon te genyen yon ti fanm, korve bare nan bobo l, ah hey, a yo*, which translates into English as 'Dieu Bon had a little woman, a work crew got stuck in her vagina, a hey, a yo'.

In the village, pilgrims clutching rosaries or dressed in Erzulie's red and blue colours were walking the streets singing and asking for offerings while noisy street bands played drums and horns made of sheet metal. A lot of people were very drunk on rum (or possessed, one of the two). The streets were full not only of drunk people, but also of donkeys, carts selling food and rum, and makeshift restaurants. Well, when I say restaurants, there were diners sitting on plastic stools in the dark. They would have had no idea what they were eating (which was probably a good thing).

We wandered the streets past 'discos' that had been set up in corrugated tin sheds that looked as if they'd been put together by me (which is the worst compliment you could ever get). Loud Rara music (a sort of drum-based hip hop Vodou music) blasted out from inside. We peeked through a gap in the wall of one shed to see people all doing the same dance. 'It's not the chicken dance,' I said to the boys. 'It's the *sacrifice*-the-chicken dance.'

We stopped at another Rara music shed. This one just had tin walls and a large open tarp as the roof. As we tried to peep through a gap in the door, a big *mambo* stuck her head out and said, 'Come inside my friends.' A band of eight drummers, with bongo players and three singers, was up on a stage belting out a song using the different drums sounds as a melody. It sounded extraordinary. There seemed to be one member of the band, however, whose sole responsibility was to wander up to the other band members with a bottle of rum and give them long swigs while they were playing. Our big mamma *mambo* led us to the bar and gave us two beers each. She then dragged us to the front of the stage, threw some old people out of their chairs, and said, 'You sit!' The music was deafening. The PA system would have looked more at home at a Rolling Stones concert. We sat there mesmerised by the band, but that was probably because the music was so loud that our brains had shut down.

An hour later the band was still playing the same song. We'd had enough (well, my ears had at least), so we nonchalantly got up and made our way to the exit. We'd thought no one had noticed us leaving until we turned around to see every single person in the place staring at us.

'Let's go back to our 150-dollar-a-night room (the price of our room had slowly been creeping up during the day) and order room service,' Mike said as we stepped out onto the still-crowded street.

I slept on the floor in my clothes with my ears ringing. All four mats didn't quite fit into the room, so I had Roger's feet in my face. Jean-Robert was already asleep.

·

I slept surprisingly well. When I woke up a little after four for a piss on the banana tree, the path at the front of the house was already full of people trudging noisily up to the waterfall. When I got back to the room, the roosters started.

'Hey, Jean-Robert!' Mike said. 'Go sacrifice those fuckin' roosters will ya?'

By four-thirty we were all awake. Jean-Robert suggested we leave before the human traffic jam on the path to the waterfall built up any further.

'Does our 200-dollar-a-night room include breakfast?' I asked Jean-Robert. Not surprisingly, it didn't.

As we were leaving, Mike said, 'Let's take some furniture. We paid for it.' As I was loading up the car, Mike turned up with a massive bag of husked coconuts.

'What are you going to do with them?' I asked.

'I don't know,' Mike shrugged. 'But at 300 dollars a night we have to take something!'

Fifteen minutes into our bumpy drive out of the village, the car stalled. Then Jean-Robert couldn't start it. Pilgrims clambered over the bonnet to get past us as Jean-Robert tried frantically to get the car going. First gear had shat itself. Jean-Robert had to start it in second, lurching into a guy on a mule in the process. Worried that he might stall the car again if he slowed down, Jean-Robert barrelled over bumps (and the odd person and donkey) as we got thrown around in the back. By the time we'd reached dust mountain, the engine was sounding not dissimilar to an old washing machine on spin cycle.

'Hey Mike, pass me the bag of coconuts,' I said casually. 'I've got a brilliant idea!'

Without even asking what my brilliant idea was, Mike dragged the large bag from the rear of the car and plonked it on the seat next to me. As we rounded a bend, and I spotted the first group of begging dust children, I threw out a pile of coconuts onto the road. The children's faces lit up as if it was Christmas (or whatever the Vodou equivalent is). The coconuts immediately started bouncing down the steep mountain road and the kids bolted straight down the road after them. Out the back window, we watched as the kids performed the most impressive rugby tackles to stop the coconuts shooting off the mountain's edge. After I'd thrown out a few more coconuts, we came upon a huge group of begging dust children. I grabbed the end of the bag and emptied all the remaining coconuts out of the window to the delight of the children. Mind you, if I'd done this only 10 seconds later I would have been responsible for the mass murder of about a dozen kids. As they charged down the road, a large truck careened around the bend and the coconuts bounced under the truck. The kids only just dived out of the way in time. I felt so bad that I threw our mat-cum-beds out the window as well. And Mike's bottle of Coke—so the bad spirits would be happy as well. By the time we reached the highway, the car was screaming like a banshee. We'd now lost fourth gear and Jean-Robert was thrashing the engine in third.

'We've been cursed!' I said. 'The owners of the Ritz-Carlton discovered we stole their coconuts, so they've put a Vodou curse on the car.'

Just as I said that, we lost third gear. Jean-Robert said, 'Terri-bull! Terri-bull!' then simply dropped it into second. The car now sounded like a 747 with a large bird stuck in the engine.

If the folk of Port-au-Prince, who are well used to clapped-out cars, look at your car because it's making a lot of noise then, boy, is it making *a lot* of noise! On top of that, whenever Jean-Robert took his foot off the accelerator, the car backfired—sounding for all the world like a gunshot. If people weren't staring, they were running away thinking they'd just heard the sudden return of the Tontons Macoutes.

Jean-Robert was possessed. He was driving straight through intersections without even slowing down. Not that technically he had to stop, I might add. Port-au-Prince, with a population of over two million people, doesn't have any traffic lights. Or stop signs, for that matter. The city is basically just one big free-for-all smash-up derby.

When Jean-Robert happened upon some traffic, he swung the wheel wildly and turned off down a side street. There was more traffic there, too, so off we went down another street. Within five minutes, Jean-Robert was officially lost. Finally, there wasn't another side street to turn down and the car stalled. We were stuck smack in the middle of a major intersection. I'm sorry, but I couldn't help but piss myself laughing. Particularly when we got out to push the car and looked down the street. A long line of traffic was backed up behind our stricken car and all the drivers were feverishly beeping their horns. As we pushed, Jean-Robert, who was losing his body-weight in sweat, chanted his mantra 'Terri-bull! Terri-bull!' over and over.

By the time we pulled into the Hotel Oloffson I was limp, ragged, dirty, sweaty and speechless (but that was mainly because I was still laughing so much). We only just made it as the car spluttered and groaned up the drive to the entrance of the hotel.

We then had a big argument because we'd payed for two days' guiding and it was only nine-thirty in the morning. Finally, Jean-Robert agreed ('You are terri-bull, terri-bull!') to come back with his car and take us to the market. As he drove off, frightening the hotel's guests, Mike said, 'Imagine his friend's face as he thinks "What the hell is that noise?" then Jean-Robert pulls up in his car.' I was still laughing as I stood in the shower washing off two days' worth of dust and grime.

After an early lunch, Jean-Robert turned up in his well beaten-up Toyota. There wasn't a single panel without a dent in it.

'How was your friend?' Mike asked teasingly.

'Terri-bull! Terri-bull!' Jean-Robert said shaking his head.

I'd just like to add here that, although Mike constantly took the piss out of Jean-Robert, he'd actually known him for over a year. He had used him on all his previous visits and had even sent money from the States so that Jean-Robert's 10-year-old daughter could go to school (without Mike's help he couldn't have afforded to send her).

•

The Marché de Fer (Iron Market) looked as if it belonged on the set of *Arabian Nights*. Built of red pre-cast iron, complete with minarets, the whole market was manufactured in Paris in 1889 and transported in bits to Port-au-Prince. That was all very well, but the place stank. The fetid aroma of rotting fruit, raw meat and urine was suffocating. We went straight to the Vodou craft section and were immediately greeted like long-lost brothers. The stallholders probably hadn't seen a tourist for weeks and were soon all flapping around us like moths to a flame. While we stood in one tiny stall looking at sequined Vodou flags (Mike wanted to buy one), proprietors from painting, straw hat, wood carving and women's underwear stalls were squashed in with us trying to flog their wares. When I registered passing interest in a metallic Vodou Sun face (the mother goddess, apparently), the stall-holder followed me through the entire market: we walked out of the craft section, into the large clothes section, through the fruit and veg section and into the meat section (Mike wanted to get a nice holiday snap of rotting meat covered in flies). The price started at $10, but by the time we got to the meat section it was $1. Finally, he turned to me and said, 'Okay, have it for nothing, I don't care, I don't want it any more.' I gave him two dollars for it. I didn't fancy him sitting on my bed next to me in my hotel room still trying to sell it to me.

I spent the rest of the afternoon lounging by the pool reading Graham Greene's *The Comedians*, which is set in the Oloffson during Papa Doc's reign. As I took sips of my fruit cocktail I was reading about the manager finding a dead fellow with slashed wrists at the bottom of the pool. He probably couldn't face another char-grilled chicken.

I, on the other hand, was quite excited about eating some more char-grilled chicken. We'd earlier walked past the packed Arc-en-ciel Restaurant, which not only had deliciously plump rotisserie chickens, but also had a two-for-one happy hour. The chicken was excellent. And so was the owner—that was because his name *was* Excellent. He was so excited to have an Australian, a Swiss and an American eating in his fine establishment that he invited us into the kitchen to meet the staff and take photos. He sat with us afterwards and asked what rotisserie chickens were like in our countries. I could honestly tell him that his chicken was one of the best I'd ever had.

After eating, we did as the locals did and filled our table with bottles of Prestige beer. With only a few minutes of happy hour to go, the locals were ordering armfuls of beer to take advantage of the two-for-one deal. By the time we staggered out a couple of hours later, I was well on the way to being seriously intoxicated.

Back at the Oloffson there was a huge party going on. The owner of the hotel also happened to be the lead singer of Haiti's most famous group, RAM, and every Thursday night Richard and his 10-piece Vodou-rock band played to a packed crowd of wealthy locals. You could tell they were wealthy because the cars in the car park weren't covered in dents. We sat down at one of the many tables that had been set up around the pool and ordered rum punches. Two hours later I had my first Vodou experience. I was possessed. It was absolutely incredible. I kept stumbling over, my arms were flailing about uncontrollably and my eyes were rolling around in my head. Then again, after seven beers and seven rum punches, there was a slight chance that I might have just been pissed rather than possessed.

Hemingway Festival

Key West, Florida, USA
July 20th

Ernest Hemingway was everywhere. The first time I saw him he was sprawled out on the footpath. He looked up at me with his blood-shot eyes and asked for some 'spare change' so he could buy a drink. He stank of cheap booze and urine, and his silver hair and salt-and-pepper beard looked as if they hadn't been washed in weeks. I ignored him and walked on. Over the next three days I saw Ernest fishing off a pier, singing in a karaoke bar, asleep and terribly sunburnt on the beach, and groping a barmaid. I even saw him naked.

I should have told the smelly Hemingway that if he wanted a drink there was a $100 bar tab waiting for him at Sloppy Joe's Bar. All he had to do was win the Ernest Hemingway Look-Alike Contest. He was a dead ringer. He just needed a good wash and the ability to stay upright.

The Hemingway Look-Alike Contest, where over 150 bearded hopefuls in safari suits or cable-knit fisherman's sweaters compete to look most like 'Papa' Hemingway, is just part of the five-day Hemingway Days Festival held every year in Key West, Florida. Other events include a fishing contest, pie-eating contest, arm-wrestling contest and a mock Running of the Bulls. The whole event could also double as the Santa Claus Festival and Look-Alike Contest. Throw a red suit and hat on ol' Ernest and he could easily have scored a job in any department store during the festive season.

To be honest, I didn't know much about Hemingway until I decided to go to Key West. All I really knew was that he wore safari suits with lots of pockets, drank like a fish, liked hunting and killing assorted wild beasties, and dabbled in a bit of womanising. Oh, and that he also wrote a few books.

I may be no Hemingway expert, but at least I knew who he was. When I asked the Swedish receptionist at the Sea Shell Hostel if she had a program for the Hemingway Festival, she said, 'Who?'

'Ernest Hemingway. You know? He wrote books and stuff?' I said.

'Sorry. I am new to Key West.'

Before I go any further with my story I have a confession to make. Before I arrived in Key West, I hadn't read any of Hemingway's books. I had every intention of reading at least one of them before I arrived, but I just never got around to it. I tried to borrow one from my local library but they were all out on loan. There were other Hemingway books on the shelf, but they were written by a collection of Hemingways cashing in on his name, including Lorian Hemingway (who I later discovered was his granddaughter), Maggie Hemingway, Reanne Hemingway, John Hemingway, Hilary Hemingway and Amanda Hemingway. Maybe I should change my name, too. Brian Hemingway has got a nice ring to it, don't you think?

There are just as many Ernest Hemingway Festivals as there are Hemingways. As well as the one in Key West, there's one in Oak Park, Illinois (his birthplace), Toronto (where he lived for a couple of years), Kansas (where he died), Michigan (where he once stopped for gas) and California ('cos they always have to get in on the act). Then again, he's no one in the festival stakes compared to ol' Willie Shakespeare. In a five-minute search on the net, I found 34 different Shakespeare festivals. They were being held everywhere from his hometown of Stratford-upon-Avon to Nashville (Romeo sings 'Stand By Your Man' to Juliet), Las Vegas (Juliet kills herself because she has lost her life savings on the pokies) and Stratford in country Victoria, Australia ('Romeo, Romeo, where th' fuck are ya?').

Ernie and Willie aren't the only writers to have their very own festivals. George Orwell, Jane Austen, Charles Dickens, Hans Christian Andersen, D. H. Lawrence, Mark Twain and even Stephen King (BYO axe) have festivals dedicated to them. Luckily, there isn't a Barbara Cartland Festival. Imagine how scary the Look-Alike Contest would be.

The first real Hemingway look-alike I spotted was standing in a newsagent in Duval Street flicking through one of Hemingway's books. Actually, it wasn't a book by Hemingway; it was a book about Hemingway. There was an entire shelf full of them. As well as biographies, there were books written by people who 'knew' him, including the postman and a taxi driver who picked him up twice. I believe one of his pet cats is negotiating with a publisher as we speak.

I picked up one of the biographies and noticed the Hemingway pictured on the back was a carbon copy of the Hemingway standing next to me. Right down to the fisherman's vest, khaki shorts and rope belt. I picked up another book about the 11 years that Hemingway lived in Key West, which—according to the dust jacket blurb—was the most prolific period of his career. He wrote the novels *A Farewell to Arms*, *Green Hills of Africa*, *To Have and Have Not*, *The Snows of Kilimanjaro* and *For Whom the Bell Tolls* while drinking daiquiris in the sun.

The latter-day Hemingway bought a Hemingway cookbook. I bought *The Old Man and the Sea*. I purchased that particular book because it won the Pulitzer Prize in 1953 and, the following year, won Hemingway the Nobel Prize for Literature. Oh, and it was also a very short read and I have a very short attention span.

The rest of Duval Street seemed to be mostly made up of T-shirt shops. I hadn't yet ascertained whether Hemingway was Nobel Prize material, but if he'd penned any of the slogans on the T-shirts that filled the countless T-shirt shops then he really was a genius. There were such classics as 'I'm shy . . . but I've got a big dick', 'I don't need an encyclopedia. My wife knows it all' and, on a pair of underpants, 'A fart a day keeps the wife away'. Who buys these things and, more worryingly, actually wears them? Even more worryingly, can anyone be big enough to wear them? I've seen XXL shirts before, but these were—and I'm honestly not exaggerating here—XXXXXXL T-shirts. Gee, I had no idea elephants went to Key West for their holidays.

In between all these T-shirt shops were ludicrously expensive restaurants and gay bars (Key West is the gay holiday capital of the States). On the front window of one of these gay bars I spotted a poster for another festival going on in town. It was the Wet Underwear Festival. Maybe they could combine the two: The Ernest Hemingway in Wet Underwear Festival.

Another homeless Hemingway accosted me in the street. With wild eyes and even wilder hair he shoved his face right in front of mine and spat, 'You're a fuckin' MORON!' If there was a Mentally Deranged Psychopath Look-Alike Contest, he'd win it hands down.

I walked to the end of Duval Street and headed for the docks, where the Hemingway Fish-Off (a fishing competition for the Hemingway look-alikes) was taking place. Well, I thought it was. There was no one there. I asked a fellow who was manning a boat-chartering booth where it was and he said, 'Oh, they'd had enough so they all went to the pub.' Good idea. Across the road was The Raw Bar which was probably where all the Hemingways were. Why not, I thought? I'd join them for some naked women and a beer.

It was a raw bar alright, but only the food was raw. It was an oyster bar. I sat at the bar, ordered a plate of raw oysters, and started on *The Old Man and the Sea*. Hemingway wrote: ' . . . his hands had the deep-creased scars from handling heavy fish on the cords. But none of these scars were fresh. They were as old as erosions in a fishless desert.' Yeah, it was good, but nowhere near as crafted or poignant as his later T-shirt work—like 'Remember my name . . . you'll be screaming it later'.

It was time to do what Hemingway did nearly every night and go to Sloppy Joe's bar for a wee tipple. Sloppy Joe's was Hemingway's favourite haunt and he spent many a night there getting very sloppy with the locals. When he arrived in Key West in 1928, he spent his first night at a 'blind pig' (an illegal bar—it was during prohibition) in Greene Street, run by charter-boat captain Joe Russell. The melting water from Russell's iced fish left the floor wet, so Hemingway allegedly told the owner, 'You run such a sloppy bar that this place should be called Sloppy Joe's.' And so it became. Eventually Russell needed a bigger place, so he moved in 1937 to the current site in Duval Street (the bar never closed and thirsty patrons, including Hemingway, simply carried their drinks from one bar to another).

Sloppy Joe's was Hemingway City. Half a dozen of them were propping up the bar, while another one was hoeing into a hamburger the same size as his head. One wall of the bar was plastered with framed photos of the previous winners of the Look-Alike Contest. They looked like identical octuplets. After downing a quick beer, I sidled up to one of the Hemingways and introduced myself. His name was John Clifford and he was a neurosurgeon from Baton Rouge. He had participated in the Hemingway Look-Alike Contest for the first time in 1995 (he hadn't won yet—previous winners can't compete again so they become the judges).

'One of my patients came out from under anaesthesia,' he said in between large gulps of beer, 'and the first thing he said was "You look like Ernest Hemingway", so I figured that was a good excuse to take a summer vacation in Key West.'

Another Ernest Hemingway waltzed into the bar and John squealed with delight when he spotted him. They hugged like long-lost brothers and went straight into an animated conversation about the comparative size of their guts. I let John get on with his stomach analysis and decided to call it a night.

On the way back to the hostel I passed a karaoke bar. Ernest Hemingway was up on stage singing 'Chantilly Lace'. I never knew Papa sang. He had quite a good voice, too. Never shy when it comes to karaoke (okay, I'm a little bit obsessed with it), I waltzed on in just as a guy who could have won the Sean Connery Look-Alike Contest got up to sing. After Sean, another Hemingway got up to sing. Well, when I say sing, I mean howl. He howled his way through 'Lady' by Kenny Rogers and was so pissed he almost fell off the stage. His name was Tom Grizzard and, besides having a very red nose, was a realtor (American for real estate agent) from Leesburg, Florida. I wonder if his house-selling spiel was done à la Hemingway: 'Walk into this room that is the ensuite. The toilet is desired by everyone until the new winds draw close. And the bath beholds the very gentle and the very strong by the new French windows.'

Tom had brought his fan club along. All 20 people sitting at a long table were wearing yellow T-shirts with 'Tom Grizzard— Wannabe Pop' printed on them. This was his third attempt at winning the title. I asked him what he thought his chances of winning were.

'As Hemingway would say,' he slurred, 'the fun is in the hunt, not the catch.'

I told him I was writing a book about festivals.

'What's Hemingway got to do with vegetables?' he asked looking very confused.

'No! Festivals!' I shouted over a fat bloke's boisterous version of 'Rhinestone Cowboy'.

'What sort of vegetables?' he said looking even more perplexed.

'Hemingway loved carrots,' I shouted.

'Really? I didn't know that.'

•

Oh, the joys of dorm accommodation. At four-thirty in the morning I awoke to the sound of someone humming in my ear. The shaven-headed fellow from the bed opposite me was sitting cross-legged on the bedside table right next to my head doing some sort of meditation thing. He was totally naked. I'd left my Hemingway book on the bedside table, so his bum crack must have been resting right on Hemingway's face.

In the morning, after meticulously wiping my Hemingway book clean, I decided to find out more about the man himself by visiting his house. Hemingway paid $8000 for a two-storey Spanish-colonial house at 907 Whitehead Street, Key West, in 1931 and lived there for almost 10 years.

Our guide for the tour was (surprise, surprise) a Hemingway look-alike. He had glazed eyes and was frantically chewing gum in an attempt to get rid of morning-after-getting-pissed breath. 'I'm sorry about my voice,' he croaked. 'I had a big night at the karaoke.'

During the tour, I found out that Hemingway wore safari suits with lots of pockets, drank like a fish, liked hunting and killing assorted wild beasties, dabbled in a bit of womanising and also wrote a few books. Okay, I did learn some new things about our Ernie. Like what a nice little life he had. He would rise at six am every day and head straight to his studio, which was located on the second floor of the little cottage behind the house (he built a catwalk between the studio and his upstairs bedroom so no one could disturb him). He would write until lunchtime (or until he'd done 700 words, whichever came first), then he would go marlin fishing on his private boat (where his very own captain would be waiting for him). He'd get back in time for Happy Hour at Sloppy Joe's and, more often than not, stay there downing whiskies all night. Sounds like a pretty ideal life. Maybe I should employ a similar writing regime. Except I hate getting up early, I can't stand fishing and the smell of whisky makes me feel sick. Oh, and I haven't won the Nobel Prize for Literature (although I've been practising my speech just in case).

Our croaky-voiced guide really loved his Ernie and regaled us with many anecdotes about his life (Ernie's life that is, not the guide's). I'm not a cat person (okay, I can't stand the bloody things), but I was impressed with the fact that the house was home to 61 cats which were all descendants of Hemingway's six-toed cat called Snowball. Over half of the cats had inherited Snowball's six toes.

Inside the house, the photos on the walls showed Hemingway catching fish, standing over dead large beasties and posing with a succession of women. He did all right, too, by the look of it. When

Hemingway arrived in Key West he was in his early thirties and looked more like Clark Gable than the later Father Christmas version. Although he was married (to his second wife, Pauline), he didn't mind the odd extra-marital shag as well.

Funnily enough, the fact that he was bonking other women wasn't the major reason for Hemingway's falling out with Pauline. In 1937, while Hemingway was away in Spain (as a war correspondent covering the Spanish Civil War), Pauline decided to surprise him by building the first swimming pool in Key West. It was dug out of solid rock by hand. With no running water, a saltwater well had to be dug as well. When it was finally completed, Pauline had spent $20 000. The house had only cost $8000. That's the equivalent of buying a $400 000 house today and spending a million dollars on a swimming pool.

He got his own back, though. When Hemingway and Pauline divorced (and he ran off with his mistress to Cuba), he couldn't take his (and Pauline's) collection of some of the finest wines in the world (worth almost as much as his house) with him. So what did he do? He organised a party with a few friends (as in the drunks from Sloppy Joe's) and, in the space of three days, drank every single bottle.

Our guide looked like he needed a drink by the time he'd finished the tour. Quite coincidentally, he finished it under a large sign saying 'TIPS ARE WELCOME'. 'I'll give you a tip,' I was tempted to say. 'Don't drink so much.'

I was a bit disappointed by the souvenir shop. They had the usual pencils, cups, hats, key rings and Hemingway snow domes, but it just wasn't tacky enough for my liking. Where were the Hemingway toilet brushes, the Hemingway glow-in-the-dark condoms and the Hemingway whoopee cushions?

It was time for lunch and another visit to Sloppy Joe's. The bar had the usual smattering of Hemingways milling about. They were all wearing identical white pants, white shirts and red bandannas. They were dressed up as the locals of Pamplona, Spain, do for the Running of the Bulls. (Hemingway had taken part himself.) The local version of the running of the Bull was due to start at one-thirty. One of the Hemingways, however, stood out larger than life. But that was probably because he was. He looked as if he'd eaten the real Ernest Hemingway. He also looked like one of the bulls as he was wearing a Viking-horned helmet.

I wandered over and introduced myself. His name was Tom Chadwick and this was his 20th year competing in the Look-Alike Contest. 'And you haven't won yet?' I said, trying to sound surprised.

'I don't want to win,' he chuckled. 'I'd have to become a judge and stay sober and that's no fun.'

When I told him I was from Melbourne, Australia, he grabbed my hand and bellowed, 'We're from Melbourne too, Melbourne, Florida! You have to join us for lunch.'

His fellow Melburnians were as large as him and were all wearing T-shirts with 'Vote For Tom—The Horny One' printed on them. When I told one of the ladies I was writing a book about festivals she said, 'We went to the Liberace Festival in Las Vegas last year.'

'Oh, that would have been fantastic!' I said. Secretly, though, I couldn't think of anything worse. Even the Judy Garland Festival (held in Grand Rapids, Minnesota) would be more fun—although one journalist advised that you should 'Bring your heart, but leave your brain at home'. Talking about leaving your brain at home, if you went to the Dukes of Hazzard Festival ('inspired' by the abysmal eighties' TV show) in Covington, Georgia, you probably didn't have one in the first place.

Not only do minor TV shows have their own festivals, but even the most minor star of a minor TV show can have a festival devoted to him. In Heber Springs, Arkansas, they have a Grandpa Jones Festival. Grandpa who? You know, he was the star of the TV series 'Hee Haw'. Gee, I wonder if Tiger, the dog from 'The Brady Bunch', has a festival devoted to him.

People will find the smallest of celebrity links to hold a festival. The Gene Autrey Festival is held in a town he didn't even visit. But then again he did save it. Literally. In the mid-thirties, the Kenton Hardware Company in Ohio, which employed over half the town, was on the verge of bankruptcy when they received a contract that saved the company (and the town). They got the gig to produce a Gene Autrey toy cap gun. It soon became the hottest toy in America and went on to sell over six million. The festival is a way of saying thank you. Oh, and to make some more money out of him.

The biggest of all the celebrity festivals, however, belongs to the King. Elvis Presley Week in Memphis, Tennessee, attracts tens of thousands of people with sideburns every year. Among the 74 events at the 2003 festival were an Elvis Fashion Show (isn't that an oxymoron?), Elvis Pool Party, Elvis Art Contest, Elvis Luau, Elvis Moonlight Cruise, Meet Elvis's Former Sweetheart Dinner and an Elvis Fun Run (over a distance of 30 yards!). The festival is sponsored by Pepsi—'The official soft drink of Graceland'. I wonder if they have a deep-fried-peanut-and-banana-sandwich-eating competition.

I'd ordered some deep-fried artery-blocking food for lunch at Sloppy Joe's. I had a basket of Conch Fritters (a conch—pronounced *conk*—is a mollusc). When the waiter put the small basket of fritters down, Tom said, 'Is that *all* you're eating? What's a matter with you, boy?' He sounded just like Foghorn Leghorn. Under considerable pressure from Tom (he was worried I'd starve to death), I ordered some dessert.

'You can't come to Key West without having a slice of the world famous Key Lime Pie,' Tom said. It's so famous, in fact, that there is even a Key Lime Pie Festival in November. The 'pie' was a cheese-cake sort of thing made with, um, limes from Key West.

'Aren't you having any?' I asked Tom as I scoffed down the deli-cious pie.

'No, I'm in the Key Lime Pie Eating Contest later and I'll prob-ably eat about 20 slices.'

A pen had been set up for the bulls on the street outside the bar. Inside it there were five really big scary bulls. Actually, they weren't *really* that scary—they were wooden bulls on wheels. It wasn't quite Pamplona. And instead of bulls being released and chasing people, a Hemingway mounted each of the bulls and teams of four other Hemingways pushed them in a race around the block. I don't think they took it that seriously, though. For a start, the riders (and some of the pushers) were drinking large mugs of beer and smoking even larger cigars. One of the riders was Tom Chadwick. Pushing Tom would have been like pushing a bus. Another of the Hemingways sitting atop one of the bulls was wearing a red silk robe, proper black lace-up boxing gloves and boots (apparently Hemingway liked boxing). He was having quite a bit of trouble holding his mug of beer.

But the real give-away that the race wasn't that serious was when the Hemingway Days' Official Photographer stopped it halfway through by shouting, 'Stop! Can all you Hemingways move back so I can get you all in the shot?'

Quite a crowd had gathered and it soon turned into more of a photo-taking frenzy than a race. At one point Tom screamed out, 'Hurry up! I've almost finished my beer.' Amazingly, Tom came second. (What made it amazing was that one of the Hemingways pushing him had a walking stick and a huge metal brace on his knee.)

All the Hemingways were soaked with sweat. In fact, it was so stinking hot that I decided to skip the Key Lime Pie Eating Contest and hit the beach for a swim and a bit more reading. Tom was a shoe-in anyway. He'd probably finish his allocated pies and start on the other competitor's share before the time was up.

Key West must be the skin cancer capital of the world. Chocolate-brown and lobster-red bodies paraded up and down the beach. It was hard to concentrate on my book when scantily clad ladies kept sauntering by in front of me. Particularly when there wasn't much action happening on the page. The 'Old Man' had spent two very long days trying to haul in a rather stubborn marlin he'd hooked at the start of the book. The 'Old Man' sure was keen. I get bored fishing after an hour.

As I left the beach I passed a Hemingway flaked out—more than likely hungover—on a banana lounge. He was glowing so red with sunburn that he looked like a bearded safety beacon.

I freshened up back at the hostel and rushed down to Sloppy Joe's for the final of the Look-Alike Contest. The bar was packed and the crowd spilt out onto the street where a massive screen was relaying what was going on inside. The finalists were all inside posing and swaggering about in safari suits, rope belts and fishing vests. Some had even gone for the authentic, but incredibly hot and uncomfortable, thick woollen roll-neck fisherman's jumpers. Some of the Hemingways were fatter than others, some younger, some older, with and without hair. There was a sea of old men trying to look like the author did when he wrote *The Old Man and the Sea*.

Chris Storm from Amarillo, Texas, looked—and I mean *really* looked—like Hemingway. He even had one of those safari jackets with a hundred pockets. The photo of him on his cheer-squad's T-shirts looked identical to the picture of Hemingway on the front cover of the *Life* magazine that was mounted on the wall of the bar. I pushed my way through the crowded bar to tell him he looked like Hemingway. 'Have you read Hemingway's books?' I shouted over the chanting of the cheer-squads.

'I'm a huge fan and I'd read all his books before I even knew about this event,' he shouted back. 'I've been to Africa 10 times, Cuba and the Running of the Bulls in Pamplona. I also like fishing, hunting, drinking...'

'...and womanising?' I added with a grin.

He looked around to make sure his wife wasn't looking then gave me a cheeky wink.

'I do everything Hemingway did except write.'

As I stood drinking my 'Hemingway Hammer' (151-proof dark rum, banana and strawberry liqueur, blackberry brandy and a dash of white rum), a middle-aged woman with curly hair placed a yellow balloon in my hand. On one side, inscribed in black marker was 'Prime Time 4 Paul'. On the other side was a smiley face. 'Paul's the young, good-looking one tonight,' she told me. In her wake, she left a long trail of yellow balloons, rising above the crowd, like the heads of absurdly tall spectators, jockeying for a clear view of the impending action. Paul wasn't the only one campaigning for audience support, though. In the next 15 minutes I acquired a set of gold-coloured plastic beads with a large red-and-white button pendant bearing the slogan 'Phil's the Thrill', and a small orange-coloured plastic garland with 'A Lei from Larry' on a yellow strip of paper stapled to it.

The start was delayed because one of the Hemingways was missing and hadn't registered yet. It was probably the sunburnt fellow. They should have tried the burns unit of the local hospital.

Each one of the 24 finalists took it in turns up on the stage trying to win the crowd and judges over with witty dittys and tall tales of their exploits. When big Tom was called, the crowd roared. He staggered up and mumbled into the microphone. He was well sozzled. No one could understand a single word he was saying, but they gave him an almighty cheer anyway. Another Hemingway went the poetry route. 'Ernest was called a wussy. Just because he liked to play with pussy. I'm talking about the cat. Where in the hell was your mind at?' Chris Storm did half of his speech in Swahili. Either that, or he was more pissed than Tom.

The sunburnt Hemingway finally turned up and stepped up onto the stage. He could have won first prize in the Ripley Tomato Festival.

One of the 12 judges got up and called out the names of the final five. Neither Tom Grizzard nor Big Tom made the final cut. Chris Storm was still in there, though. The chanting of the cheer-squads was now deafening. Everyone was getting excited, including the large lady in front of me who kept rubbing her more than ample bottom up against my groin. It all seemed like a lot of hard work for not much (that's the contest, not the groin rubbing). You don't get rich if you win the contest. The winner gets a $100 bar tab, a return flight to anywhere in the USA, plus three free nights at a dodgy Key West motel.

The winner was announced. Up jumped a Hemingway who didn't look much like Hemingway at all. I thought Chris Storm would have stormed in, but Mike Stack, an electrical contractor from Eastchester, New York, took the big prize. There weren't a lot of Hemingways around to congratulate him, though. Most of them, because of the recently introduced smoking ban in Florida bars, were out on the street smoking cigars like naughty schoolboys.

·

I rushed 400 metres down the road to Mallory Square to catch the sunset. This is the last place the sun sets in continental USA and a huge crowd gathers to applaud as the sun drops over the horizon (yes, only in America). I missed the actual drop, but sat on the crowded waterfront and watched the sky go from orange to red to purple as silhouetted 'sunset cruise' sailing ships crossed in front of me. I'd been to Key West 14 years earlier and clapped along as the sun sunk over America, so I wasn't too disappointed on missing it. I was, however, surprised to see the same buskers from 14 years ago. Less surprisingly, there wasn't a single Hemingway to be seen. They were all back at the bar.

Most of the Hemingways back at the bar were red-faced now. A few of them looked like they were on the verge of a heart attack. A whole bunch of stocky, bearded 60-year-olds were dancing uncontrollably in the street to 'You Shook Me All Night Long' by AC/DC. I had one more Hemingway Hammer, then headed to the karaoke bar (I'm sorry, it's a disease. I can't help myself).

I sat down and chatted to one of the Hemingways who hadn't made the finals. 'That's because you look more like Grizzly Adams,' I wanted to say. I sang a few songs from my extensive karaoke repertoire, then went to see what the rest of the Hemingways were up to. I found one of them totally in the nuddy. I had popped upstairs at the Bull Bar, where 'clothing is optional', to have a wee look (for research purposes of course, not to look at naked women). There were no gorgeous naked girls (not that I was looking out for them, mind you), however, just gangly naked men. That's when I spotted the naked Hemingway. Even the real Hemingway wouldn't have found the words to describe the scene in front of me.

Back in my hostel dorm I piled everything I owned on the bedside table. I didn't want to be woken up by my meditating friend again. And besides, I'd had enough of naked men for one night.

•

I hit the beach early. I wanted to finish *The Old Man and the Sea* before I left Key West. I did finish it and, I have to say, it had me on the edge of my seat—or towel in this case. The 'Old Man' eventually caught his giant marlin, but in the long haul back to port he had to fight off schools of sharks that were tearing at the marlin he'd tied to the side of his small boat. What started as a slow story had turned into *Jaws* with Nobel Prizeworthy prose. It must have been good, because as the morning turned into a hot day I forgot to actually go in for a swim.

I dropped back in to Sloppy Joe's for a farewell beer and to watch the Arm Wrestling Contest. I thought big Tom would win it hands down, but he went out in the first round. 'My head hurts,' he groaned. 'I need a drink.' The guy who looked like Grizzly Adams won. I think he was the only one who wasn't hungover. I didn't hang around for the prize presentation (a 12-pack of beer!), though. I had a long drive to Miami and, to be honest, I was Hemingwayed out. As I walked back down Duval Street for the last time I passed a Hemingway in one of the T-shirt shops. He was holding up a shirt with 'It's not a beer belly. It's a fuel tank for my sex machine' on it. Hemingway couldn't have said it better himself.

Hogmanay

Moffat, Scotland
December 31st

During Hogmanay (New Year's Eve), every house in Scotland holds an open party. Traditionally, you may enter anyone's home as long as you bring a lump of coal, some oatcake and a bottle of whisky. You may then join your hosts in a celebratory toast to the New Year. I didn't quite make a 'traditional' entrance to the first house I dropped into. I tottered in clutching half a can of Tartan Special lager and stumbled upon two old couples having a quiet drink in the lounge room, listening to Engelbert Humperdinck records. I lurched into the room, tripped on the rug and collapsed in a heap on the floor. Well, at least it solved the problem of where to crash for the night. I couldn't remember where I was staying.

Despite my lack of orientation and balance, I was having a grand old time. In fact, I'd say I've had a grand old time at just about every New Year's Eve celebration I can remember. You see, I figured it out years ago. Most people have such high expectations that they'll have an amazing time on New Year's Eve that when they just have a good time it's not good enough. I go into New Year's Eve with low expectations so that if I just have a good time then, as far as I'm concerned, it's a raging success. Mind you, I've also had a few absolute humdingers. Indeed, New Year's Eve holds a special place for me. It was when I had my first real kiss, got drunk for the first time, had sex for the first time and got together with my wife (not all in the same year or with the same partner, I might add).

I had my first real kiss when I was 14 years old. And I mean a *real* kiss, not just when grandma tries to give you a big sloppy kiss on the lips. I was on a camping holiday with my parents on the coast and, as midnight approached, all the teenagers congregated around the main street of the campsite waiting to get a kiss. I spent the first 15 minutes of the New Year watching other people kiss. It was mostly the older, blond, cool surfie types doing all the kissing. No girl was interested in shy, young, short, scrawny me. Then it happened. This much, much older girl (well, at least 16) staggered up to me, bellowed 'Huppysnewyeers' into my ear (she may have been a trifle drunk) and kissed me. It was one of the grossest things I'd ever experienced in my life. She stuck her tongue in my mouth and sloshed it about. I remember thinking—besides 'What the HELL is going on?'—that this couldn't be normal. I spent the next 15 minutes frantically spitting, worried that I might have caught diphtheria or something similar.

The next New Year's Eve, I got drunk for the first time. I spent the entire evening with my friend Paco Francisco Gomez busking for beer (as his name suggests Paco was a bit of a maestro on the acoustic guitar). We actually didn't try to get drunk, but as we wandered around the campsite in Victor Harbour, South Australia, serenading campers, each group we sang to would give us a sip of beer. We played to about 30 groups of people over the course of the evening, so by midnight we were singing with drunken gusto. At least we had no trouble remembering lyrics. We played the same song all night. Over and over again. It was the current no. 1 hit, the annoyingly catchy 'Mull Of Kintyre' (in retrospect, we were lucky people didn't *throw* beer at us). I remember waking up in the morning with a terrible throbbing head thinking, 'This can't be normal'.

A couple of years later, I had sex for the first time on New Year's Eve. My girlfriend and I had planned it for a month before the big event. (We wanted it to be perfect. Oh, and we also had to wait till her mum went away on holidays so we could use her double bed.) And despite the fact I had no idea what I was doing, I really did have a grand old time that New Year's Eve.

And, lastly, New Year's Eve was when I got together with my wife. We were working together in a ski resort in Switzerland and had known each other for less than three weeks when I saved her life. Well, not quite, but I did carry her home after she'd fallen down an embankment and onto some train tracks. We were shuffling home through a field of snow after the big NYE Fancy Dress Party and, as we crossed the train tracks in front of our house, Natalie slipped and landed hard on her bottom. She couldn't walk, so I carried her the rest of the way home. I seized the opportunity and said, 'I think I deserve a New Year's kiss for that.' We had a good snog (tongues and all), then toppled into bed. We woke up in the morning still fully dressed. Natalie was cleverly disguised as a bottle of Moët et Chandon (a cunningly converted large black garbag), while I was still in my full Russian naval uniform.

•

Going into my first Scottish Hogmanay, however, I did have high expectations . . . Hogmanay is huge (400 000 people partied in the streets of Edinburgh in 2002 alone). In fact, for many centuries, Hogmanay in Scotland was far more important than Christmas. Best of all, though, when every house is hosting an open party and the entire population has a penchant for getting totally *plukey-faced* (Scottish for drunk), then I had a very good chance of having a *hoot* (Scottish for hoot).

Hogmanay's less boozy origins are in pagan rituals that marked the winter solstice. The Romans' hedonistic winter festival Saturnalia (which was basically one big orgy) and Viking celebrations of Yule (the origin of the 12 days of Christmas—and more orgies) both contributed to celebrations in Scotland around the New Year. These celebrations and other ceremonies evolved over the centuries to become the Hogmanay holiday celebrated in Scotland today (with the addition of a few hundred thousand pints of lager and, sadly, minus the orgies).

No one in Scotland seems to know, or agree on, the exact derivation of the word Hogmanay (a few too many pints of lager may have had something to do with that). Some say it's a Gaelic word, while others think it's Celtic, Flemish, Dutch or Old French. At least the Austrians know how their New Year's Eve got its name. They call their New Year's Eve Sylvester—after the cartoon cat. Actually, it's named after St Sylvester (the feast day of St Sylvester falls on December 31st). The Greeks call theirs, and I kid you not, Basil. I think Australia should make their New Year's Eve stand out from the crowd as well and give it a name. 'Come to Australia to celebrate . . . Kevin!' It could work, you know.

I was on a flying visit to London on a freelance advertising job staying with my friend Stuart who, along with a few of his flatmates, were heading up north for Hogmanay. When I say a few flatmates, there were 15 of them. And, when I say flat, I mean a *flat*. It was a two-bedroom flat. One couple shared a room as big as a cupboard (in fact, it might have actually been a cupboard), eight were squished into the other bedroom (with three on the floor) and the other six, including me, slept in the lounge room. I did all right, though. I had one of the best sleeping spots in the house—under the dining room table. It was a particularly good spot because when drunk people came home (which happened *every* night) they couldn't stand (or fall) on my head.

Mind you, the population of the flat at that stage was quite low compared to peak figures over the years. Amazingly, the landlord had no idea what was going on. He knew that the four official tenants had a 'few extra' friends staying there now and again, he just didn't realise that the equivalent of the population of a small country had moved in. Here is an example of how little idea he had: when I was staying there a couple of years ago we decided, one uncharacteristically sunny Sunday in summer, to have a barbecue. We dragged an old bathtub out onto the street, threw some metal fridge shelves over it and fired up some snags. The landlord turned up and smiled and waved at us as he walked inside. He just assumed that the tenants were having a group of mates around. Little did he know that all 26 people at the barbecue were actually living in his flat. Those 26 Aussies and Kiwis were crammed in so tightly that there wasn't room for them all to bunk down at the same time. Two couples were sleeping in their vans parked out the front.

There was no such thing as a quiet night in. Over 20 people would be sitting on top of each other in the lounge room every night watching the evening news (with cigarette smoke pouring out of the one and only lounge-room window as if from a chimney).

The flat was nicknamed the 'Shabby Flat'. That's what the real estate agent had called it. When four people returning from a bus tour around Europe went to a London real estate agent in search of a flat they were told that for their budget there wasn't much about. They could only offer them a basement flat in Inverness Terrace, Bayswater, that, although it was in a great position, was 'a bit shabby'.

They moved in the next day. With half of the other passengers from the tour. To be fair, the flat was no longer that shabby. In fact, it was almost verging on five-star. With the extra money made from all the visiting 'guests', the original tenants had, among other things, painted the place, installed a new kitchen, a new shower, satellite TV and a large bar. Over the years, literally hundreds of itinerant travellers have passed through (and passed out in) the Shabby Flat.

Among the recent motley crew of flat-sardines was Phil, a New Zealander who came from a town with a smaller population than the flat. He was on such a strict budget that he had been eating nothing but steamed potatoes for the last six months. Honk was another New Zealander. You didn't want to tease him about his nickname, though. He was the size of a bathroom (but not the Shabby Flat one—that was tiny). Dave was from Sydney. That wasn't his real name, however. His girlfriend, who he'd met on the tour, had decided that he looked more like a Dave than a Paul. My friend Stuart had originally planned on staying in London for six months. That was almost nine years ago. He did have the 'good' room (or cupboard), though. There was also a girl called Rubber. I had assumed she got that name because she often pulled condoms over her head, but it was because she wore a rubber raincoat. Well, when she wasn't flashing her tits at least. After a few drinks (and sometimes after only half a drink), her breasts would make a sudden and wobbly appearance. Still, she could drink me under the table. Literally. I collapsed in my bed under the table one night while she continued partying—and flashing her boobies.

It was a bit cold for boobie flashing on the morning we left to drive to Scotland. I was sharing a hire car with Phil and his girlfriend Clare (and a large bag of potatoes). There was a convoy of cars heading north, but we were all taking different routes and leaving on different days (we were leaving the day before New Year's Eve). We planned to drive the entire 700 kilometres in the one day. I told an English friend we were doing just that and he thought I was mad. I told him we drive that far in Australia just to get a pint of milk.

We stopped for lunch at the oldest pub in Britain. Ye Olde Trip To Jerusalem in Nottingham was built in 1189. The turkey sandwiches we had for lunch were made not long after that. Actually, to be fair, they were quite nice. You would never have guessed that it was five days after Christmas, though. Also on the menu was a turkey salad, a turkey stew and turkey 'surprise'.

A little after eight, we pulled into the main street of the little mill town of Moffat ('The town to stop off at') in the Southern Uplands of Dumfries and Galloway. We parked across the road from the statue of the Giant Moffat Ram in the main square. The much-less-than-giant bronze ram was perched on top of a slab of ragged rock five metres high. There aren't too many real rams wandering around nowadays, though. The glory days of Moffat's wool trade are well and truly over and the surrounding wool mills are now mostly tourist attractions.

We went straight to the pub. We were meeting the rest of the crew at the Black Bull. Compared to Ye Olde Trip To Jerusalem, the Black Bull was virtually brand new. It was built in the 16th century. The gang were in the Robert Burns room (the famous Scottish poet often frequented the pub). They were all very plukey-faced indeed. Phil suggested that we do our very best to catch up in the drinking stakes. He was quite happy to stretch his budget when it came to beer.

I got a wee bit excited when I realised we were in the Robert Burns room. It was he, after all, who wrote the New Year's Eve standard 'Auld Lang Syne'. As I stood reading the lyrics in a framed picture on the wall, it dawned on me that not only did I only know the first verse and chorus, but I'd also never in my life sung the song sober. Mind you, by the look of the complete set of lyrics I don't think ol' Robbie was quite sober when he wrote it, either. Actually, looking at verses two to four, he must have got progressively drunker as he went:

And surely ye'll be your pint stowp!
And surely I'll be mine!
And we'll tak a cup o' kindness yet,
For auld lang syne.

We twa hae run about the braes,
And pou'd the gowans fine;
But we've wander'd mony a weary fit,
Sin' auld lang syne.

We twa hae paidl'd in the burn,
Frae morning sun till dine;
But seas between us braid hae roar'd
Sin' auld lang syne.

The way a couple of people from the flat were talking was not dissimilar to that. We'd just about taken over the bar. Also joining us Shabbyites for the big trip to Scotland was another bunch of Kiwis from a rival Shabby Flat in London (we now had almost half the population of New Zealand in Moffat) and a Liverpudlian called Hoop, who was so drunk I could almost understand what he was saying. In less than three hours I managed to get quite pished (not a printing error, by the way, but another Scottish word for drunk— or the work of a drunken Scottish lexicographer).

We were staying in the Well Road Centre, a large Victorian house that had been converted into a 'budget' guest house and conference centre just out of town. All 22 of us were staying there. The good thing was that it didn't matter how drunk we got, finding a bed wouldn't be too difficult. That was because we had three beds each. The house has 13 dorm rooms and 65 beds. Compared to the Shabby Flat it was like the Queen Mary (after those few quick pints it was swaying like the Queen Mary, too). And, much like a large ocean liner, the place even had a half-size indoor basketball court. On the return from the pub, most of the drunken revellers decided to take part in a game of basketball. However, with 10 people a side and not a sober person among us, it soon turned into more like a game of basketbrawl. It wasn't long before I learnt an important lesson from this hybrid and dangerous version of the game. If Honk comes towards you with the ball, you get the fuck out of the way very quickly. The game ended when someone threw up underneath the ring. No one knew who won, but that was because no one was capable of counting. And, inevitably Rubber brought *her* basketballs out to join in the fun. She even let one of the boys test them to see if they bounced all right.

•

I had a sore head in the morning. And a sore back, arm and ribs where Honk had steam-rolled me. Phil, Clare and Stuart were waiting in the car as I hobbled out into the dull and cold day. We drove two hours north to St Andrews and its world-famous golf course. We parked near the clubhouse and wandered over to the first tee. We stood there for a second and Phil said, 'Gee, it's cold.'

'. . . and windy!' I added.

We then turned around and drove back to Moffat.

After a wee nap (it took me a few minutes to find my bed from the night before) and a long bath (in one of the 10 bathrooms), I wandered down for dinner. I could smell the delicious aroma of something obviously scrumptious cooking downstairs. I was famished by the time I'd found the dining room. That soon changed, though. The lads had bought, and cooked up, that traditional Scottish New Year's Eve fare . . . haggis. Although it smelt quite nice, I didn't think I had the stomach for stomach. 'This is exactly what you need just before you go out and drink 20 pints of lager,' I mumbled to Stuart. Anyway, I ate one. Well, most of it at least. With all the spices and herbs, it tasted quite nice. If I'd known what was actually in it, however, I think I would have rather eaten Phil's steamed potatoes. Or Honk's socks. The recipe for haggis is a boiled sheep's stomach stuffed with minced sheep heart, sheep liver, sheep lungs and beef kidney fat. One recipe I found reminded you to scrape the membranes and excess fat from the stomach before boiling it.

Mind you, the Scots aren't the only ones to eat offal on New Year's Eve. In Austria, the locals eat an entire roasted pig's head, while the folk in the Philippines head down the other end and eat crunchy pigtails. In Nigeria, they eat an entire roasted antelope (not *each*, though, I imagine). If we'd eaten an entire roasted antelope, we might not have been able to fit into the pub.

We started our New Year's Eve in, according to *The Guinness Book of Records*, the 'Narrowest Hotel in the World'. The Star Hotel, at only 20 feet wide, was so narrow that it made all the occupants inside look fat. The locals were surprised (to say the least) when 22 rowdy antipodeans waltzed in. I have it on good authority that it only took Rubber an hour to get her tits (or *Coopy baps* as the Scots would say) out. I missed them (which, with their size and sheer blinding whiteness, wasn't easy) as I was having a pint of Chiffel Ale and chatting to, or doing my best to understand, a local sheepshearer called Bram (although, with his strong Scottish accent, I can't be absolutely sure that was his name). I figured I'd better speak to some of the locals early, before they got drunk and started speaking Hungarian.

Bram was originally from the island of Lewis. 'As in Jerry,' he told me. For the next 10 minutes I had to use every ounce of concentration I had in me to understand what he was saying. The story he told me went something like this (I think): When he was a wee lad the local boys would form themselves into bands (or buns?) during Hogmanay. The leader of each band would wear a sheep-skin, while another member would carry a sack. The bands would then move from house to house, reciting a Gaelic rhyme. On being invited into the home by the woman of the family, the leader would walk clockwise around a chair while everyone else hit him with sticks. The boys would be given some oatmeal bread for their sack, before moving on to the next house. He said it was a hut. Or a hit. Or a hoot. I couldn't be absolutely sure. He also told me that having only one day to recover from a Scottish New Year's Eve just isn't enough, so January 2nd is an official holiday as well. Bram said he needed three days.

By eleven o'clock, everyone was rubbered. And, no, I don't mean everyone had their tits out. It's just another Scottish word for drunk. You know a nation drinks a lot when it has so many slang words for being drunk. (As well as the ones I've already mentioned, examples include gubbed, blootered, guttert, mingin', dugless, smeekit and reekin—and I'm sure we're still not even close to the bottom of the barrel).

By eleven-thirty the entire bar was speaking Hungarian. Time had just flown by. 'Maybe it's because the pub is so narrow,' Phil said, 'that time is condensed.' Stuart suggested it might have had more to do with the copious amounts of beer we were drinking. Just before midnight we made our way, mostly stumbling, to the Main Square. A large crowd of folk wearing tartan tam o'shanters and jester hats was gathered around a blazing bonfire. The lighting of a bonfire at Hogmanay brings the knowledge and wisdom of the old year into the new one. By the dazed looks on the faces of people staggering around, it hadn't exactly been a vintage year.

Standing right next to the bonfire, with the warm air rising up their kilts, was a Scottish Highland band complete (of course) with bagpipes. I never thought I'd be so excited to hear the sound of dying cats. We joined some of the locals who were doing a jig—or in desperate need of the toilet.

As the town clock struck twelve, the band broke into 'Scotland The Brave'. Bottles of whisky were passed around and, just like when I was 14, I watched everyone else kissing. Stuart did give me a quick peck, though. On that note, I attempted to mount the ram. I didn't get too far up the monument, however, before a burly policeman screamed at me to get down. Or asked me for a kiss—even the police spoke Hungarian. I'd had much better luck a few years earlier with my attempts to mount a monument. I was staying with my friend Monty in Paris for New Year's Eve when we climbed up onto the first level of the Bastille monument. That was silly enough, but we decided to be even sillier and strip off. We then proceeded to do a bit of ballet around the narrow ledge while flashing our bottoms to Paris. And very cold bottoms at that; it was only three degrees. We further embarrassed ourselves later on as our gang of drunken misfits caught the Metro back to Monty's apartment. And when I say later on, it was six-thirty in the morning and the train was already half full of commuters on their way to work. While these quiet (and sober) people sat reading their morning papers, Monty and I had a game of Australian Rules football. With a tin can. With accompanying loud and incoherent commentary, we chased each other up and down the carriage. The game ended in a drunken wrestling match on the dirty floor. At least we didn't shame our country—by then we were speaking fluent Hungarian.

Back in Moffat, my Hungarian was working an absolute treat. Somehow, and to this day I don't know (or remember) how, I talked my way into the town's one and only nightclub. The surly bouncer had denied our entire party entry until I stepped up. He told me it was a ticket-only party, so I showed him a London Underground ticket, a laundry ticket and a ticket stub from a West End musical. Actually, when I think about it, it was probably when I started singing 'Oklahoma, where the wind comes sweepin' down the plain' that he let me in. After all that I didn't stay long in the nightclub as I couldn't understand a single word anyone was saying. Oh, except a large and pasty-looking English girl who asked me for a 'kish'. None of my fellow Shabbyites made it inside (maybe they should have tried a couple of numbers from *South Pacific*).

Not long after leaving the nightclub I staggered into the first house I spotted with its lights on and unceremoniously, and rather painfully, collapsed onto the lounge-room floor. It was lucky for the occupants I didn't die. It's bad luck to leave a dead body lying about the house into the New Year.

As with Tet in Vietnam, the first person to cross a Hogmanay-celebrating home's threshold after midnight (known as 'first-footing') determines the homeowner's luck for the entire year. And, again as in Vietnam, it is crucial that the person is deemed suitable. In Scotland, that person should be a man with dark hair. Why dark hair? The answer harks back to the 8th century, when the fair-haired Vikings invaded Scotland. A blond visitor was not a good omen—particularly when he sliced off your head with an axe and raped your wife. The 'first-footer' also shouldn't be a doctor, minister or gravedigger. It is also customary to bring a small lump of coal and drop it on the fire and say, *'Lang may yer lum reek'.* I believe I said something similar to that as the two kindly gentlemen helped me up and ushered me rather unkindly out the front door.

I was still singing Engelbert's 'Please Release Me' as I entered the next house. It was only a small party, but the music was ear-shatteringly loud. Still, the noise didn't stop me from falling asleep in the comfy and capacious lounge chair in the corner. I dozed off for I don't know how long dreaming of haggises dressed in kilts. What I should have been dreaming about, though, was eggplants. At least that was what I should have been dreaming about if I'd been in Japan. All dreams on New Year's Eve in Japan are thought to have a special meaning. In characteristically Japanese numerical order, the three subjects that will bring you good luck are: (1) Mount Fuji; (2) Hawks; (3) Eggplants. I can't say that I can ever remember having a single dream about eggplants (although I have had a few about artichokes and one about a cucumber).

I stumbled upon (and into) the guesthouse a little after three. To follow on from the previous night's sporting pursuits, a table-tennis tournament was in full swing. There was certainly a lot of swinging going on. Just not much hitting. Ten pints of lager tend to wreak havoc on one's hand-eye co-ordination.

Hoop staggered into the room and proceeded to drip blood from his arm onto the table-tennis table. He'd 'first-footed' through someone's lounge-room window but didn't really have much of a recollection of what happened. 'I think I was trying to dance,' he said. At least he knew that he actually fell through a window. I awoke one New Year's Day totally covered in deep scratches, dry blood all over my pillow and no idea what had happened (I was 18 and at that very unwise let's-get-so-drunk-we-don't-know-what-planet-we're-on stage). My brother had to fill me in on the night's events. We were spending New Year's Eve camping with his mates at a surf beach to the east of Melbourne when, apparently, I tried to dabble in a bit of ornithology. I attempted to catch a mutton-bird in the bushes. Naturally the mutton-bird wasn't too happy about getting tackled to the ground so it cut my hands and face to bits with its claws.

There was a bit of cutting going on in our guesthouse. We'd all been warned that if you didn't make it (as in weren't capable of making it) back to your bed then your eyebrows would be shaved off. Rubber had already lost hers. Poor Stuart had spent half an hour crawling up the stairs to make it to his bed only to be dragged out into the hallway. Technically he wasn't in his bed anymore, so he lost his eyebrows. Some brave and misguided fool shaved off Honk's eyebrows. He in return would more than likely shave 10 years off the fool's life.

I awoke in the morning with my eyebrows intact. And I hadn't even made it to my bed. They hadn't shaved me because no one could find me. I'd fallen asleep in the corner of the basketball court, hugging a basketball as if it contained my entire store of earthly knowledge and wisdom.

Acknowledgements

Probably the biggest debt I owe is to the book itself. Having an excuse to research, attend and write about festivals made me realise not only how much fun they can be, but also how many insights they provide into the local culture. Whenever you are going overseas (or even on a holiday in your own backyard), I strongly suggest you do a quick search on the internet before you go. You never know, you might have timed your holiday perfectly to experience something as memorable as the Bald Beaver Festival in New York.

A friend of mine was heading off to Thailand and after a quick search on Google and a slight rearrangement of her itinerary she was able to attend the country's largest festival (and water fight) in Chang Mai—the Buddhist New Year or *Songkran*. Not surprisingly, it turned out to be the highlight of her trip and she is now planning her next one around festivals. I've now got the festival bug in a big way, too. In planning the journey for my next book, I did searches for all the places I'm visiting. Simply by changing the order of my stops, I've managed to time my visits to coincide with three major festivals (sadly, though, I will miss the Bald Beaver Festival by one week).

Now back to the human acknowledgees. First and foremost, I'd like to thank my wife Natalie for her encouragement and patience, and for putting up with an AWOL husband and father. Thanks also to James Richardson for his advice and liberal use of red pen on my rough-and-ready prose. Special thanks for their hospitiality and assistance during my travels to Kaz Pickett and Chris Davies in Tamworth; Matt Daves and Nick Hotton in Vietnam; and Julie Thompson who got me through Mardi Gras. Last, but certainly not least, many thanks to the crew at Allen & Unwin, including Jo Paul, Joanne Holliman, April Murdoch and Christa Munns.

If you'd like to see photos of me in a nappy or Pigsy throwing beans or a chicken getting sacrificied, you can check out the photo album of my trip at <www.brianthacker.tv>. You will also find useful links to help you locate festivals all over the planet, including all the festivals in this book and other favourites such as the Broomstick Beating Festival and Penis Festival. Or just drop me a line and tell me about your must-do festival. I'd love to hear from you.

Brian Thacker
East St Kilda, August 2004